Praise for
BEGINNERS WELCOME

"As delicate and powerful as a sonata,
Annie Lee's story of music, magic, loss,
and love should not be missed!"
—Jessica Day George,
New York Times bestselling author of *Tuesdays at the Castle*

"Targeted to kids who sometimes feel invisible or afraid,
Baldwin's prose challenges them to be the bravest and wisest versions
of themselves, delivering the message that it is our brokenness
that makes us beautiful, not our perfection."
—*School Library Journal* (starred review)

"Southern charm and ghostly magic bridge
the loss of eleven-year-old Annie Lee's daddy.
Once again, Baldwin crafts a solid story of hardship
tempered by community and resilience."
—*Kirkus Reviews*

"Genuine and hopeful, Annie Lee's story is
one of finding courage in tough circumstances,
of love and vulnerability, and of the power of music,
despite one's imperfections."
—ALA *Booklist*

"Intermingling themes of grief and loss
with moments of unexpected, joyful connection,
Baldwin depicts character growth with particular grace."
—*Publishers Weekly*

Praise for
WHERE THE WATERMELONS GROW

An Indies Introduce Title
An Indie Next List Selection

"Della's story is a reminder that even under
the toughest rinds of troubles, we can find the cool,
sustaining sweetness of friendship."
—Kirby Larson, author of the Newbery Honor Book *Hattie Big Sky*

"Della's voice will tug at readers' heartstrings as she tries to hold
her family together. Middle grade stories about mental illness,
particularly those that focus on empathy and acceptance, are rare.
This heartfelt story will stay with readers. A top choice."
—*School Library Journal* (starred review)

"Baldwin has written a heartbreaking, yet heartening,
story that explores mental illness and its effects on an entire family.
Readers will connect with the novel's well-formed characters
and be absorbed by the plot, which pulls no punches
but doesn't overwhelm."
—ALA *Booklist* (starred review)

"Cindy Baldwin's graceful debut is an ode to
family and community. Hints of sweet magical realism touch
Where the Watermelons Grow, balancing this exquisite novel's
bittersweet authenticity."
—Shelf Awareness (starred review)

"In her debut novel, Baldwin presents a realistic portrayal of life
with a mentally ill parent."
—*Publishers Weekly* (starred review)

"This has a tenderness that will appeal to fans
of DiCamillo's *Because of Winn-Dixie*."
—*Bulletin of the Center for Children's Books*

Beginners WELCOME

Beginners WELCOME

a novel by
CINDY BALDWIN

Quill Tree Books
An Imprint of HarperCollinsPublishers

Quill Tree Books is an imprint of HarperCollins Publishers.

Library of Congress Control Number: 2019944066
ISBN 978-0-06-266590-4

Typography by Erin Fitzsimmons
21 22 23 24 25   PC/BRR   10 9 8 7 6 5 4 3 2 1

First paperback edition, 2021

For Dad, who showed me how important daddies are,
and who has always been the #1 fan of my writing.
Thank you for believing in me until I believed in myself, too.

And for Mom, who taught me to love music and spent a decade
supporting my dreams. For every afternoon spent waiting through
a lesson, for every battle over practicing, for every musical you took
me to, and for every John Denver CD you played in the car:
Thank you.

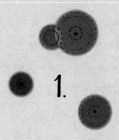

1.

I woke on the first day of sixth grade to the sound of Mama crying in the bathroom.

Before my eyes were all the way open, I was reaching over to my nightstand to grab the two-headed quarter that sat there, cool to the touch even on this warm late-August morning, the kind of morning where summer had its claws so deep into everything it felt like it might never let go. Those two faces of George Washington were twice as shiny as a regular coin from rubbing— first Daddy's big fingers, and then my smaller ones. He'd carried that magic-show quarter around in his pocket as long as I could remember.

It always pays to carry your own luck, Al, he'd say whenever he showed it to me, flipping it from heads on one side to heads on the other. *You never know when it might come in handy.*

"Annie Lee?" Mama's voice was tight and stretched, but at least she wasn't sniffling anymore. Mama had cried every single morning for more than two and a half months. *I'd* hardly cried at all. Sometimes it felt like Mama had sucked up all the space for grieving in our family so there wasn't any left for me.

A minute later Mama knocked on my bedroom door. "You awake in there?"

"Yeah," I said, and closed my fingers around the quarter.

By the time I was dressed—the two-headed coin in the pocket of my denim shorts where it belonged—Mama had scrubbed all the tears off her pale face and turned the fan on loud in the bathroom, so that there was only the tiniest hint of Daddy's aftershave in the air. She'd washed the sink out, too, so I couldn't see the foam and stubble that appeared there every morning like clockwork.

"You excited to start at your new school?" Mama asked while I dragged a hairbrush through my hair. Every year I was alive, my hair moved further away from yellow and closer to that not-really-a-color that happens to blond hair when it gets bored.

I shook my head.

"Do you have your key to get in here after school is over?"

"It's in my backpack already."

"Good. And you remember which bus number you're on?"

"I'm almost twelve, Mama."

Mama sighed. "I just hate knowing that I won't be here when you're home from school. I don't like thinking about the things that could—never mind. I'm sure you'll be fine."

Every day for the last six weeks I'd been treated to her worries about leaving me alone. *A latchkey kid*, she'd said the day she'd gone full-time at the housekeeping company. *I'm sorry, Annie Lee. I never wanted you to have to fend for yourself like this. I wish there was any other choice.*

Now Mama sighed again, something she did almost as much as crying these days. Sometimes I thought maybe it was just the way she breathed now, like the world was pressing too hard on her shoulders and she could never get a deep-enough breath. "I'm gonna go figure out some breakfast."

She scooted past me out the bathroom door and was gone before I could blink, just like she'd never been there at all.

When I came into the kitchen, she was crying again. Not the regular, sniffly tears that appeared every morning when she got up and found the bathroom smelling so strongly of Daddy he could've left it only seconds before—these were big, shocked sobs that shook her whole body. She was standing with one hand over her mouth, her skin white, staring at the kitchen table.

It was a little table, the only size that would fit into the little kitchen of our little apartment, and it was so old and dinged up that you couldn't even tell what color the stain had been in its old life, before Mama and I had found it during the Independence Day sale at the Goodwill. And on top of it, smelling like sugar and memories, there was a box of old-fashioned donuts from The Hole Shebang.

My daddy had been dead for eighty-three days, and still, somehow, there was a box of the exact same donuts he'd brought home on the first day of every new school year since I started kindergarten, sitting right there on our kitchen table.

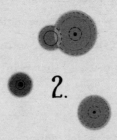

2.

The apartment was quiet and dark when I got off the school bus that afternoon. My phone—the cheapest plastic flip phone that Mama could find at Walmart—buzzed from my backpack with Mama's check-in text. I imagined her paused in the middle of vacuuming, her bubble-gum-colored Mary's Maids polo smudged with dust and sweat, pulling out her phone the second she knew I'd be back.

you get home okay?

yep, I typed back. I'd asked for a phone for what felt like years before Daddy died, but he and Mama had always agreed that I was too young.

But afterward, when Mama had to call her boss at the cleaning company and say that she wanted to work full-time, as many days a week as they had available, she'd given me the phone. *For emergencies,* she'd said. *And to let me know you're safe.* She hadn't even let me give Monica and Meredith my phone number, back when we were friends, because she didn't want them running up my texts.

My phone buzzed again.

good. see you in time for dinner. stay inside. xoxo

I closed it and stuck it into the pocket of my shorts. That was the one good thing about that phone—it was nice and small.

I left my backpack where it was on the doormat and went right back outside, making sure I'd locked the door behind me, my silver fold-up scooter tucked under my arm. I turned my brain off so that it couldn't think about Mama's instructions to stay inside, or how panicky she'd be if she knew what I was actually doing. Mama, who had stayed with me at the bus stop that morning until the bus came, even though I was eleven and not six. Mama, who checked the locks on the doors three times when we went to bed and never let me open the windows in case I forgot to lock them again.

Mama, who'd always been a *little* anxious before Daddy died, but lived in a constant state of terrified these days.

I unfolded my scooter when I got down the wrought-iron stairs of our apartment complex, and hopped on. I didn't worry about scootering through the probably-not-so-safe parts of town by myself, the way I knew Mama would've. I was good at being invisible—I knew how to stay small, so that eyes would slip right past me like I wasn't there at all. If I concentrated hard enough, if I closed my eyes and imagined that I had Harry Potter's invisibility cloak, I was pretty sure I could make myself fade away into the world around me so that my skin took on the look of grass or brick or cinder block. So that nobody looked over and saw Annie Lee Fitzgerald at all.

Invisible people couldn't be seen, and people who couldn't be seen couldn't be hurt. My heart had cracked right down the middle the day that Daddy died, and then cracked all over again when me and Monica and Meredith drifted apart and stopped talking.

I couldn't take any more cracking.

Durham was a big city, one that sprawled out over so many miles that it felt like two or three cities all joined up together. There was a little bit of everything in Durham—shining shopping malls surrounded by new subdivisions where every house had the same floor plan, endless suburbs that stretched out as far as the eye could see, towering glass buildings that glittered in the sun.

And then there was where we lived, Old North Durham, where everything was either old and falling-down or old and fixed up to be trendy. Where Mama and I lived was definitely the first kind of old. The sidewalk I rode down, the one that ran along our road, was broken up and lined with weeds and sagging Victorians wrapped around with chain-link fences. It only took a minute of riding for the houses to disappear and give way to squat auto shops and churches with weather-stained signs and bars on their windows. I rode along our street until it widened and then widened again, and I reached the part of town with cute little coffee shops and imposing office buildings and stores where rich hipsters went to buy groceries.

I stopped when I got to Brightleaf Square. Brightleaf was a mall, but not the kind shoved into the middle of a parking garage and filled with Sears stores and smoothie shops. It was built into a pair of old redbrick buildings with a fancy courtyard between them. Once, when Daddy and I had come here for ice cream, he'd explained where the buildings came from and how they'd been around longer than even Gramps Fitzgerald had been alive.

A long time ago, before there were regular roads or

anything like that in Durham, the whole city was ruled by people who grew tobacco and made cigarettes, Daddy had said, dragging his spoon through his rocky road and licking it off. The whole ice cream store smelled like cream and sugar, which meant it was one of Daddy's favorite places, because he loved anything sweet. *You know. Before D.A.R.E. or anything like that. Before doctors knew that smoking caused cancer. Anyway, all these old buildings around town—they were tobacco warehouses.*

He'd paused then, looking at me with an excited gleam in his eyes, what I always thought of as his Teaching Face. *If you try hard enough, Al, I swear that when you're wandering around this mall, underneath the high wooden ceilings and past the big tree-trunk beams and through the golden light falling from the window glass, you'll be able to catch a glimpse of those olden-day tobacco workers hurrying back and forth to the sound of horses' hooves thumping on the dirt roads outside.*

Now, I hurried past the ice cream shop so I couldn't smell that cream-and-sugar smell, trying to close my heart to all those memories of Daddy that hurt like needles. I stopped a few minutes in front of a shop with curling golden writing on the window that said *QUEENIE'S CUTS* in big letters and *Queenie Banks, Proprietor* in smaller ones. Queenie was inside with one of her employees and a couple of customers, cutting a blond woman's hair with fingers that dipped and dived like jumping fish. It was hard to miss Queenie—she looked the way I imagined a goddess must look, big and beautiful, with deep brown skin and purple-streaked black hair done up in braids.

Queenie was the opposite of the person I'd turned myself into. I didn't think there was a magic cloak in the world that could turn Queenie invisible, and not just because she was what older ladies referred to as "plus-size." You couldn't help *seeing* Queenie, because even watching through the glass of her shop window, love rolled off her in waves. It was there in the way she smiled at her customers, in the way she talked to them in a loud, joyful voice when they were excited and a quiet, comforting one when they looked sad. It was there in the way she hugged them as they left, like they were her best friends.

I touched the ends of my own hair. I'd never had a haircut in a salon like Queenie's; Mama had always cut it in our kitchen, draping me with a purple plastic cape and cutting with slow, careful strokes. Her haircuts looked good, though—she could do cool layering and things like you might see on the cover of *Seventeen*, even if it took her a long time to finish.

Sometimes, when she was done cutting and stood back to look at her work, she'd say, *You know, Annie Lee, way back before I married your daddy, I always used to think I'd like to go to beauty school.*

Why didn't you? I'd asked her once, grumpy at hearing that same story over and over again. *Why don't you just go now?*

Mama had shrugged. *I met your daddy, honey, and then you came along and kept me busy. And besides, Daddy's teaching salary is never going to be good enough for me to stop working part-time for Mary's Maids. I just don't have the time or the energy or the money to do both.*

Would Mama have been like Queenie if she'd gone to beauty school the way she'd meant to? I couldn't imagine her laughing and grinning, the way Queenie did with her customers—Daddy had always been the laughing one in our house, while Mama was quiet and serious. But still, if I squinted hard enough, it was like I could almost see her through the glass there, a black apron tied around her waist.

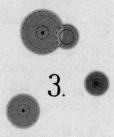

3.

It was while I was watching Queenie that the music began.

It was quiet at first, piano notes floating to me in wisps and whispers that made the hair stand up on my arms. I hadn't heard the sound of a piano in months. After Daddy died, Mama had sold the little upright piano tucked into our living room, along with our house and nearly all the other furniture we'd owned.

When I'd protested that she couldn't sell the piano, Mama had scowled. *You made the choice not to care about the piano a year ago, Annie Lee*, she'd said. *When was the last time you even touched it?*

The music got louder and stronger, until it had wrapped its fingers all the way around me, and without even knowing what I was doing, I'd turned and was following the sound.

I followed it all the way to a shining grand piano, set up in the middle of an atrium near the building's front entrance. At first I thought that there was a skylight, letting in sunlight to pool and dance in the air above it, but then I realized that it was the opposite—the light was rising up off the keyboard, swirling with gold and silver and flecks of other colors, too, like the music coming from that piano was so powerful it couldn't help but burst out of the keys in more ways than one.

I stood still in the shadow of a pillar, just watching and watching, my eyes and ears and every part of me swallowing that music like water.

Music had been one of Daddy's *things*. That was what Mama called Daddy's hobbies, usually in an exasperated voice when she'd tripped over a pile of sheet music or found the kitchen table covered in playing cards and books of magic tricks. *Fitz, you've got way too many* things. *Wouldn't it be better to just take the time to be really good at one thing?*

Daddy always laughed and said that there were too many exciting things to learn in the world to confine himself to just one. Still, music had been a part of him in a way the others hadn't—like it was written into his

DNA as much as his red hair or the light-brown eyes we shared, eyes Daddy always said were the color of the Eno River after a flood. And piano had been his favorite. *Annie Lee, there's only one instrument that can switch in a heartbeat from Bach to John Denver and make them both sound amazing. Only one instrument that can rival a whole orchestra, all by itself.*

He could play a little, and loved to plunk around on our piano, but he'd quit taking lessons when he was a kid and never had the time or money to start up again as a grown-up. It was one of the reasons he'd been so upset when I gave it up last year.

Now, listening to the notes echoing around the wooden rafters, watching the golden lights dancing in the air like music made visible, I shivered. Daddy had never been able to play as well as the man who was hunched over the keyboard, hands moving up and down so fast I could hardly follow them. Still, it was like Daddy was all around me, like if I closed my eyes I could feel his arms pull me close and hear him sing his favorite song, the one he'd named me for—"Annie's Song." Sometimes, when he was in an especially good mood, he'd called me his mountain springtime or his desert storm, after that song.

Part of me, the part that had buried the first-day-of-school donuts in the trash this morning and eaten a Pop-Tart that tasted like dust instead, wanted to run away from anything that felt so much like Daddy, anything that sent the sharp pain of missing him into my heart.

But the music, the lights, held me there.

I'd seen things that couldn't be explained before, of course. There was no way to wake up every morning to stubble in the bathroom sink when nobody had been in there all night and not think *magic* every now and again. But that was a sad kind of magic, while this—this was pure happiness, dancing there above those piano keys.

Sometimes the man played fast and thundery, and then the light above him sparked and spun and turned blue and purple and deep sea-green. But other times he played gentle, so quiet and still that the notes reached right inside me and made me feel calmer than I had in months, and the colors faded and became pure and simple and sweet as the end of a summer's day.

I lost track of how time was moving, standing there watching and listening, the seconds stretched out so thin I could almost see light through them. When the pianist finally stopped, the whole high-ceilinged building felt hushed, like it wished he'd keep on playing forever.

And the piano man was looking right at me. He was old, with a mostly-gray beard and pale skin like the bark on the birch tree by my apartment, as thin and saggy as if it had seen a hundred years of sun and wind. The baseball cap he wore was ripped at the brim, loose threads waving as he moved.

His faded blue eyes looked right into mine. Like he could *see* me, invisibility cloak and all.

"Hi there," he said, and his voice sounded kind of like tree bark too, rough and scratchy. "What's your name, girl?"

My heart gave one enormous *thump*, and before my brain had even caught up with my ears I was turning around and running, running to the glass door and the sizzling August heat outside.

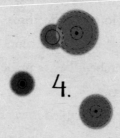

4.

Mama was tired when she got off work that evening, big dark circles painted under her eyes.

"Thanks, baby," she said when I brought her a slice of the frozen pizza I'd stuck in the oven earlier. It was the cheapest one she could find at Harris Teeter, and it tasted exactly like the cardboard it came in. Mama rubbed a hand across her face. "I don't think I'm ever gonna get used to these hours. And I've got laundry to run tonight, too, else you'll be wearing dirty clothes to school tomorrow."

In the other room the television gave a staticky popping sound, and then I could hear the voices of Mama and Daddy's favorite goofy mystery show, the one with the guy who pretends to be psychic to solve crimes.

Before Daddy died, Mama had spent all of Monday running clothes through the washer and dryer, and then after dinner on Mondays the three of us had hauled laundry baskets into the family room and folded everything while we watched TV. It made the chore almost fun, doing it that way.

Mama's shoulders crumpled inward. "That show isn't even on TV anymore," she whispered, her eyes unfocused, like she was saying it to somebody I couldn't see.

Mama and I hadn't talked much about the strange things that had been happening since Daddy died—the shaving cream in the sink, the first-day-of-school donuts, the way sometimes the radio or TV flipped on to Daddy's favorite stations without anyone being near them. Every now and then, the coffeemaker would start its own self up, burbling and clicking as it brewed a cup of Daddy's favorite Panama coffee.

Sometimes I wondered if it meant that Daddy was having just as hard a time letting go as Mama and I were.

We'd both freaked out a lot more there at the beginning, right after Daddy had died, and then again when we'd sold our house and moved to an apartment and the strange things had followed us here. But we'd mostly freaked out by ourselves, in our own separate worlds. And because we didn't talk about it, neither of us had said that word that was always on my mind:

Ghost.

"I'll turn it off," I said now, jumping up and hurrying in to find the remote.

When I came back, Mama had finished her pizza and was loading dishes into the dishwasher, her face as expressionless as if the whole TV incident had never happened. "You mind getting the wash going, Annie Lee?"

I shrugged and went to gather up the dirty clothes from my room and Mama's. Somehow, even though there were two of us left, we only had half as much laundry as we did before Daddy died. Because his clothes were so much bigger than mine and Mama's, I guessed. I missed the feel of his soft button-down shirts, the way they smelled like shaving cream and sugar.

I had just closed the washer lid when the machine started making a weird noise—kind of a grinding, groaning sound, like I'd thrown a wrench into the washer along with the clothes.

"Annie Lee, what's that?" Mama called from the kitchen.

Before I could answer, the washer gave a loud pop and ground to a stop. With a *whoosh*, water flooded the hallway so fast that my feet were wet before I even registered what was happening.

Mama appeared around the corner, her mouth round

and horrified. "Get towels!" she yelled, splashing toward the washer. "I'll get the water turned off."

I ran to the linen closet a few feet away, my wet feet slapping on the linoleum, and pulled out all the biggest towels I could find before running back to spread them across the floor. Mama had the water off and the washer pulled out of its alcove. The whole hallway smelled like burnt rubber.

Mama's fist clanged down on the top of the broken washer. "It's toast. I think. I have no idea, really." She laughed, a sound that was almost like crying. "I don't know how to fix a washer, Annie Lee! I don't even know where to start! We'll be lucky if we can scrounge up enough cash to pay somebody to haul this down to the Dumpster for us. And a used washer would cost more than a hundred bucks! If that life insurance payment doesn't come through soon—"

She stopped, like the alternative was too awful to think about.

I finished sopping up the water; all the towels were soaked and heavy now, not to mention covered in sticky laundry soap. "Where should I put these?"

"The bathtub, I guess. Hand-washing stuff in the tub isn't exactly how I expected tonight to go, but it's not like we have options."

"What about the Laundromat?"

"When would we cart our stuff to a Laundromat, Annie Lee? It's not like I've got oodles of spare time and money lying around. Besides, it costs at least three dollars to wash a load at a Laundromat. It makes more sense to save that money and put it toward a new washer. If we take what we'd spend once a week on the Laundromat and put it into a Washer Fund, we could have a washer in . . . less than a year. Sooner, if we can figure out what happened with the insurance money, though who knows how much longer that will take."

Less than a year sounded like a pretty long time to me. From the way Mama scowled as she did the math, I was pretty sure she felt the same way.

I rolled up the towels and carried them, armful by armful, into the tub. By the time I'd finished, the shirt I was wearing was soaked through. Mama sat in the hallway next to the busted washer, her head in her hands, shoulders shaking with sobs.

If Daddy had been here, even the washer breaking down might have been fun. He'd have cranked "Splish Splash" up on the CD player and tied bath towels to his feet, swishing around in the water and pretending to sing into an invisible microphone. He'd have challenged Mama and me to a water fight, maybe, and even though me and Mama weren't as good as Daddy at being spontaneous or silly, we all would've ended up grinning.

Before Daddy died, Mama had loved the way he could turn anything into a celebration. Even when she was frustrated with him, she had a hard time staying mad too long. Daddy had a way of making her laugh so hard her face would turn red and tears would squeeze out of the corners of her eyes. Sometimes, when Mama was stressed, Daddy would come up behind her and put his arms around her and say, *It's going to be all right, Joanie*, like he was protecting her from the world.

Annie Lee, Mama used to say to me, *someday, when you're looking for somebody to settle down with, you make sure to find a person who makes you laugh.*

Now I stood and watched Mama cry, my arms crossed over my wet shirt. How had one June day changed everything so much?

The Bad Day hadn't just taken away my daddy. It had taken Mama, too. On nights like this, watching Mama cry on the floor beside a washer full of wet, soapy clothes, I felt more alone than I'd ever been in my life.

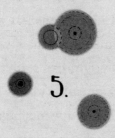

5.

The bus brakes squealed as we pulled into the middle school parking lot the next morning. I sat up, trying to ignore the queasiness in my stomach. Yesterday had been okay—I'd just kept my head down and my invisibility cloak pulled tight—but Tuesday classes were different from Monday classes, which meant that everything was new again today. I rubbed the two-headed quarter in my pocket.

I'd barely made it up the steps and through the front entrance of the school when there was a *whir-thud-scrape* behind me. Some kid nearby screamed and dropped the books she was holding as a freckle-faced girl I vaguely recognized from the bus slid her skateboard right up the railing beside the front steps and landed with a bang on the shining linoleum.

She hopped off the board and kicked it so that it flipped neatly into her waiting hand, all the while looking as careless and unconcerned as if she didn't know that an entire hall full of students was staring at her with wide eyes. The skater girl had a white knit beanie over her wild dark curls. She didn't seem to care that it was August and hot as Hades any more than she cared about the frowning lady teacher who rushed toward her, high heels clicking against the floor.

"What in the—What's your name, girl?" the teacher asked.

"Mitch Harris," said the skater. Her cheeks were pink, but I couldn't tell if it was from nervousness or exercise.

"Congratulations, Mitch Harris," said the teacher. "You just earned yourself a trip to the principal's office."

My eyes followed them until they disappeared down the hallway.

At least my day hadn't started off quite as badly as *hers*.

I got lost on the way to science that afternoon, so turned around I was pretty sure I was going in circles but still couldn't find the classroom I wanted. I was so busy looking at my hall map, trying to figure out where I was, that I bumped right into the skateboard girl from that morning.

"Hey," she snarled. "Watch where you're going!"

"Sorry," I squeaked. A trio of older girls walked past, their arms linked. I stared after them, missing Monica and Meredith so hard that the sadness was a lump in my stomach. Back in fifth grade, we'd walked like that sometimes. If I tried, I could remember just exactly what it felt like to be between them, Meredith's red curls tickling my cheek, Monica telling a funny story about one of the animals her dad had treated at Hsu Zoo Veterinary that made us all laugh.

I hugged my notebook tighter against my chest, like a shield. Even if Monica and Meredith went to this school, it wasn't like the three of us would be arm in arm anymore, anyway.

When I looked back at the skater girl, she didn't look quite so scary anymore. Instead, her expression was thoughtful, her head tipped just the tiniest bit to one side. Up close like this, Mitch Harris was pretty. *Really* pretty. Her whole face was delicate and sweet—pale, freckled skin stretched over high cheekbones that could've belonged to a model, gray eyes, long black eyelashes underneath her frizzy hair. She looked about my age, even though she was taller, and definitely wearing a *real* bra instead of the stretchy-undershirt kind I had.

Up close, Mitch seemed like the kind of girl who

could either rule the sixth grade or destroy it.

"Where are you trying to go?" she asked.

"Science."

Mitch jerked her thumb toward a nearby door. "Me too. You're close. It's right up here."

I was pretty sure this was more words than I'd exchanged with another kid in weeks. Yesterday I hadn't said a thing, and nobody had talked to me, either.

"Thanks," I said, but Mitch had disappeared into the classroom.

I followed and managed to slide into the last seat in the room—a few desks away from Mitch—about two seconds before the teacher stood up and introduced himself. He had wrinkled brown skin and wiry gray hair that made him look old enough to have lived on the earth alongside Adam. Even his eyebrows, bristly as toothbrushes, were silvering. Still, he had enough energy to outdo any of the other teachers I'd met. He never seemed to be still—his feet tapped, his hands fidgeted, he looked like at any minute he might break into a Broadway-style song about how awesome it was to teach science to a bunch of nervous sixth graders.

Daddy would have loved him.

"Afternoon, class! My name is Mr. Barton. Who's ready to explore the wonders of the natural world?"

A few students murmured something halfheartedly.

"Excellent!" Mr. Barton said, not seeming to care. "Now, I firmly believe that the best scientific discoveries arise from dedicated communities of learners! So to begin our semester together, I'd like for us all to get to know one another better. You'll each have five minutes to freewrite about something interesting you did over the summer. When the time's up, I'll choose a few of you at random to read your essays aloud."

"Excuse me, Mr. Barton?" A girl in front of me with sleek black hair and golden-brown skin raised her hand. "What does this have to do with science?"

"As I said, Miss—"

"Kavya Lahiri," the girl supplied.

Mr. Barton nodded. "It's a community-building exercise. But more than that"—he paused for a moment, wiry eyebrows up, and I almost expected him to give a dramatic flourish—"I don't think there's any discipline out there that *isn't* part of the scientific world. For instance, since we're on the topic: writing. What do you do after completing the first draft of an essay, Miss Lahiri?"

"Um . . ." The black-haired girl shifted uncomfortably. "I guess, read it and see if it's any good?"

"Yes! You assess your initial efforts and revise until it's as strong as possible. Much like the process of testing a hypothesis."

"Okaaaaay . . ."

Mr. Barton set an egg timer on his desk and twisted it. "Begin! You have five minutes."

I stared down at the notebook in front of me. How could I write about *anything* that had happened that summer? How could I sit there and write down the story of how my daddy died without warning one day playing pickup basketball with some friends—one second going in for a basket, and the next second crashing to the ground? *Hypertrophic cardiomyopathy*, the doctor had told Mama when we'd made it to the hospital, where Daddy was lying with a sheet over his face. It was a fancy way to say *a disease nobody knew he had until he was dead*.

How could I write about how my two best friends weren't my friends anymore?

How could I write about how Mama sold our house in the suburbs and we moved downtown to a horrible apartment with mice and ants and, now, a broken washing machine? How could I write about the way she hadn't finished washing our clothes in the tub the night before, so I was wearing the same T-shirt and shorts I'd worn yesterday, the feeling of them gritty and gross against my skin?

I'd spent the whole day trying harder than ever to be invisible, so nobody noticed those clothes. I could just imagine the way some kids would stare and whisper things behind their hands. *Look at that Annie Lee. So disgusting. Doesn't she have anything else to wear?*

"I want to see everyone writing," Mr. Barton said, looking right at me.

I took out my pencil and started tracing a spiral on the paper in front of me. Small at first, then bigger and bigger, until it was swallowing my page whole and the edges of the biggest rings floated off the notebook. It was soothing, drawing that line that went on and on, swirling endlessly across my desk. It meant I didn't have to think about anything else at all.

After Mr. Barton's timer had dinged and we'd listened to four different kids tell us about their trips to Disney, he gave us our homework assignment and dismissed us, asking us to hand in our summer essays on the way out.

"Miss Fitzgerald, wait a minute," he called as I tried to slip out the side of the door farthest from his desk. "You're not going to hand anything in?"

"No, sir."

He cleared his throat and stood, coming around the desk. "Is there a reason why you weren't able to complete the assignment?"

I shrugged, looking at my shoes—glittery silver knock-off Toms that had duct tape on the inside where the sole had started to peel away from the top. I needed new ones, but when I'd brought that up to Mama a few weeks back, she'd just pulled her lips into a tight line and said, *We'll see*, which was code for *There's no money for new shoes*. Just like there wasn't money for school clothes that fit, or a backpack that didn't have a big iron-on patch to cover the hole on the bottom, or a washer that actually worked.

Or maybe it meant *as soon as we figure out the life insurance*, because that had become our mantra: every-thing, *everything* was going to happen *as soon as we figure out the life insurance*.

"I hope it isn't inappropriate for me to say, Miss Fitzgerald, that I knew your daddy," Mr. Barton said. It wasn't a huge surprise. Daddy hadn't taught at this school, but he'd been awarded Durham Teacher of the Year once and always arranged slam poetry contests for all the high schools in the district, so lots of Durham teachers knew him. "I was very sorry to hear of his passing."

I wiggled my right toe, watching the way the shiny stuff on the outside of the shoe caught the light.

"Well. I won't make you do this assignment today, Miss Fitzgerald—Annie, right?"

"Annie Lee," I muttered to my shoes.

"Annie Lee. It might be worthwhile to consider seeing the school counselor a time or two. She's a very good listener. And please know that you can come to me if you need anything through the school year."

"I won't," I said, and ducked out of the classroom before he could say anything else.

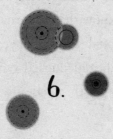

6.

It didn't take long for all my teachers to stop paying attention to me if I turned in my work on time. Most kids didn't notice me, either. Sometimes, getting stuff out of my locker or handing in an assignment after class, I wondered if I really *had* gone invisible. In homeroom, I sat next to a pair of best friends who wore matching necklaces and even had names that sounded alike— Tonya and Shonda. Friday morning I'd dropped a pencil and asked Tonya if she could hand it to me, and she'd looked at me with round dark eyes like she'd never seen me before in her life, even after sitting next to me for five days in a row.

On Friday at lunch, I picked a seat in a corner of the cafeteria next to Juan Diego Herrera and Malik Larson, who were always too busy fake-burping and throwing tater tots at each other to pay attention to anything else, and then I took out my book. I'd been sitting in this exact spot and reading this exact book every day all week long—it was my favorite part of the day, because I could let the whole noisy, smelly room fade out around me and pretend like everything in my life was normal and happy and good.

Today I was reading *The Book of Three*. It was the best kind of book, because it was about a different time and a different place and it wasn't anything at all like my life. It was made even better by the fact that it had been Daddy's, and every now and then I'd come across a little note he'd made to himself in the margins, and the sight of his handwriting would be fire and ice all at once.

I had just gotten my lunch tray situated and opened the book to where I'd left off, where the Assistant Pig-Keeper has run away to find his missing pig, when someone sat down in the empty seat across from me.

"Hey. Reader girl."

It took me a minute to realize that she was talking to me, because nobody had ever, *ever* talked to me in the lunchroom before except to say, "Enjoy your lunch, dear" or "You dropped your napkin," and those had always been adults.

"Well? You gonna answer me, reader girl?" It was the skater girl, Mitch Harris, who'd made such a stir riding her board up the front steps railing on Tuesday. I'd heard plenty about her in the last four days. Like how she'd already racked up three lunch detentions—one for the skateboard stunt and the other two because she'd gotten a bunch of dress code violations for refusing to take off the white-colored beanie she wore over those wild curls, even though indoor hats were against the school rules.

Sure enough, that hat was sitting on top of her hair right now. Had the teachers finally given up?

"Can't you talk?" There were a lot of different accents at this school—people who talked a little bit Southern, like me and Mama; some whose voices carried the memory of Spanish or another language when they spoke; others whose parents had moved to Durham from some other place and spoke in those neutral TV accents that didn't sound like much of anything. Mitch was in the last group, her gruff voice giving no hint about her history.

"Yeah." It was a little mouse of a word, more squeak than anything. I cleared my throat and tried again. "I mean, yeah."

"Huh. Okay." There were sparkly little diamond studs in Mitch's pierced ears. I wondered if they were real. Even before Daddy had died and pressed pause on everything, leaving me and Mama waiting and waiting for that life-insurance payment, we'd never had the money for real diamonds. I was pretty sure even Mama's wedding ring was fake.

"Well," Mitch said, "I'm sitting here today. All the other seats are taken."

I shrugged. "Okay."

"I'm Mitch. You got a name?" Nobody in school knew if Mitch was really the name on her birth certificate, or if it was short for something, or a nickname. I'd heard some of the eighth-grade boys in the hallway yesterday, though, calling her something that rhymed with *Mitch* and laughing like hyenas with a cornered antelope. Mitch hadn't seemed to notice or care, just pushed her way past them like she was tough enough to take all three at once but couldn't be bothered to try it.

A few years back Daddy and I had read *Pippi Long-stocking* together at bedtime, and it struck me now that that was who Mitch reminded me of—she may have been just a girl brand-new to the sixth grade like me, but it wouldn't have surprised me at all to learn she could lift a full-grown horse over her head.

Mitch snapped her fingers in front of my face. "I asked if you had a name."

I started. "Annie Lee Fitzgerald."

"Ooh, fancy," said Mitch, but her eyes were crinkled like she was laughing inside. "Good book?"

"It's one of my favorites."

"So. You read a lot."

I nodded, not sure what to answer. If I said, *My daddy loved books*, it would just open things up to questions I didn't want to answer. So would saying, *I used to sit with my two best friends at lunch every day and we called ourselves the Three Musketeers, but they're at a different school now, and they're not even my best friends anymore, so it probably wouldn't matter anyway.*

I slipped my fingers into my pocket, feeling the comfort of that shiny two-headed lucky quarter, rubbing it with my thumb.

"I read a lot, too," Mitch said.

"Yeah?" Mitch didn't exactly seem the reading type.

"Sure. My mom's a journalist and my dad teaches political science at Duke. Our house is practically *made* out of books. Once my little brother got lost in the office and we didn't find him for a week because the books were stacked up taller than him. A lot of them are pretty boring, though. I mostly like the ones where people die or figure out that magic is real."

I was *pretty* sure that story about her brother wasn't

true, but Mitch said it with such a straight face I half believed her.

"Anyway," she went on, "is there some law against a girl who skates *and* reads?"

"No," I said with a shrug, and Mitch's eyes crinkled up again as she smiled.

I smiled back.

Mama worked late that evening—which meant it was just me all afternoon until after dinnertime, with the stacks of moving boxes that still sat, taped up and untouched, where they'd been put when Mama and I moved more than a month ago.

I finished all my homework but stayed on the computer, scrolling through my news feed, looking at start-of-school pictures from all my old friends: sassy selfies in front of lockers, big posed smiles underneath *Welcome Back* banners. Off in Oregon, where Daddy's only sister lived, my cousins were still on summer break, posting photos of pedicures and writing that they'd slept in till ten in the morning.

My finger paused when it got to one picture—two girls, one with wavy red hair and one with shining black, arms around each other, faces smooshed close together, holding up a package of M&Ms.

Monica and Meredith.

It was Mer's account. *So glad to be starting the year with my BFF*, the caption underneath the picture read. *M&M forever!!!! My drama class is a-MAZE-ing and try-outs for the fall musical will be soon. Eek! Wish me luck!*

I reached forward and pushed the computer's off button, watching as the screen sparked into nothingness.

I lay in bed for a long time after Mama got home, holding a pillow over my ear so that I couldn't hear her crying while she hand-washed clothes in the bathroom. I thought about the man I'd seen at Brightleaf on Monday and the way his hands had flown like birds on the keyboard. That music stayed with me, somewhere deep inside and close to my heart, like it was whispering that if I just looked hard enough, I could find the key to fix all the broken things in my life.

That night, I dreamed about Daddy. He was in a place where the sun and sky sparkled like glass, and dozens of colorful umbrellas—cherry red and popping pink and key-lime green—hung suspended in the sky so that it felt like we were wrapped up in a rainbow. The air itself was full of music, the kind of music the piano man at Brightleaf Square had played, the kind that sank deep into your heart and threaded itself right into your soul.

Daddy sat at a piano, his fingers flying over the keys, colorful light pouring from his hands, just like the man at the mall. The air in that rainbow place smelled like Daddy—like aftershave and Hole Shebang donut glaze and the dusty scent of books.

I watched him for a long time, watched while he played fast and then slow and then fast again, the way he never could play when he was alive, just waiting for him to turn and look at me. I knew that when he did, his face would be filled up with so much love that it would light the world more than that glitter-glass sun and those rainbow umbrellas ever could.

But he didn't turn. Even when I called out to him, shouted his name over and over and over, he just kept on playing and playing some more, like he was all alone in that strange bright place, like he couldn't hear me over the sound of the music he'd always wanted to be able to play.

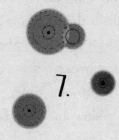

7.

Mama left early the next morning, the way she always did on Saturdays. When she'd first started working full-time, before she'd sold our house in the suburbs and we'd moved downtown, I'd spent most Saturdays and plenty of weekdays too at Monica's house, feeding cockatiels and cuddling with kittens and helping Monica walk their pony-size yellow Lab. Monica's daddy, Dr. Hsu, was a veterinarian, and their house was better than visiting a pet store. They had a bunch of their own pets, and sometimes Dr. Hsu would bring home an animal from the Hsu Zoo Veterinary office if it was in really bad shape and needed around-the-clock care.

On days I wasn't at Monica's, I'd gone to Meredith's.

The two of us would lay on her bed and talk about what middle school would be like and if the boys would be cute while we listened to *Les Misérables* and *Hamilton*. Sometimes, Monica and Meredith and I had all gone somewhere together.

But those days had slowed down to a trickle as the summer dragged on, and then they'd dried up altogether, like the water in the little creek in the woods behind Monica's house.

Now I had Saturdays to myself, and they stretched on and on.

By afternoon, boredom had set in. The apartment was too small, too hot, too unfinished-feeling, and so I got my scooter and locked the door behind me. The apartment next door was open, too, and our neighbor, Mrs. Garcia, was coming out with a bulging trash bag in one hand. Mrs. Garcia was the only other person in the apartment complex that we'd ever really talked to, mostly because she loved to talk to anyone who would listen and also because it made Mama feel better to know that another grown-up was keeping an eye out for me while she was gone. When we'd first moved in, Mrs. Garcia had even offered to let me come over to her place when Mama was gone at work.

It gets so quiet there, Joan, she'd said. *I have to put talk*

41

radio on all day just to make it feel like my thoughts have some company. Annie Lee would be welcome.

Hanging around all day with Mrs. Garcia was about the last thing I wanted. No offense—she was nice enough—but the only thing worse than spending the days by myself while Mama was working would have been making small talk with my elderly neighbor. Lucky for me, Mama had just smiled her tight smile and said, *No, thank you, we'll be fine, but we appreciate the offer.*

The couple of times I'd snuck out in the afternoon before, I had tiptoed past Mrs. Garcia's apartment, praying she wouldn't open her door and ask questions I didn't want to answer. Her offer to watch me was always hovering right there on the edge of my thoughts. I knew that if it came down to leaving me with a neighbor or leaving me to go all over Durham by myself in the afternoons, Mama wouldn't take a hot minute to decide.

"Hi, Annie Lee. You going somewhere?"

"Just for a walk," I said, clutching my scooter. *Please don't ask anything else. Please don't ask anything else.*

"Nice day today," Mrs. Garcia said, looking up at the cloudless sky. She had grown up in Ecuador, and her accent made everything she said sound extra interesting. "Stay safe, *mija.*"

I nodded. As soon as we both got to the bottom of

the stairs and she headed off toward the trash can, I unfolded my scooter and zoomed off as fast as I could, trying not to think about what Mama would say if she knew what I was up to.

You know what the crime rate is in Durham, honey?
You know why they put bars on the shop windows?

Every evening during dinner, Mama would ask me what I'd done that afternoon while she was at work. And every evening, I'd make up some lie. *Just homework. Read a new book, yeah, it was pretty good. Played on the computer most of the time. Listened to music.*

The summer heat was finally slacking off, the sun backing away from the Carolinas and dipping the temperature down into the low nineties, sometimes even cooler on a nice day. There was a breeze in my hair as I rode, the little kind that carried the tiniest hint of the autumn that was still a month or two away here in the South. Brightleaf was busy when I got there—people talking and laughing as they strolled around the red-brick avenue between the two sections of the mall.

But the second I opened the glass door, I couldn't hear anything but the music.

The piano man's fingers were laughing today, tripping in light, funny notes up and down the keyboard—giggles, chuckles, guffaws, the kind of music that had a smile creeping up onto my face before I even realized what my lips were doing. The atrium that had been so empty Monday was busy now. People hurried back and forth, toward shops and restaurants, talking in voices that echoed off the high rafters above us. The glass door on the far side of the space swung open and shut every few minutes, carrying with it the smell of the heat and the restaurant next door.

Mostly, though, people crowded around the piano, smiling just the way I was, leaning forward like if they got close enough maybe the music would swallow them up and remake them as bigger, braver, more beautiful versions of themselves. Some of them had put coins or bills into the piano man's baseball cap, which was upside-down on the floor at his feet.

Nobody but me seemed to notice the lights floating up from the piano man's fingers, winking and twinkling today in pinks and yellows that perfectly matched the laugh of the notes. I'd never seen anything like it. He didn't have sheet music in front of him; the notes poured from his fingers, out of somewhere deep inside. I could've watched him play all day—maybe all night, too—without feeling tired or hungry or thirsty, unable to look away.

On the pillar beside me, a white brochure fluttered in

the breeze made by somebody walking past. I turned my head just a tiny bit to look.

HOLIDAY EXTRAVAGANZA! it shouted in bold-faced capital letters, with smaller ones beneath: *Durham Piano Teachers Association will be hosting its yearly competition December 14. Compete against pianists at your level for cash prizes in performance, accompaniment, and composition. Beginners welcome.*

Underneath, in even smaller letters, the first-place prizes were described. *Junior A and B: $100. Senior A and B: $150. Young Artists: $200.*

On the bottom the paper had been cut into neat little slices that all said *DPTA HOLIDAY EXTRAVAGANZA!* and an email address to send in applications.

Not even quite knowing why, I slipped my fingers up and tore one of those little strips off.

Cash prizes. Beginners welcome.

A hundred dollars could buy a whole winter's worth of clothes that fit. Shoes without duct tape on them. A backpack without a hole in the bottom.

I had started piano lessons when I was eight. Daddy had made a big deal out of it, how I was old and mature enough to learn an instrument. He'd pulled out the record player he'd found at a thrift shop when I was in first grade and played me record after record—Beethoven's

"Moonlight Sonata," Scott Joplin ragtime, a bunch of piano arrangements of songs by his favorite oldies singers. By the end of it, I was just as excited as he was, picturing me and him at the piano together, a golden string of music between us.

But piano lessons hadn't exactly gone that way. I'd taken them for two years, but I'd never gotten to the point where I could play anything as cool as those old records—barely gotten to where I could stumble through "Minuet in G Major" with both hands. I hated practicing, and every time I sat down to play it was like a spiderweb of anxiety spread over my skin, whispering that I'd never be able to make my fingers do what I wanted them to, so I might as well give up trying.

Why don't YOU take lessons instead of me? I yelled at Daddy one afternoon when he was getting on my case about practicing. Daddy could plunk around with simplified piano arrangements a little trickier than what I could play, and of course he'd taken lessons for a while when he was a kid, but I didn't know why he'd stopped.

My words had made him crumple in on himself. He'd sat down next to me on the piano bench and put his arm around my shoulders, planting a kiss on the top of my head. *Al*, he'd said, sounding like an old man, *I've struggled my whole life with following through on things.*

Don't be like me, baby girl, okay?

When I'd quit piano a year ago, right after a recital where I forgot the whole second half of the piece I was supposed to be playing and just sat there on the bench until I finally burst into tears and ran off the stage, Mama had hugged me tight and said it was okay. But later that night, when I was falling asleep, I'd overheard her and Daddy in the kitchen.

I wish she hadn't quit in the middle like that, Daddy had said, and Mama had been silent for a long minute before asking, *Do you mean you wish* she *hadn't quit in the middle, or that* you *hadn't quit, honey?*

Now I closed my fingers around the piece of paper with the competition email address on it and stuck it into my pocket. *Cash prizes. Beginners welcome.*

A minute later, the song filling the atrium ended and the magic lights winked out.

The piano man straightened up, shaking his hands out and then rubbing them, like his hands hurt him. All the smoothness and speed he'd had while playing was gone. Now there was only the pain that I could see sitting on his shoulders, running through his fingertips, and bending his neck. He coughed once, a cough that rattled deep inside him. For the first time, he didn't seem like some wise ancient guy who knew the answer to everything—just like a regular old man who could've been a rougher, scragglier version of Gramps Fitzgerald down in Florida, dressed in clothes that looked like they'd all seen too many trips to Goodwill.

"Real nice, Ray, like always," said Queenie Banks from across the atrium, where she was leaning up against the wall of the hallway with a grin on her face. "Wish Margie could've heard it. She would've loved to hear you play like that."

Ray put a curled, painful-looking hand to his heart. "You and me both, Queenie. Hope you and Elijah will come to dinner at my place soon. Things have been too quiet there lately."

"Mm-hmm," said Queenie. "Let me talk to him and I'll let you know." Queenie gave a little wave before she headed back into her salon.

I was still standing by my pillar when Ray picked up his hat, poured the change inside it into his pants pocket, put the hat on his head, and turned around to look straight at me. Just like last time.

He smiled. It was a nice smile, even if some of his teeth were gray and uneven.

"You again," he said, getting up off the piano bench, slow and steady like his legs and back hurt him. "You enjoy that song? What's your name? I'm Ray Owens."

In that moment, I didn't care about my invisibility cloak. I couldn't think of anything except the way Mr. Owens had played and the way it had felt to listen. Like being back with Daddy again, listening to all those thrift-store records, music knitting us together.

For just that moment, I let that old invisibility cloak fall to the polished floor.

"It was beautiful." I took a deep breath, clutching my scooter tighter. "And my name's Annie Lee."

Before Ray Owens could say anything else I was already halfway to the door. I didn't stop until I was outside and my scooter was open and I was riding, *whir-whir-whir*, along the sidewalk toward home.

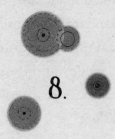

8.

I woke up Tuesday morning to thunder that rattled the windows in their frames. I felt kind of thundery about going back to school, too. Weekends were boring—especially a long weekend, since the day before had been Labor Day, so it had been me at home all day long while Mama worked. But at least then I was able to do my own thing and pretend like I had lots of friends who just happened not to be with me right at the moment.

I didn't think I could take a whole school year of tater tot wars in the cafeteria or watching Tonya and Shonda be best friends in homeroom. It was hard, when I was around the two of them, not to think about how things used to be with Monica and Meredith, when we'd all been in the same fifth-grade class and passed notes whenever the teacher wasn't looking. Meredith had been really good at origami folding, and she'd taught me and Monica how to fold up our notes so that they looked like little pieces of art.

Back then, it hadn't mattered how boring a class was or how stressed I might be about a test, because I could feel that best-friend love filling up the room like a shimmering net that wouldn't ever let me fall too far.

Mama was still sleeping when I got up, which meant that the bathroom sink was filled with shaving cream and ginger-colored stubble, and the whole bathroom smelled so much like Daddy had the morning before he died that my heart forgot how to beat.

Sometimes in these mornings, with the feeling of the ghost all around me, I almost thought I could reach out and find my daddy there, whole and healthy and just the way he'd been in the hours before he'd left for that game of church ball. I'd even opened my mouth once or twice, ready to whisper something, hoping maybe Daddy would hear me if I did. There were so many things I wanted to tell him—so many things that had piled up inside me all summer long.

A few days before Daddy had died, he'd taken me to my favorite park for a picnic dinner. After we finished eating, he'd pulled out his phone and a set of earbuds, and we'd lain on our picnic blanket with one earbud in each of our ears, listening to a Chopin recording with piano notes that went so fast they sounded like the rushing of a waterfall. We lay there until night fell and the lightning bugs came out, winking their lights one after another after another, until the whole world felt like it was filled up with music and light and the warm feel of Daddy's shoulder against mine.

Sometimes I thought the worst thing about Daddy's heart attack was that I'd never gotten a chance to say goodbye.

I brushed my teeth hard, like I could brush away the taste of the memories that were rising up to choke me, and then I washed my face and got out of that aftershave-scented bathroom as fast as I could.

"I don't feel well," I said at breakfast, while Mama scrubbed a couple of our shirts in the kitchen sink before tossing them into the dryer, and I pushed store-brand toasted oat cereal around my bowl. "Can I stay home today?"

"No."

"But—"

Mama came over and put the inside of her wrist against my forehead. Her skin was damp from the wash water. "You're fine. Have you packed a lunch?"

"But—"

"That's *enough*, Annie Lee!" Mama shouted, banging the container of laundry soap onto the counter. "You don't have a choice, okay? School is—school is all you have. You have to go, you have to do *well*, you have to go to high school and graduate and go to college so that you can make yourself a different life than—"

She closed her eyes and took a deep, shaky breath, like she could will herself into being less upset if she tried hard enough. "I want a different life for you, baby. I don't ever want you to be stuck like me, depending on a life-insurance payment that's taking forever to come, okay? Just get ready and let's go down to the bus stop."

We didn't say another word to each other all morning, even when Mrs. Garcia knocked on our door and asked if we had any margarine and stayed for almost ten minutes, telling Mama a story about the time she'd left a whole tub of margarine in her car in the summertime and how it had taken six months to get the sour, oily smell out. Mama tapped her foot while Mrs. Garcia talked, until finally Mama smiled politely and told Mrs. Garcia we *really* had to go or I'd miss my bus.

When the bus came, Mama wrapped one wooden arm around my shoulders and gave me a quick peck on my hair, but I wriggled away after half a second and dashed up the bus steps. I made sure not to look out the rain-soaked window, so that I didn't have to see how her hands swiped at tears.

All my life, Daddy had said that our family was like an orchestra: we all played important roles, we all depended on each other to make our music beautiful.

But if we were an orchestra, Daddy had been the conductor. He'd been the glue that held me and Mama together, and with him gone, I wasn't sure there was anything else on earth that could.

For just a minute, as the bus pulled away from the apartment complex, a traitorous little voice whispered inside me:

It would've been better if it had been her.

I hardly had time to pull my book out at lunch that day before I heard Mitch's voice cutting across the cafeteria chatter.

"Hey. Reader girl."

She squeezed onto the bench next to me, elbowing a belching Juan Diego out of the way. "How come you didn't save me a spot?"

My stomach churned uncomfortably, a whole lot of feelings I didn't really know how to name tumbling around inside me. I was still the tiniest bit afraid of

Mitch—and even more afraid of what it might mean to keep on letting her past my invisibility cloak. Hadn't this summer taught me that liking people just made it harder when they left you?

But even so, there was something tangled up in that mess of emotions that felt an awful lot like hope.

"Sorry," I said finally.

Mitch shrugged. "I figure it's not like either of us has anyone else to sit with. Pretty sure half the student body thinks I might *actually* hex them. The rest just snap my bra straps and call me names."

I was surprised by how breezily she said it, like she was commenting on the weather or asking me to pass a napkin. I didn't think I could ever just *not care* like that.

Mitch leaned down and rummaged in her backpack, popping back up a second later with a book in her hand. She tilted it toward me so that I could see the cover: it was dark blue, with trees and plants and three kids drawn in black, like silhouettes, and *Echo* written along the top in big white letters. "Have you read this one? It's *really* cool so far. Especially if you like music."

"I do. A lot." For just a second, I itched to tell Mitch about Daddy and his records, or Ray Owens and his magic lights. I'd only heard him play twice, but I was already dying to go again.

"Well, maybe I'll let you borrow it when I'm done," said Mitch—and with that, she did the only thing I expected less than her coming to sit by me in the first place: she propped the book open with her tray and glued her eyes to it, reading and eating just the way I always did.

After a surprised minute, I did the same thing. But I could hardly keep my thoughts on *The Book of Three*, even with Daddy's notes in the margin, because my eyes kept sliding over to where Mitch sat. It felt nice, sitting here reading with somebody else. Before June, Daddy and I had done that sometimes, sitting at opposite ends of the couch and sharing a blanket. It always made me feel safe and warm and happy.

Reading with Mitch was a little like that.

Like being with a friend.

I felt my invisibility cloak slip down my shoulders, letting Mitch just the tiniest bit in.

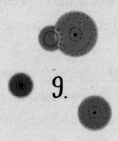

9.

I set my four-dollar bunch of purple chrysanthemums into the little brass vase on Daddy's grave, making sure they were all standing up straight and tall. Mama and I came out here at least twice a month, usually on Tuesday afternoons when she got off work early, but it still didn't feel real, seeing *ROBERT FITZGERALD, BELOVED HUSBAND AND FATHER* written out in fancy lettering across a granite headstone.

"Wish you were here, Daddy," I whispered, touching my finger to the *F* in Fitzgerald. "I need my conductor."

It was weird, talking to him like this. Hadn't I learned my whole life at church that heaven was somewhere far off, out of my reach? But being here, seeing his name written out with a birth date and a death date like his life was wrapped up and closed, I couldn't help it.

At least when I was at the cemetery I had something to talk *to*. It was better than trying to whisper to the ghost at home.

I stood up slowly and stepped back, looking at my bouquet of mums. They were bright, each petal catching the sunlight, the purple deepening and sparkling like a prayer. I thought suddenly about the dream I'd had last week: Daddy playing the piano underneath a rainbow of colorful umbrellas. It was nice to think of him that way, somewhere off in a beautiful place, doing the thing he loved best in the world—even though the memory of the dream was shot through with how much it had hurt when I'd called to him over and over and he hadn't seen me, like my invisibility cloak was too strong, even inside a dream.

"I'm gonna walk around," I said.

"Be safe!" Mama's voice was thin and anxious.

"It's a *cemetery*, Mama. It's *all* safe." What did she think, that somebody would come abduct me in a place where most people didn't even raise their voices?

Maplewood Cemetery was huge, like a little city made of grass and headstones and winding drives. There were sections that went all the way back to the Civil War, graves with little blue-crossed red flags on them to show that a Confederate soldier was buried there. Daddy's grave was in the newer section, where all the headstones were flat and set into the grass, and the green awning that meant that somebody new had been buried was up a lot.

I wandered through the short-clipped grass, over the curving road and toward the woods that hugged the edges of the cemetery. It didn't seem right, thinking of Daddy in this quiet, perfectly-kept-up place. Daddy had been more than the life of the party—he'd been any party's heart and soul. He'd been the one who'd kept our house full of music, who'd made me and Mama laugh. He'd been the one who loved to turn on the radio loud on a Friday night and polka Mama around the kitchen until she could hardly breathe and her face looked ready to crack with smiling.

Even being at home in our lonely apartment, with Daddy's ghost turning Simon and Garfunkel on his thrift-store record player when the place got too quiet, was better than this solemn cemetery.

I took out my lucky quarter as I walked, flipping it over and over in my fingers. Heads. Heads again. And again.

Daddy had been carrying his own luck with him the day he died. How much good had it done him?

I'd made it to the woods when a joyful bark startled me so bad I nearly ran into a tree. There, trotting toward me with its tongue hanging out of its mouth, was a white dog with golden patches and eyes the color of honey on a warm day. It had a collar on, but no leash.

"Hey there, sweet doggy," I said, dropping into a crouch so I could hug its neck. "Where'd you come from, huh? Are you lost?"

"No, ma'am, she's not lost," wheezed a voice from the direction the dog had come from. "She's mine."

I looked up to see someone coming toward me through the trees, a tattered baseball cap on his head.

It was the piano man.

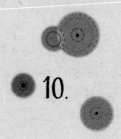

10.

"Hello again, Miss Annie Lee," he said, stepping forward and sticking out a hand so I could shake it. His white skin was dry and scratchy, his fingers covered in calluses. "Remember me? Ray Owens. We met at Brightleaf Square t'other day."

My eyes felt like they'd grown as big as balloons, but I didn't know how to stop staring. I stood up slowly, keeping one hand on the dog's head, the warm softness of her fur was the only thing that made sense right now.

Ray nodded toward the dog. "That there's Clara. Named her after Clara Schumann. You know who she was?"

I shook my head no.

"Probably one of the greatest female pianists who ever lived, that's who. Figured it was a good name for the dog. I got her after my wife, Margie, passed on, to keep me company. She lives over in that cemetery now—Margie, I mean."

"Oh. Sorry."

"Missing people's a part of life, Annie Lee. I expect since you're here, you've got cause to know that."

I looked down at my fingers, still resting on Clara's head.

"I always wanted a dog," I said softly. "My best friend—I mean, one of my best friends—I mean, my old best friend . . . well, anyway, one of my friends' dads is a veterinarian, and their whole house is full of animals. I used to go there all the time to play with them. But Daddy is allergic. I mean, was. And we had to move to a place that doesn't allow pets."

"Your daddy's the one buried here?"

I nodded, swallowing past the thickness in my throat. "He died at the beginning of the summer."

"I'm sorry to hear that, child. You're awful young to carry that kind of burden."

I shrugged, wanting to change the subject. "How'd you learn to play piano the way you do, Mr. Owens?"

"Call me Ray. Don't think I've ever been Mr. Owens in my life. It would be strange to start now." Ray chuckled. "I learned the piano same way anyone ever learns anything—with plenty of practice. I've been playing since I was smaller than you. These days, I can only play so long, though. The arthur won't let me keep going as much as I might."

"Arthur?"

Ray flexed his hands. "Arthur-itis. Been getting bad lately. It always is, when the weather's about to change, and my old mattress don't help any. But I'm grateful to have a roof over these old bones—my house is back that way," he added, jerking a thumb at the woods behind him. "I used to be a roofer, but I took a bad fall and now my joints are too creaky to get up there. Now it's just the tips from Brightleaf and some disability payments that keep me afloat."

"I'm sorry." Money troubles were something I could understand. Everything had been so tight for me and Mama since Daddy died—no new clothes, no working washing machine, just the two of us crammed into an apartment full of moving boxes and ghosts and promises that things would get better when Daddy's life insurance got sorted out.

We'd already had a payout from them. That, plus the Social Security payment you get when your parent dies before they can retire—a tiny one, since Daddy had been so, so young—had covered enough to pay for a funeral, and moving costs, and a week or two of rent in the new apartment before Mama took on more hours at Mary's Maids. But Mama had said at least a dozen times that the insurance payment should've been a lot bigger, should've been big enough that we could have lived on it while she went back to school so she could get a job with better hours, big enough that we could buy me clothes that fit and replace our washer.

Twenty thousand dollars? Mama had said when the insurance check had come, her white skin turning paler than ever. *It was supposed to be a hundred!* She'd gotten on the phone with the life insurance company that day, insisting that they'd gotten the numbers wrong and should've sent us five times as much as they did. The money they sent, Mama had explained, was the insurance money Daddy got automatically for being employed by the school district. But he'd had the option to pay for more, a *lot* more, and they'd decided together when he started at the school that it was worth doing that, so if something ever happened to him, me and Mama would be taken care of for a little while.

But the life-insurance person said they didn't have any record of those payments being made, so he was sorry, but he couldn't authorize any more checks until they got it figured out. Mama had been on the phone about it at least once a week ever since. The first guy had gotten his manager, and then that manager had gotten *his* manager, and then that woman had suggested contacting the school district to get a copy of Daddy's pay stubs, which would give proof that Daddy had bought the bigger insurance policy all those years before. But the school district hadn't been able to find anything like that yet, and so me and Mama were stuck.

"I thank you for your sympathy, Annie Lee," said Ray solemnly. "But even when things are tight, I'm blessed. I've got Clara, and my music."

Just then, I heard Mama calling. "Annie Lee! Annie Lee Fitzgerald, where've you got off to? It's time to go get some dinner!"

"That's my mama," I said, my heart thumping hard. What if Ray tried to introduce himself? There was no way I could explain to Mama the way I'd been sneaking off while she was at work. "I've gotta go. Thanks for letting me pet your dog, though."

I gave Clara one last pat and then turned, running up toward the cemetery, where Mama waited.

"Were you talking to somebody?" Mama asked. "I thought I saw somebody down there. A man. And I heard a dog."

I glanced back, but all I could see where Ray had stood a minute before were a few branches waving in the wind. What was he doing, ghosting in and out of the trees by Maplewood Cemetery?

"It was just me." The lie tasted funny in my mouth, sharp and as sour as the hard candies Daddy used to buy me, the kind that made your face pucker and your eyes water. I'd spent plenty of time lying to Mama about what I did all day while she was working, but somehow this time was different. It was bigger, scarier, because from that very first day Ray had seen right through my invisibility cloak. All the excuses I'd always had in my head about why it was okay for me to sneak out when Mama was at work (*nobody notices me anyway, I keep to myself, I never talk to anybody*) fell to pieces if somebody else noticed me—especially a grown-up. A stranger.

I was smart enough to know that I'd be in trouble if Mama ever knew I sometimes snuck out while she was at work. But if she knew I'd snuck out *and* met up with a strange man who knew my name? That might break her trust in me into so many little tiny pieces that I'd never, ever get it back.

"I don't want you going down that way, by the woods," said Mama, putting her arm around me and herding me toward the car. I squirmed out of Mama's grip and slid into the passenger seat. My heart felt like it was climbing up into my throat at the idea of Mama learning about my trips to Brightleaf Square, about Ray.

Whatever else happened—with the life insurance, with school, with Mama's job—I couldn't let her find out about that.

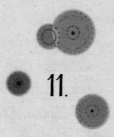

11.

The next morning at breakfast, Mama cleared her throat. "I ran into Carol McBride at the bank yesterday morning. She asked how you were doing. Said she misses seeing you around her house."

I pulled my spoon through the milk in my bowl, the little whirlpool dragging cereal into its depths. One of the things I missed about the Before Time was getting name-brand Cheerios, the kind that didn't dissolve into mush when they hit the milk or taste more like cardboard than honey and nut. My family hadn't ever been *rich*, but before Daddy had died, we'd never bought off-brand cereal.

"I've been wondering about that, myself," Mama went on. "You haven't seen Meredith or Monica in a long time, have you?"

"They've been busy."

Mama sighed. "I guess we have been, too. If I could just find that life insurance! The school district's looking into it for me again." She looked up at me, brown eyes pleading. "Once we've got that, I can cut back my hours a little bit. Go back to school so I can get a better job—maybe even beauty school. Things won't be like this forever, I promise."

I nodded, my eyes drilling into my cereal bowl. My fingers itched to reach into my pocket and rub the quarter, but I didn't want Mama to see.

After the doctor had told Mama and me that they couldn't save Daddy, the ER nurse had given us a little bag with Daddy's clothes and things that he'd had with him when they brought him in. That night when Mama wasn't paying attention, I'd snuck into her room and fished the quarter from the pocket of Daddy's basketball shorts.

Somehow, that quarter was like a symbol of everything my daddy had been—the kind of person who was so sure he could make things go his way that the only coin he'd carried on him was a magic-show prop, one where the only answer was yes.

Keeping it in my own pocket felt like carrying a tiny little part of him with me. And maybe it was selfish, but I didn't want to share that with Mama. Ever since the Bad Day in June, it had felt like Mama had filled our apartment with her tears and sadness and memories. Selfish or not, the quarter was something I wanted to keep just for me. Besides, Mama had packed all Daddy's magic stuff into boxes after he died, planning to sell it on eBay as soon as she had a spare minute.

I sighed, just the way Mama had a minute ago, and put my spoon down. "I think I'm full. Gonna go finish getting ready for school."

I didn't know how to tell Mama about Monica and Meredith. I hadn't talked to either of them in more than a month. What could I even say? We hadn't had a fight, not exactly. Mostly, after Daddy died, none of us knew quite how to act. Their questions about how I was doing had felt like thorns in my bruised-up heart, and when they got excited about starting middle school or talked about what it might be like to kiss a boy someday, I'd been mad at them for forgetting Daddy so quickly.

One day, Meredith had been upset about getting grounded for something she figured was unfair. We'd all been sitting on her bed while she went on and on about how mean her parents were. *Are you even listening right now, Annie Lee?* she'd snapped, and I'd snapped right back that at least she got to *have* both parents, alive and well.

The more time passed, the more it felt like they were in a world I couldn't share anymore.

The world of the M&Ms. Best friends forever.

And slowly, just about as slowly as autumn comes to Durham, they'd pulled away, so that by the time August rolled around it almost didn't matter that I'd moved downtown and that we were starting different middle schools, because I hadn't talked to them in weeks anyway.

I missed Monica, the way she could give hugs that made you feel as loved as you could ever be. I missed her house, the way nothing was ever quiet with all those pets.

I missed Meredith, the way she took up a whole room with her personality, the way she could get on a stage and convince anybody in the world that she was Annie or Dorothy or Cosette.

And maybe most of all, I missed the me that I had been when they were around. I'd never been loud and dramatic like Meredith or fun and funny like Monica— but back then, I'd known how to be *happy*.

Mitch ate lunch with me every day that week, in the corner beside noisy Malik and Juan Diego. Sometimes we talked, and sometimes we just ate in silence, and sometimes she pulled out a book of her own and read alongside me—but she kept on coming.

By that Friday, it wasn't even a surprise when she plopped her tray down by mine.

"So," I said, slurping chocolate milk through a straw, "what's your real name? Is Mitch short for something?"

Mitch scowled, spearing a piece of broccoli with her fork like it was a lethal weapon. I swallowed. I mostly didn't feel scared of her anymore, except when her face looked like *that*.

"Never mind," I mumbled quickly.

"Listen," said Mitch, looking up at me with an expression that could've stopped the heart of a small animal, "because I like you, reader girl, I'll let you in on a secret. Nobody else in the whole school knows this, you hear?"

She leaned across the table, casting a furtive look at the totally clueless kids near us. "Mitch *is* short for something."

"Oh yeah?" My heartbeat started returning to normal.

Mitch nodded slowly, gray eyes round. "Yep."

I waited for a long minute, pushing chicken tenders around my plate.

"But," said Mitch at last, sounding more dramatic than Meredith at her very best, "if I told you that, I'd have to kill you and dump your cold, dead body into the Eno, so my lips are staying sealed."

At the sight of my face, she started laughing. "You should see the look in your eyes right now, reader girl. You should just see the look in your eyes."

And for the second time that month, that long-gone smile inched back onto my face, whispering all the way down to my heart.

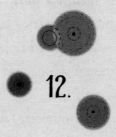

12.

That afternoon, I went to Brightleaf.

I knew it might be a bad idea. Both times I'd gone before, Ray had noticed me—and we'd had a real conversation on Tuesday when I'd run into him at the cemetery. If things kept up like that it wouldn't take long for him, or somebody else, to start asking me where my mama was. And I knew deep down in my bones that if Mama ever found out how I'd been sneaking out, she'd be madder than I'd ever seen her.

But I couldn't stay away.

When I got to Brightleaf Square, Queenie was gone from her salon. The only people inside were one of Queenie's stylists—an older white lady with gray hair cut short and gelled up into a fauxhawk—and the customer she was working with. Queenie herself was in the atrium, leaning against a pillar and watching Ray with one hand up over her heart. I could tell, just from that hand and the way her head tipped to one side like she was drinking the music in, that she felt it as deep down as I did.

"Sorry, sugar," she murmured as I slipped past her, but even Queenie, who noticed every little detail about the people in her salon, couldn't see me right now. I wasn't sure if it was my invisibility cloak or just that the music was impossible to look away from, but I was grateful.

Once, a year or two ago, when I was upset about some test I'd taken at school, tears had leaked out of my eyes before I could stop them and I'd started crying at the dinner table. My hair had fallen forward, waving in front of my face until it was wet with my tears. I felt about as pathetic as I possibly could have been.

But then Mama had reached over from her seat next to me and gently, gently tucked my hair behind my ears for me, her fingers soft and light like butterfly kisses on my face. And somehow, that one little touch had started to heal all that sadness inside of me.

Today, Ray's fingers on the piano were like that— gentle, sweet, slow, so full of goodness and kindness that the notes that came from them were like warm rain. The magic lights swirled and shifted above the keys, silver and gold and a particular shade of rich yellow-brown that was like sunlight through honey.

I reached my hand into my pocket, rubbing my fingers against Daddy's two-headed quarter and the slip of paper I'd been carrying around since I'd been to see Ray play last weekend. *Cash prizes. Beginners welcome.* I watched and listened until Ray's fingers had stilled, and the last echo of the last note had faded away, and the light had winked out and left behind empty air.

"Hello again, Miss Annie Lee," Ray said before he'd even turned all the way around to see me.

"Mr. O—I mean, Ray. Could you—" I said at the same time that Queenie came forward and grabbed Ray's hand and said, "Oh, Ray, you play like you are straight out of heaven."

For a minute all three of us stood, frozen in surprise. And then Queenie looked over and saw me—really *saw* me, this time. "Hello, child. What's your name? Any friend of Ray's is bound to be somebody special."

My face went so red that even my hairline prickled. *Please, please, please, don't ask about my parents.* "Annie Lee," I whispered.

Queenie nodded, her amber eyes looking straight into mine, serious and warm. Her hair wasn't in braids today; it was loose, in crinkly waves that made the purple streaks stand out even more. "I'm Queenie Banks. It's lovely to meet you, sugar."

Ray cleared his throat. "You had a question, Annie Lee?"

My tongue felt thick as a boa constrictor. "Yeah. I mean. Could you teach me? Piano. Can you teach me to play, like you do? So beautifully, and—" I stopped. I wanted to wave my hands at the space above the keyboard where the lights appeared whenever he played, and ask him to teach me that, too, but just the thought of it made me feel hot and embarrassed. Could Queenie see the lights? Would she think I was making them up?

Ray reached down and picked up his baseball cap from the floor beside him; today it had a handful of coins and one lone bill, I guess from people who'd trickled by before I did. He poured the coins into his hand and then shoved them into his pocket. His movements were slow, his fingers clawed and crooked as he pulled them back out of his pockets. I wondered if his arthur was hurting him.

"Your mama around here? She okay with this?"

He and Queenie both looked at me, waiting. My stomach dropped from my middle all the way down to my toes.

"Yeah. She'd be fine with it. She'd be excited! She works near here. At—" I thought fast. Not a restaurant, and definitely not anything inside the mall. And not a gas station, because even though I didn't know if Ray had a car, he might've gone to the convenience store. "She's a housekeeper."

Queenie's face relaxed. "At the hotel?"

I nodded real fast.

"Poor thing. Those are long hours."

She didn't even know the half of it. At least I hadn't had to lie outright. It felt like every lie I'd told this summer was piling on top of me, heavier and heavier.

"How 'bout your daddy?" Queenie asked.

I rubbed the quarter in my pocket. It never, ever got better, having to say those words aloud. It was like ripping off a Band-Aid—no matter how much you prepared your brain for it, it still hurt. "He's dead."

"Oh, Lordy, I'm sorry to hear that," said Queenie, and I could tell from her voice just how sorry she really was. Her *sorry* was different, somehow, from the way other people said it. In June, after the funeral, Meredith had come up to me and wrapped her arms stiffly around my shoulders and said, *I'm so sorry, Annie Lee*, with this face that looked like she was a girl in a play whose best friend's dad had died—hollow, somehow, like as soon as the curtain went down she'd be back to laughing and smiling like normal.

Right in that moment, it had hurt almost worse than seeing Daddy's coffin lowered into the ground. How could my whole world have shattered, and Meredith didn't even know how to look for-real sad?

Queenie knew. I could see in her eyes that she understood a thing or two about the kind of sadness that could split you in two. "I expect that's been hard on you and your mama both," she said.

"Yeah." There was something about Queenie, with her warm voice and her scent of hair spray, that made it easy to tell her things. "You'd like Mama. She used to want to go to beauty school. So she could cut hair. Like you."

The surprised grin on Queenie's face was like the sunrise. "You don't say!"

"Yeah."

"Well, I'm real glad to have met you, Annie Lee." She reached out and gave my hand a little pat. Her dark-brown skin was warm and soft. "If Ray here agrees to give you lessons and your mama needs somebody to vouch for him, you tell her to come stop by and say hello. I've known Ray almost two decades, and he's one of the finest, gentlest human beings I've ever had the pleasure to spend time with."

"Queenie's who got me this volunteer gig in the first place," Ray interjected.

Queenie laughed. "Pure selfishness, I promise. I just liked the idea of being able to hear his glorious music while I was working. This man's got more magic in his little finger than most people have in their whole bodies."

Ray shook his head, putting the baseball cap on. "Y'all are such flatterers, my head will get too big for this hat if you don't stop."

"Good," Queenie said, then leaned in and kissed his cheek. Queenie liked to touch people, I could tell. I wondered what it would feel like for her to wrap her arms around me in a hug.

"So—will you teach me?" I asked Ray again, as Queenie hurried back to her shop.

"Hmm." Ray looked at me for a long minute.

My fingers snaked into my pocket to rub the quarter, and I imagined my daddy saying, *Sometimes it pays to carry your own luck, Al.* Wasn't that what I was doing, right here and now? If I could learn to play like Ray, maybe it would be a little like bringing my daddy back. It would make me feel close to him. Certainly closer than when I went to Maplewood Cemetery to put chrysanthemums on his grave.

And maybe, just maybe—

Cash prizes. Beginners welcome.

"All right then," said Ray, putting the cap on his head. "What day do you want to do 'em? I still gotta have time for playing myself, since it's close to all the income I've got. But if you tell me what day works for you, we can figure it out."

"Um," I said, panic rising in my throat. I hadn't even thought about a schedule when I'd asked him my impulsive question, but he was right; when I'd had lessons with my old piano teacher, they'd always been on the same day at the same time. Still, how could I sneak off to Brightleaf at the exact same time each week without Mama noticing something was up, or Mrs. Garcia asking too many questions about where I was going? It was hard enough getting past her apartment now without her popping out to say hello or ask me what I was doing. It would be worse if she could tell I was always gone at the same time, since anything she said to Mama about my regular appointment could destroy my whole house of cards.

And if Mama figured out what I was up to, I could kiss my lonely afternoons goodbye. It would be me and Mrs. Garcia every day until Mama got off at dinnertime.

"Yeah?" Ray prompted.

"Could we maybe, like, change up the days?" I said, my thoughts racing. "Sometimes I have, uh, school projects I have to work on in the afternoon. And Mama's shifts aren't always the exact same. If things are slow at the hotel, she can't pick up any shifts. And sometimes she covers for other people if they need, so she can earn extra."

"All right, I guess we could make that work. How 'bout each lesson, we'll figure out when to meet the next week. We could start tomorrow. Does your mama work Saturdays?"

I nodded.

"What time does she start?"

"Um—nine," I said, hoping that sounded like a realistic time for a person who worked in a hotel to start at.

"You meet me here tomorrow at nine, then, Annie Lee, and we'll dive in."

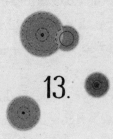

13.

Ray was at the piano when I got there the next morning. Even that early, the atrium was filling up with people. This morning the music was the kind that made your feet itch to dance. All around the piano, people clapped their hands in time and smiled at each other, and I didn't think I'd ever in my life seen so many people looking so *real*, like all their secret armor was down and only their truest selves were left.

Maybe Ray did that to everyone, saw right past the invisibility cloaks we all pulled around us.

The magic lights rising from Ray's fingers sparkled blue, like sunlight on a lake on a summer's day. I stood hugging my folded scooter to my chest while he finished. He didn't hurry—he let the song go and go as long as it wanted to, getting bigger and then smaller and then bigger again, finally thundering down into the bass notes for a grand finale before he played one last sharp, crackling chord and lifted his hands off the keys like they had wings.

The clapping turned from rhythm to applause. People were laughing, rushing up to fill his cap with change. Ray stood and turned to face his audience, his gnarled hand on his heart.

"Thank y'all very much," he said. "I've got to go now, but I sure do appreciate your time."

He hadn't once looked at me yet, but I knew he could feel me there just as surely as I could feel Queenie down the hall, cutting hair in her big-windowed shop and calling people honey and sugar. She'd waved at me as I'd walked by this morning, and I'd been split down the middle between anxiety that she'd find a way to unwind all my lies like a cat with a ball of yarn, and happiness that she knew who I was.

Letting people see past my invisibility cloak meant they could hurt me. But I guessed it meant they could love me, too. I still wasn't quite sure which was most worth it.

"That was amazing," I said when Ray came over, leaning on a wooden cane.

Ray's grin stretched wider. "Thank you, Miss Annie Lee. That means a lot to me. Now, you ready to start learning?"

I looked around at the atrium, feeling the airless anxiety you get right before a test. Most people hadn't lingered after Ray finished—they'd disappeared into shops or restaurants, or left through the glass doors into the heat of outside, where I could hear laughter and chatter and the sound of a guitar being strummed in the brick-lined courtyard between the two buildings. But still, it felt like anyone could walk by at any time. What if I sounded awful? I hadn't touched a piano in more than a year.

Maybe I hadn't quite thought this lesson idea all the way through.

Ray looked at me steadily, the birch-bark skin under his eyes sagging sympathetically. "I promise, child, nobody pays much attention to this old piano most of the time—I should know."

"You're sure?" I squeaked.

"Sure as sure."

I rubbed at the quarter in my pocket, my fingers brushing up against the paper I'd stashed in there, too.

Cash prizes. Beginners welcome.

I thought of the way the washer had dumped water all over the hallway on the first day of school, the way my clothes had smelled a little funny ever since, like Mama's sink-washing wasn't ever quite as good as the real thing. Yesterday in gym class, a girl had looked sideways at me and wrinkled up her nose. I'd never been so aware before of the way I smelled, of how even though Mama had washed it the night before, my T-shirt smelled of sweat and the laundry detergent Mama hadn't been able to quite rinse out.

Maybe that prize money could even buy a new washer.

"Okay." I slid onto the piano bench. I'd have to pull my invisibility cloak extra tight, if I wanted to keep being overlooked while I was practicing out here.

"Your mama already gone to work? I figured she'd bring you today."

"Oh, uh—no, she had to get in early today. Maybe another time, though."

"But she'd be okay with us having a lesson, even without her here?"

The real answer would be *definitely the heck not*, but I nodded anyway.

Ray shuffled back to the piano, walking with a funny sort of rolling high-step-low-step action, his cane clicking against the shining floor. He sat down on the opposite end of the bench and sighed heavily. "Got the arthur in my hips, too. I tell you what, Annie Lee, getting older is for the birds."

I thought about Daddy, how he'd never be an old

man with skin sagging into papery wrinkles.

Ray coughed. "I guess I should start by asking you if there's anything you already know."

"I took lessons for a while. My daddy really, really loved music. I can read music okay, and I used to be able to play with two hands at once. But it's been a long time. We don't even have a piano anymore." I paused, then rushed on before I could chicken out. "I've never seen anyone play the way you do. The way your music makes those lights appear."

Ray's eyebrows shot up. "Oh? You can see those, huh?"

"Yeah. They're real, aren't they? Why can't everyone see them?"

"Oh, they're real, Miss Annie Lee. But I don't know why some people can see them and others can't. It isn't something I control—people seem to see them when they *need* them most."

"Can you . . . can you teach me to play like that? With the lights?"

Ray pursed his lips. "I can certainly try. But really, that's up to you. The lights come from in here." He tapped a curled hand to his chest. "That magic, it comes from honesty, Annie Lee, from letting people see who you really are inside."

I swallowed. "I don't know if I can do that." *Invisible people can't be hurt.*

"We'll work up to it. For now, let's start with this." He pointed at the keyboard, with its bright ivory and gleaming ebony keys. "I'm guessing you know the names of the notes."

I nodded.

"Then you know that the black keys are special. They're how you find your way around the keyboard. There's more to black keys than geography, though. They've got a secret. Any combination you play on those black keys, if you keep away from the white keys, it's going to sound great."

He put his hands on the keyboard and played something short, a few seconds of music that sounded like it should have a sax breathing behind it and be played in an elevator.

"Now it's your turn," he said, looking at me with an encouraging smile.

I balled my hands up in my lap. "I can't play that!" Nothing I'd ever done in two years of piano lessons with a gray-haired lady named Mrs. Kline had prepared me for anything like what Ray had just done. I couldn't just make things up and expect them to sound okay. Before I'd quit, I hadn't even been able to make things sound okay after practicing.

A familiar tickle of anxiety spread itself over me, starting at the top of my head and working its way down. I was starting to remember exactly why I'd quit piano lessons. But I thought of the sadness on Daddy's face when I'd told him I wasn't going back to Mrs. Kline.

Maybe even though Daddy was gone, this was my chance to reach out for him just the way the ghost in the apartment reached out to me. Maybe this was my chance to have that golden string of music connect us one more time.

"Well, no, you can't play *that* song," Ray said. "That was *my* music. But go on, child, play me some of yours."

"I don't *remember* any music! Shouldn't we be starting with something like scales?" Mrs. Kline had loved scales and made me learn new ones each week. They were boring, but not as scary as the real music. It was harder to play the wrong note when you started with scales.

"Sure, scales are good to know. But the most important music comes from inside you. And you don't need scales to figure that out."

I reached a hand out, tentatively, and played one black note and then another. They were harder to press down than I remembered, like they were waiting for my fingers to get serious, and once I finally did get them all the way down, they were loud and ugly. I put my hands back in my lap, fast. There was no way I could stay invisible out here in the atrium if I was making sounds like that.

I had to keep my playing small, quiet, the kind of thing that could fade into the background.

"I'd rather start with scales," I said, not looking up at Ray.

Ray was quiet for a long minute, then nodded. "All right, Miss Annie Lee. Scales it is."

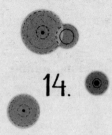

14.

Mama's hands on the steering wheel were tight. Ever since Daddy died, Mama was scared of everything—driving, leaving me home alone while she went to work, the big high school boys who thumped basketballs on the court outside our apartment complex. It was like Daddy's heart stopping in the middle of a game of church ball had filled her up with fear that absolutely *anything* could be dangerous, maybe even deadly.

Sometimes, the way she'd look at me with her mouth pulled together and her eyebrows down, I thought maybe she was even scared of me.

We were on our way to Harris Teeter the day after my piano lesson. Before Daddy died, grocery shopping was a regular thing: Mama would go to the store every

Monday morning after I'd caught the bus to school, buying exactly as much food as we needed for seven days of breakfasts and lunches and dinners.

These days, like everything else, it was different. We went grocery shopping whenever we ran out of food and had enough money, and whenever Mama had enough energy. Since Sundays were the only day Mama didn't work for Mary's Maids, that meant it was usually Sunday.

It always gave me a little twist of discomfort behind my belly button, because I knew it would've made Daddy sad, us being at the grocery store and not at church. But Mama hadn't been able to step foot in that building since the day she got the call from the paramedics. She'd never said so, but I knew it was because too much of Daddy lingered there. Like the walls and floors and ceilings of that church building had held on to wisps of the moment when Daddy's heart had stopped working, and they couldn't let go.

At the beginning, right after it had happened, our doorbell had rung over and over with church ladies bringing casseroles and cookies and hugs and making Mama and me promise to call if we needed anything. Now, though, the stream had trickled off to a call or two a month, an anxious church person on the other end asking please, please, wasn't there something they could do, and Mama always saying, *No thank you, we're fine.*

Mama turned the car into the store parking lot careful and slow, like any sudden movement could make us roll right over into the roadside ditch, and then pulled us into a parking space so far away from any other cars it might've been on the other side of the world.

I slouched out of the car. Grocery shopping was boring, and I would rather have stayed at home (or even better, run off to Brightleaf and practiced some of the things I'd learned yesterday, the way my fingers were itching to do). But since it was the one place Mama went where I could come, too, she always made me.

"So," said Mama as we walked into the store. Without Daddy here to be the bridge between us, every conversation with Mama felt like a walk uphill. "What have you been doing while I've been gone this week, Annie Lee?"

"Nothing," I mumbled. "Just homework. And stuff."

Mama's mouth pressed into a pale little line against her skin.

We were heading toward the milk section when we saw them. I tried to slink back behind a display of canned beans, but I wasn't quick enough.

"Annie Lee?"

Dr. Hsu was smiling the way he always did. Even though I'd spent plenty of time at his house and seen him wear all kinds of things, it always seemed strange to see him wear a regular T-shirt and blue jeans, like a normal dad—they looked like somebody else's clothes, like he should only ever wear a button-up shirt and his white vet's coat with *Hsu Zoo Veterinary Clinic* written in blue letters.

Monica and Meredith were behind him, their arms linked together, Mer's pale freckly skin blurring into Monica's sandier gold. They were laughing at the tank of huge, gangly lobsters who were all fated to become somebody's dinner. Monica and Meredith hadn't seen me yet.

"It's been so long since you've been over to our place," Dr. Hsu said. "We've missed you. Right, Monica?"

The M&Ms looked up now, their faces frozen into identical expressions of guilt and awkwardness.

"Yeah," Monica said finally, the word skinny and quiet and easy to spot as a lie.

I had met Monica on the first day of kindergarten. I'd cried so hard when Daddy dropped me off that morning that I could hardly see out of my puffy eyes. Even six years later, I could remember exactly how lonely and scared I'd been, and how excited I was when Monica came over to my desk and asked in a no-nonsense voice with the tiniest bit of a lisp, *Will you be my best friend?*

Every time we went out to recess that day Monica held my hand, like she knew how much I needed somebody to hold on to in the swirl of strange kids and new rules I didn't understand.

Monica and I had been best friends for two years, and when Meredith moved to Durham when we were all in second grade, the three of us had snapped together like Legos. We were all different: Monica was funny and outgoing and kind, perfect at taking people under her wing, just like she'd done with me on that first day of school. Meredith was dramatic and emotional, the kind of person who was either *entirely happy* or *devastatingly sad*. She liked using words like "tragical" and had had her sights set on Broadway since the first time her mom took her to a community production of *Beauty and the Beast*. I was quieter, calmer, the one who listened to all of Monica's and Meredith's big plans and then suggested ways to actually make them work.

You're like the glue, Annie Lee, Monica had said once when we were all sitting on her porch swing. We'd been eating Creamsicles—Meredith had a line of orange ice cream stuck to her top lip, and Monica was breaking off bits of hers to feed to the cockatiel on her shoulder. *You're the one that keeps us all together.*

Until that day in June when Daddy's heart had

stopped, and it turned out the M&Ms didn't need me to hold them together, after all.

"How are things, Joan?" Dr. Hsu asked now, his smile disappearing into the kind of concerned look that Mama and I had brought out on everyone's faces ever since Daddy died.

"Oh, we're doing fine. We've had some trouble with Fitz's life insurance, but otherwise we're not too bad."

Somehow I didn't think that *not too bad* meant *I cry all the time and our apartment is haunted*.

I reached over and tugged on Mama's hand where it was holding the cart. "We need to go get our milk," I said through my teeth, looking anywhere but at Monica and Meredith. Behind them, the lobsters scuttled along the bottom of their tank, their antennae waving. I wondered if it made them mad, being put in there with a bunch of other lobsters when their claws were tied up with rubber bands.

"Well," said Mama, her voice even brighter, "I guess we'll see y'all sometime soon. Take care, and say hello to Jenny for me."

Dr. Hsu nodded, and Mama finally let me drag her off toward the milk.

"That was rude, Annie Lee," she scolded under her breath when we'd gotten a little ways away from the

Hsus and Meredith. I didn't say anything, just picked out a gallon of milk and plopped it into the bed of our cart.

"I mean it," said Mama. "I understand that you've been through a lot this summer, honey. You and me both. But that's no cause to be unkind. You can't let the way you're feeling dictate the way you act."

She was one to talk, with all her tears and the way we hardly spoke at home and how scared she was of everything on God's green earth.

Mama sighed, and when she spoke again her voice was still quiet, but this time it was sad instead of mad. "You know what, Annie Lee, some days I worry that when your daddy died, he took with him whatever it is that you and I need to carry on an actual conversation."

I picked up a box of margarine and held it until my fingertips went numb from the refrigeration.

Sometimes, I worried the exact same thing.

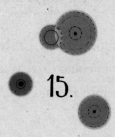

15.

"Hey! Reader girl!"

It was the Thursday after Mama and I had run into the Hsus at Harris Teeter, and Mitch was running toward me across the bus lane, her dark curls bouncing. "Save me a seat!"

I hurried up and slid into a seat near the front of the bus, rubbing my two-headed quarter while I waited.

"Hey." Mitch slid in next to me.

"Do you ever take that hat off?" I asked, looking at her beanie.

Mitch shrugged. "Sometimes. If it gets too hot. But I dunno, I like wearing it. It's my uniform, I guess. Or maybe my armor. So, hey. Your mom works, right?" I nodded. "Want to get off at my stop today?"

I squeezed the quarter in my shorts pocket, till I could imagine the pattern of the ridges imprinted against my skin.

"I mean," Mitch looked down at her feet. "You don't have to. But my mom could drive you home."

"Yeah," I said before I could chicken out. "I mean, yeah, I would."

"Cool," Mitch mumbled, still looking down at her Chuck Taylors, but I could see a little smile sneaking its way into the corner of her cheek.

"Who is this again, Annie Lee?" Mama asked when I called to get her permission. "A boy? Mitch?"

"Oh my gosh, Mama," I said into the phone as quietly as I could, my face flaming so red it hurt. "No. Mitch is my friend from school here. *She* eats lunch with me every day. She's really nice."

"I don't know, honey." I could practically see Mama chewing on her lip, squeezing her hands together till the knuckles turned white. "I don't know if I feel okay letting you go off with somebody I've never met . . . how could I even know what her parents are like?"

"We'd just be at her house the whole time. Her mama and daddy seem real nice. They're professors and stuff."

Mama was quiet for a minute. "She there on the bus with you right now, honey?"

"Yeah."

"Can you put her on for a second?"

I groaned and covered the microphone with my hand. "She wants to talk to you," I said to Mitch, *still* blushing. "You don't have to if you don't want to. She's kind of a worrier."

Mitch took the phone from me and put it to her ear. "Hi there, Mrs. Fitzgerald," she said, and her voice sounded like she was getting ready for some kind of fancy party, it was so polite and not at all gruff like normal. "Yes, ma'am. Of course. Yep. My daddy works at Duke. My mama's a journalist, though. Yeah. My grandma lives with us, too. Mm-hmm. One little brother."

I listened to the one-sided conversation, chewing on my own lip, till Mitch finished and handed the phone back to me.

"You text me if you want me to come get you, no matter what," Mama said, and though her voice sounded worried still, there was a little bit of hope, too, like maybe I wasn't the only one who was excited that I had found a friend.

Mitch's family lived in a green, tree-lined checkerboard neighborhood near Duke campus—the kind of place where the lawns were all mowed and the turn-of-the-century houses were fixed up and shining, not falling to pieces like they were on my street. Her house was tall and made of brick, the kind of place you'd see in a fairy-tale book, where a princess slept surrounded by roses.

I tried not to stare as we went up the sidewalk. Compared to me and Mama, Mitch's family might as well have been Bill Gates's.

"Mom! I'm home!" Mitch shouted as soon as we'd banged in through the front door.

"Okay," a voice echoed from somewhere down the hall.

"Her study," Mitch said, pointing at one of the closed doors. "Usually she tries to be done by the time I get home, but today she's hot on a new article and can't pull herself away. My grandma's around here somewhere, though, and—"

Before Mitch could finish talking, a brown-haired streak in a red shirt shot toward her, barreling into her stomach and wrapping its arms around her.

"Oof. And this is Jacob," Mitch finished, hugging the little boy back. He had high cheekbones and freckles, just like Mitch. "The human torpedo."

I smiled, wondering what it would be like to have a little brother who liked me enough to run at me like that the minute I got home from school. Meredith was an only kid like me, and Monica had two sisters, but the three of them all drove each other crazy.

Mitch unstuck Jacob's arms from around her waist and let her backpack drop to the floor with a *thunk*. It tipped and hit her skateboard where it was leaning up against the wall by the door, sending the skateboard sliding down and crashing onto the gleaming hardwood so loud I jumped. Mitch's skateboard was infamous—it had been banned from school ever since that first trip to the principal's office.

"Micheline Adele!" A wrinkled old lady, whose hair was tied back by a leopard-print bandanna that matched her shirt, puffed down the stairs, her eyebrows way up almost to her hairline. "You trying to give an old woman a heart attack?"

Micheline? I mouthed, and the fire in Mitch's gray eyes could've lit up all of Durham. It wasn't like I would've told, though—even if Mitch hadn't been my only friend in the world, I would've been too scared of what she'd do to me to dare breathe a word about it to anyone.

Still, the name tickled around inside my mouth, and I had to work hard not to grin. *Micheline*. It was a little like *Michelle*, except that the *een* on the end made it sound like it was a name that belonged somewhere with lacy tablecloths and *escargots* and oozing French accents. I was pretty sure I had never heard a name that was more girly, or less Mitch-like.

"Tell anyone, you die," Mitch whispered as her grandma made it to the bottom of the stairs.

"Eternal secrecy," I whispered back.

"Well," said Mitch's grandma once she was at the bottom, her hands on her hips, "are you going to introduce me to your friend?"

"Yeah, Nana," Mitch said in a long-suffering kind of way, "this is Annie Lee."

Nana put out a hand and shook mine, her pink fingers squeezing tight enough to make me think she couldn't really be as old as she looked. "Pleased to meet you, Annie Lee. I'm Micheline's daddy's mama. You can call me Nana or Mrs. Harris, 'specially since that daughter-in-law of mine didn't see fit to take my son's name when they got married." She sniffed like she was full of scorn, but her eyes twinkled with laughter.

"Nice to meet you, too," I said. I wiggled my toes in my taped-up silver shoes. Mitch's entryway wasn't spotlessly clean or fancy—dirt-covered shoes sat haphazardly around the door, and the skateboard had left a streak of mud on the warm-honey wood floor, but underneath all the day-to-day mess of a big family, it was so much nicer than anywhere I'd ever lived that the whole place seemed to whisper *poor girl, poor girl, poor girl.*

No life insurance check would ever make it so me and Mama were living like Mitch's family.

"I hope you girls are going to spend some time on your homework!" called the disembodied voice from Mitch's mama's office.

Mitch rolled her eyes. "Yep!" she called back, but then in a normal voice she added, "But not yet. We're going outside, Nana." Mitch rubbed Jacob's head until his hair stood straight up, and then leaned down to flip her skateboard up into her hand. "C'mon, Annie Lee, want to learn how to be cool?"

"Uh—" I said, but Mitch was out the door and on the sidewalk already, motioning for me to come.

"You," she said, setting the board on the ground and pointing to it. "There. One foot forward, one foot back, like this."

"Are you sure?" I asked, because all I was sure of was falling on my butt if I tried to get up on that thing.

Mitch gave me a don't-make-me-tell-you-twice look that made her transform right into her grandmother, and I swallowed and put one foot up on the sandpaper surface of the skateboard.

"Good," said Mitch. "Now the other, nice and slow.

You can hold on to my arm if you need. The main thing is you have to keep your knees bent so your center of gravity stays low."

So slowly that the grass might've grown faster than I moved, I pulled my other foot up after the first, leaning hard on Mitch. The skateboard rolled a little, but she was right: as long as I stayed still and kept my knees bent enough, I didn't fall.

"See? You got it!" Mitch crowed, and a split second later she'd shaken my hand off her arm and reached out and given a good hard *push* on the skateboard that sent me rocketing down the sidewalk.

I might've screamed, or let out one of those cuss words I'd heard Mama shout every once in a while when she stubbed her toe, or even hollered Mitch's real name to the whole dang neighborhood—but all the air had been sucked right out of my lungs by shock, and all I could do was keep my knees bent and pray and think about how I was gonna kill Micheline Harris just as soon as I got off that death trap.

But to my surprise more than anyone else's, by the time the skateboard had swerved into the grass and I'd stumbled free and just barely managed to keep myself from spread-eagling onto the pavement, I was laughing. Real, deep, belly laughing, the kind that makes tears pop up at the corners of your eyes, the kind that feels like it's never going to stop and that's okay because you don't want it to. I laughed so hard that I sat right down on the lawn and kept on laughing.

"You are the weirdest girl I've ever met," Mitch said, stalking forward to stand over me with her arms crossed.

But I'd learned enough to know that in Mitch language, that was as good as saying *I like you a lot* or *Thanks for being my friend*, and so I didn't bother to stop laughing.

I just let that laughter fill me up, all the way down to my toes, the way the sun comes up in the morning and fills the whole sky with brightness, till I felt lighter and happier than I had in a long, long time.

And when Mitch tapped her foot and pursed her lips, I just kicked my legs out and knocked her off-balance so that she toppled into the grass next to me, laughing her squeaky-door laugh, too.

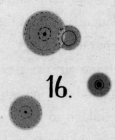

16.

That floaty, light feeling lasted all the way until Mitch and her mama—a nice lady with Mitch's curly hair and a no-nonsense voice, who liked to use words like *predilection*—drove me home and I stepped into the apartment.

It was gloomy, the curtains closed and all the lights off, which meant that Mama wasn't home yet. But that wasn't what I noticed as soon as I put my foot in the door.

What I noticed was that Daddy's old record player was whirring like there was a record inside it even though I knew for sure it was empty, and James Taylor was singing sadly about how he was gone to Carolina in his mind.

Daddy's music.

Before I'd so much as gotten the rest of my body inside the door, that song had reached right inside me and squeezed so that I couldn't even swallow.

They say that when you're about to die, your life flashes in front of your eyes. This was like that—I could see images like ghosts all around me, times that Daddy had let me stand on his feet when I was little and danced me around the kitchen of our old house, or hummed along to the car radio, or sat at the piano picking out the notes to "Annie's Song" and singing, *"You fill up my senses, like a night in a forest . . ."*

Except it wasn't *seeing* so much as it was *feeling*, feeling it so strongly all the way through to my bones that I could have reached out my hand and it would've met Daddy's big warm one.

"Annie Lee?"

I startled, blinking like I was waking up from a dream. Mrs. Garcia was standing on the landing next to me, her face wrinkled up in concern. "You okay, *mija*?"

"Uh. Yeah. Fine. I just was remembering a homework assignment I gotta go do. See you!"

"Let me know if you need anything!" Mrs. Garcia called as I bolted inside.

"Yep!" I closed the door behind me with a quick snap and went right to the record player and pulled the plug.

James Taylor stopped midsentence, and only silence

was left, holding me tight, its arms wrapped around me like it wouldn't let me go no matter what I did.

That night I had the dream again.

I was back in the rainbow-umbrella place, my senses filled up with the smell of my daddy and the sound of his piano—playing "Carolina in My Mind" this time, just like the record player had been when I'd gotten home from Mitch's house. He looked strong and happy, his red hair catching the glittery sunlight and making his skin glow, so that he seemed almost like one of those Greek gods that we'd studied last year in school.

I reached into my dream-pocket, but the quarter wasn't there, so I just twined my fingers together instead. How could he look so happy, so *all right*, without me and Mama there by him?

After last time I was afraid of what would happen if I opened my mouth and called out to him, but I did anyway.

"Daddy?" My word hit the sparkling air around me and sizzled. But Daddy stopped playing and turned around anyway.

"Al?" He squinted, like I was standing in front of the sun, like he couldn't quite make out where my edges began.

I'd spent three months wishing every single day that

I'd had a chance to say something to my daddy before he died. To tell him that I loved him, that I needed him. To tell him that being without him to bridge the way between me and Mama scared me. To beg him to stay, stay, stay.

But here, in this dream, with Daddy in front of me at the shining black piano and the air that smelled like aftershave and paper and love, I couldn't make any of those words come out.

"Daddy, I love you."

But this time, my voice was reedy and hard even for my own ears to catch.

"Annie Lee?" Daddy said, his mouth tightening up, his eyes looking worried. "Al? Baby, where'd you go? Annie Lee?"

I looked down at my hands, except my eyes didn't land on pink skin and knuckles and stubby fingers with nails trimmed short. They went right through to the grass below that sparkled in the sun as it came through the umbrellas in shades of green and red and gold.

Ever since the day Daddy died, I'd done my best to be invisible, to let myself fade into the world around me, to hide in plain sight.

It looked like I'd finally succeeded.

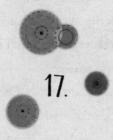

17.

Waking up one Sunday morning a month after school started to the sound of Mama crying and rinsing out the bathroom sink, I realized that I didn't know whether or not I wanted the ghost to leave.

I closed my eyes and settled back against the pillow. That week in English we'd been working on argumentative essays. The teacher had explained to us that an argumentative essay was a little bit like a formal pro-con list: weighing competing opinions and picking a side. We'd done a few exercises in class, drawing a line down the center of a piece of paper and writing bullet points on each side, to help us brainstorm through arguments on either side of our assigned issues.

Now, I imagined that my mind was lined like

notebook paper. At the top I'd written *The Ghost in Our House*, and then I'd pulled the pen straight down the middle of the paper, one side labeled *Pros* and the other labeled *Cons*.

PRO: With the ghost in the house, it was like a tiny piece of Daddy still lived there. Sometimes when the radio or the TV flipped on by their own selves, instead of turning them off right away I'd close my eyes, pretending like it meant that Daddy would be standing right there with his hand on the dial and a smile on his face.

Of course, that always made opening my eyes even harder.

CON: With the ghost in the house, it was like the only pieces of Daddy left there were the hard parts—the parts that socked me in my stomach with missing him and reminded me how I'd never hear one of his bad dad jokes or hear his soft voice singing me to sleep at night. Never, ever again.

With the ghost in the house, I couldn't let the memories of Daddy loosen and unspool enough so that they were good things, instead of feeling like they had closed their fingers around my neck.

I opened my eyes again. The water in the bathroom sink had stopped, and I could hear Mama's footsteps padding down the hall to the kitchen.

I wasn't sure which side had won out on that list in my head.

"Let's do something today," Mama said at breakfast. "Something fun. It's been too long since we did that."

I took a drink of my water. I didn't know if Mama and I had ever done anything "fun" with just the two of us. We'd both counted on Daddy to take care of things like fun.

"How about we go to Eno River State Park?"

"It's too hot," I mumbled, laying my head down on my arms on the table. Autumn would begin tomorrow, according to the calendar, but the weather hadn't got the memo.

Besides, I'd been planning to hole up in my room and study the sheet music Ray had given me during our second piano lesson. *It'll take some time to learn*, he'd said, setting it on the piano, *but I know you can do it, Annie Lee*. It was by Beethoven, called "Russian Folk Song in G," and it had two hands on the piano and an F-sharp. When Ray played it, it sounded too complicated for my fingers to ever wrap themselves around. But he had reassured me it wasn't any harder than the "Minuet in G Major" I'd been learning a year before. *Keep trying*, he'd said. *Your fingers will remember.*

I'd had two lessons since the first one two weeks ago, but the music still felt like a foreign language, like something hovering at the edge of my understanding that I could never quite figure out.

I couldn't practice at home, but I could at least look at the music and whisper the names of the notes to myself, bringing back the memories of all those days I'd struggled to learn to read music when I was taking lessons from Mrs. Kline. When I'd told him I didn't have a piano, Ray had even suggested that I just practice the fingerings anyway, tapping my fingers against a table or a piece of paper or something. *Some teachers actually have their students do that on purpose*, he'd said, *to help train them to be able to visualize the notes more clearly.*

Plus, Ray had given me some finger exercises to do to help strengthen my fingers when I couldn't make it in to Brightleaf to practice or have a lesson.

Mama checked the thermometer that hung outside the kitchen window. "It's barely even sixty right now. It should be gorgeous. Come on."

She turned to look at me, biting her lip just a little bit, like she was the kid and I was the mom. "Please?"

I sighed. "Okay."

I looked out the car window as we drove. It *was*

gorgeous, the kind of warm Carolina September morning where the blue sky felt deep enough to swim in.

"Remember Daddy and the fuel pump?" Mama said with a sad little laugh. "I think of that every time I start this old car up."

"Yeah," I said. The year I was eight, our car spent months having mysterious problems—sometimes it would be fine, other times it would drive for a few minutes and then just shut off. Mama had asked Daddy to please take it to the mechanic and get it looked at after he was done at work, but he kept forgetting. Until finally one day it wouldn't start up again for love or money. The evening it broke for good, Daddy had gotten tickets for the Durham Symphony—two tickets, for me and him, for a special night out. Except once it was clear the car was really and truly dead, going anywhere without a tow truck was out of the question.

"Remember how he strung up those Christmas lights in the fort for me?" I asked. After he had pronounced the car dead, Daddy had gone to work on a plan B: he'd gotten practically all the pillows and blankets we owned and made them into an epic fort that took up nearly our whole living room, then strung Christmas lights all through it, so it looked like something out of fairyland. He'd pulled his record player inside and we'd lain back on the pillows while he played record after record after record, until we'd heard every single piece the symphony had been set to play that night.

And even though it cost hundreds of dollars to get the car towed to a mechanic the next day and the fuel pump replaced, and even though money was always tight, all I'd seen in Mama's eyes when she told Daddy the total for the repair was love, deep as the ocean.

"I do remember," Mama said. "He loved you, Annie Lee. He loved you more than words could say."

She lapsed into silence, and I tapped my fingers against my knees, practicing scales the way Ray had shown me: one-two-three, cross my thumb under, one-two-three-four-five. When I showed up for my third lesson two days ago, Ray had *still* wanted me to pretend I knew what I was doing and make up something to play on those black keys. But I liked the precision of the scales, the way all the notes stayed in their place. I liked the predictability of deciphering the notes in the Russian folk song so that I could know exactly what was supposed to come next and exactly how it was supposed to be played.

Thursday, before I went to have my lesson with Ray, I'd googled the Durham Piano Teachers Association competition. Their website had said you had to know how to play *two scales, one major and one minor, and two pieces from the Junior A repertoire, both memorized.*

"Russian Folk Song in G" was on the Junior A repertoire list.

Not that I was going to enter the competition. Even just thinking about being up on a stage in front of a bunch of judges made the hair on my arms prickle with nervous energy.

The paper still lived in my pocket, though, crumpled and starting to wear a little bit, but legible:

Cash prizes. Beginners welcome.

Even with those two years of piano lessons from Mrs. Kline, I'd never felt like such a beginner in my whole life.

There were lots of cars in the parking lot when we got to the state park, but the trail wasn't crowded. I hopped down the wide wood-and-dirt stairs that broke up the steep hill leading to the swinging bridge across the river. The trees around us were still green, their leaves just barely kissed with the tiniest hint of gold at the tops where their branches reached toward heaven.

"So," said Mama after we'd crossed. "Tell me more about your friend. At school. The one whose house you went to last week."

"Yeah," I said, because how could I describe Mitch and do her justice?

"Well—what's her name again? What's she like?"

"Mitch Harris. She's . . . fierce."

"That's an odd adjective to use."

"She doesn't care what anyone else thinks." Including teachers, though I didn't say that. "She just does what she wants."

"There's something to be said for a person who's brave enough to follow their own happiness," said Mama, and her voice sounded strange and choked.

"Yeah."

"Well, I'm glad you've got a friend there now, Annie Lee. I've been worried about you, starting at a new school without Monica and Meredith. Remember how the three of y'all used to call yourselves the Three Musketeers? Sometimes it seemed like y'all made up one little girl, not three."

I didn't say anything, because now I was the one feeling choked, like I'd been sprinting down the woodsy trail instead of walking. The Three Musketeers felt like a long time ago. Before the M&Ms were born.

"I'm sorry, Annie Lee. I know something's up with them, even if I don't know what. You know you can talk to me about anything, don't you, honey?"

"Mm-hmm," I said, even though I didn't know any such thing.

I thought suddenly of Queenie Banks, cutting hair in

her salon in Brightleaf, laughing so loud and strong that that laugh carried right out of the window and wrapped its arms around anyone who was passing by, like a hug. Thursday, when I'd met Ray for a lesson, Queenie had come out and talked to us for a little while, telling a story about her grown-up daughter locking the keys inside her car with the engine still running. Ray had laughed so hard he'd nearly cried, and even I had smiled a little bit.

It was impossible not to smile around Queenie. She was the kind of person who seemed to carry love around with her wherever she went. Queenie reminded me of Daddy—warm and larger than life, the kind of person you only had to see to love.

I had a feeling Queenie was the kind of person you *could* talk to about anything. When he'd been alive, Daddy had been that way.

My mama couldn't be more different.

If I had to lose one parent, how come it had been the only one I'd ever been able to talk to?

"I'm sorry. I haven't been much of a mother to you this summer." Mama paused on the trail, rubbing at her forehead like it hurt her. "Some days I don't even feel like a human anymore, like somewhere I got lost along the way. Like it was me and not Fitz who died that day."

I swallowed.

"And the life insurance," Mama went on. "It's the icing on the cake, I tell you. I just keep thinking—if we had the rest of the money like we were supposed to, then I could stop worrying so much about everything, maybe work a little less. Maybe I'd go to beauty school. Spend more time with you."

"How come you can't go to beauty school now?"

"Oh, honey. I don't know. No money for tuition, for one thing, plus I wouldn't have a paycheck while I was in school. It all feels pretty daunting, Annie Lee. I don't know if I can see beyond the current crisis right at the moment. Maybe in a few months I'll be thinking a little clearer. I just wish—"

She stopped, and I could feel her reeling her frustration back in, like a pianist who's let her speed get away from her and has to take a deep breath and start again slower.

"Well. Being prepared wasn't your daddy's strong suit. I haven't checked my email yet this weekend—maybe there'll be good news waiting for us when we get home."

Mama reached her arm out and tucked it around my shoulders, pulling me in close to her, bringing me back to the present and the sounds of birds in the trees above us. She smelled like soap and vinegar and baby-powder deodorant. Like a stranger who spent her days cleaning other people's houses.

I'd walked with Daddy like this sometimes, his arm over my shoulders and my arm around his back, me trying to match my steps to his huge ones. But it felt wrong with Mama: stiff, awkward, unfamiliar.

After a second or two, she pulled away.

We walked the rest of the trail in silence, our shadows getting longer and longer on the dirt in front of us. When we got back to the car, Mama turned to me and gave me a real hug, her arms soft around my back and her vinegar smell tickling at my nose. And before she let me go, I could hear the tiniest whisper:

"I love you, baby girl. I'm so sorry."

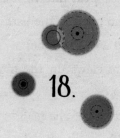

18.

The TV was on when we got home, a replay of a Duke basketball game—Daddy's favorite. And even though I kind of wanted to see the score, I went right for the remote and turned it off just as fast as I could.

Not today, ghost, I thought, clenching my teeth together so hard they ached. *Not today.*

Mama went straight to the computer. I sat on the couch while she booted the machine up, opened a browser, clicked into her email. The moment felt stretched and important, so that I was almost scared to breathe. Mama had seemed so different at the state park. She'd probably never be bubbly and happy, like Daddy had been, or like Queenie Banks—but on the hike she'd seemed like she was really *trying*, for the first time since Daddy had died.

Would whatever she found in her in-box make that stay, or would it disappear into mist again and leave me with the mama who cried in the bathroom every morning and hardly said a word to me?

Her fingers were claws on the mouse. *Click. Click. Click.*

And then silence, while she read.

Last time she'd been on the phone with the district secretary, the secretary hadn't been able to find any of Daddy's records at all. It was like Robert Fitzgerald had never even worked for the Durham school district, even though everyone knew that was wrong. So the secretary had promised to track his files down, wherever they'd got to in their computer systems. Once they did that, they'd be able to look at his pay stubs and figure out once and for all whether the insurance company owed Mama more money than they'd sent.

Without that insurance payout, Mama and I didn't have a cent besides what she brought home every other week from cleaning richer people's houses. Mama hadn't ever said it in so many words, but I knew that there was no way we'd be able to keep on making ends meet without money coming in from somewhere else before long. Pretty soon, our problems would be bigger than washing our laundry in the sink and not having school clothes that fit right.

I watched Mama now, the glow of the computer screen lighting her skin blue.

Before she said anything, before she even looked up, I could tell it wasn't good news. Her lips went thin and white, and her hand on the mouse shook.

Behind me, the TV crackled into life again, the Duke announcer yelling that RJ Barrett had made a two-handed slam dunk. Mama surged up from the computer chair and scrabbled for the remote. She turned the game off and then threw the remote at the TV; it bounced off with a clinking sound.

"Why couldn't you ever do anything the easy way?" Mama shouted at the TV. "That woman's starting to think your files got deleted completely. She can't find them. Says there will be nothing else to try soon. How could you leave us like this, Fitz?"

Mama sank back into the chair and scrubbed her palms against her eyes. I wished I was anywhere else in the apartment—anywhere else in the *world*—right then.

"You know, Annie Lee," said Mama, and I jumped a little. Her voice was strange and floaty. "I knew a girl once, back when I was in high school, who got herself stung by a Portuguese man-of-war while she was swimming out in Wilmington."

A man-of-war was a jellyfish, a horrible kind with

lacy tentacles that could be thirty feet or longer, and if it caught you it would wrap those tentacles around your arms and legs, tangling you up in it and stinging over and over again. I stuck my hand into my pocket, the warm familiar smoothness of George Washington's faces calm and comforting.

"They had to cut it off her, there on the sand," Mama went on, "and she spent the next five years getting plastic surgery over and over again to get rid of all those hard red scars. But you know the thing that's never made sense to me?"

I waited, but she didn't go on. "What?"

"She kept swimming after that day. Her family went to the beach a few weeks every summer, and she said she still kept swimming." She paused. "I don't think I could've done that."

I turned the quarter over in my fingers. Daddy had been able to make it pass over and under every finger of his hand before disappearing it, *poof*, into the air.

"Losing your daddy," Mama said, her face tired in the light of the computer screen, "it was like being wrapped up in those tentacles, Annie Lee."

She looked back at the email, at whatever she'd seen there.

"Sometimes, it still is."

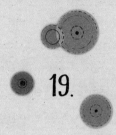

19.

That Tuesday, Mitch wasn't in school.

We didn't have any classes together on even-numbered days, so I didn't notice until lunch. I waited for almost ten minutes—practically half the time I had to eat—before I pulled my book out.

Even after I did, I could hardly keep my eyes on the pages in front of me. How had I never noticed before just how loud the cafeteria was? Or how annoying the tater tot boys were when I didn't have Mitch to talk to? Or how strange it was to sit in a room full of what felt like a million people and still be completely, completely alone?

How had I honestly thought that being invisible to everyone was better than having a friend?

* * *

At Brightleaf that afternoon, I bit my lip as I concentrated on making my hand do what I wanted it to do: happy little eighth notes, B-D-D-D, B-D-D-D, until my fingers got all snarled up and I had to stop barely two measures into Beethoven's old Russian folk song.

It was frustrating, the way my brain could *hear* how it should be played—like skipping, like dancing—but my fingers couldn't keep up. They felt like somebody else's hands, never doing quite what I wanted them to do.

Ray could play any song he wanted any way he liked: light like laughter, deep and full like tears, gentle and warm like a hug. All I could do was press too hard on every single note, wincing every time my fingers slipped from a right key to a wrong one. It was my fourth piano lesson, and even though Ray kept telling me I was doing great and moving quick, it didn't feel that way. At this rate, I didn't think I'd ever be able to get both my hands playing this song together, let alone capture any of the beautiful, elusive melodies that made their way through my heart all day and all night, just begging to slip out through my fingers.

"Everything okay, Annie Lee?" The corners of Ray's eyes were drawn down like a basset hound's. He was hunched on the bench next to me, little lines pressed into the skin around his mouth, looking tired. I wondered if the arthur was bad today.

"I just—" I took my fingers off the white keys and pulled the quarter from my pocket, flipping it over and over in my hands. "It doesn't sound the way it should."

"I'll let you in on a secret, child. It never, ever does."

I looked up in surprise. "Never?"

"Never. I been playing most my whole life, and I still have to stop myself from cringing every time something comes out different than I was expecting."

"Really?" Now that I was trying to steal away as often as I could without Mrs. Garcia getting suspicious—to scooter over for a piano lesson, or to practice by myself when nobody else was around—I hadn't had as much time to spend listening to Ray perform. Still, I'd never once heard him play a note that didn't sound like it fit just perfectly into his songs. Wasn't that what those magic lights above the piano meant, that what he was playing was all the way perfect?

"Really. I'll let you in on the secret of all music, Annie Lee: sometimes, it's not so much about playing things without mistakes as it is about *moving past* the mistakes. You'd be surprised how much most people don't notice."

I flipped the quarter some more, thinking about that.

"Whatcha got there?"

My fingers stilled, and I showed it to him—first one side, *heads*, then the other side, *heads*. He laughed. "Can't say I ever seen a coin like that."

"It's not a real coin. It's for magic tricks. It used to be my daddy's." I rubbed George Washington's face. "He always said it paid to carry your own luck. You know, 'cause it comes up heads whichever way it lands, so having it with you is making certain luck will always be on your side."

"I'd have to agree with him there," Ray said. "It just takes time, Annie Lee. That's all. You only been at this a few weeks. Music, it's a long game. It takes years to master it. Give it more time, and your fingers will relax. They'll know what to do."

I put the quarter back into my pocket, my fingers brushing up against the contest paper.

Beginners welcome.

I could do a lot with that hundred dollars—buy myself some winter clothes that fit before the cold came. Splurge on Kraft mac and cheese instead of just the store brand.

Buy that new washer.

The words were on my tongue, ready to ask: *How soon could I be ready for a competition?*

But before I could say them, Ray spoke first.

"You ready to try again, Miss Annie Lee?"

I pulled my hand out of my pocket quick and swallowed the question back down. It was silly, anyway. I didn't have a chance at that prize.

"Sure," I said, then laid my fingers across the keys and started from the beginning.

20.

Mitch was back in school the next day, white hat sitting defiantly on her head, just like normal. Science was the only class Mitch and I had together, and after the first week she'd paid some kid to switch seats so she could sit next to me. Our science teacher, Mr. Barton, had raised his bushy eyebrows, but he'd let it slide.

"Where were you yesterday?" I whispered now, while everyone was getting notebooks out at the beginning of class.

"I had to get some teeth pulled so I can start braces soon. My face was all swollen and stuff, so my mom let me stay home."

"Oh." I lined up my two sharpest pencils on the desk beside the notebook.

"You miss me?"

I stared down at my desk. "Yeah, I guess. Lunch was pretty boring."

Mitch grinned, freckles crinkling, but before either of us could say anything else, Mr. Barton stood up and cleared his throat. Today he was like a turned-on lightbulb, his mostly bald head almost shining with how thrilled he was to be telling us about our first big project of the year. Behind him, he'd drawn *EGG-DROP PROJECT!!!* in huge letters on the whiteboard, complete with an illustration of a little egg sailing down to the floor with a parachute overhead.

"This is science at its best, ladies and gentlemen," he said, sweeping his arms wide, brown fingers spread out like he was throwing invisible glitter. "Making theories, creating prototypes, recording results, sharing lessons learned! It's one part physics, one part fun!"

Mitch rolled her eyes and slid her head onto her arms. When Mr. Barton was looking away, she caught my eye and mouthed, *One part FUN?* I swallowed a giggle.

Mr. Barton grabbed a stack of papers from his desk. "We'll be dividing into pairs for this assignment. Your objective will be to build a vehicle for your egg that enables it to be dropped from the roof of the school without cracking. I'll pass out these rule sheets so that you know what materials are off-limits. We'll be working on this for the next three weeks. After that, we'll start two weeks of demonstrations, where each team will be required to test the integrity of their contraption from a two-story height, as well as give a joint oral presentation. This means that it is imperative that both partners be there on presentation day. My dear friends, stop groaning. I assure you this will be your favorite part of the year."

"At least we can work together," Mitch muttered as we filed out of the classroom. "Want to come over Friday after school and get started?"

I slowed. I'd already been to Mitch's house once. If I went again, would that mean I had to invite her to my apartment, too? I thought about trying to explain all the unpacked moving boxes, or the mildew smell everywhere you went, or how Mama's eyes always looked either like she'd just been crying or was about to start.

What would I say if Mitch saw Mama washing our clothes in the sink? Would she think we were like those people on reality TV shows who yelled and slapped each other around and lived off beer and McDonald's?

And what if the ghost did something while we were there?

"Hello?" Mitch said. "You alive in there? Do you want to come to my house or not?"

"Okay," I said, not meeting her eyes. "I'll come."

I tried hard to ignore the nervous little flutter in my stomach as I said those words.

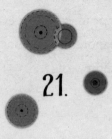

21.

Mitch's mom was sitting at the kitchen table with Mitch's nana when the bus dropped us off Friday afternoon. They were laughing at something, hands cupped around glasses of iced tea, and there was a sweet, yeasty smell in the air.

"Mmm," said Mitch, kicking off her shoes and backpack and homing in right away on a cutting board on the counter. "Want some bread with honey butter, Annie Lee? Nana makes bread every week and it's *amazing*."

Mrs. Harris smiled. Today she was wearing a zebra-print jacket and glasses with thick frames the color of ripe bananas. "I was never much good at a lot of things, but I know my way around a kitchen."

I took the slice of bread Mitch was waving at me

and bit into it. It was soft and warm and wheaty, the sweetness of the honey butter soaking into it like syrup. "Delicious. Thanks."

Mitch's mom patted the chair next to her. When she'd driven me home after the last time I came over, I'd said *Thank you, Mrs. Harris*, but she'd laughed and said Mrs. Harris was Mitch's nana, and that I could call her Lisa or Ms. Johnson.

"Come on, girls," she said now. "Sit down a bit before you get started. Annie Lee, how are you?"

I shrugged. It was strange sitting there with somebody else's mama and grandma who I hardly knew, after a whole summer when I'd hardly talked to my own mother. Last time I'd come over, Mitch and I had spent most of the time outside, and even when her mom drove us home, she'd talked *at* us more than *with* us.

"I'm fine."

"I never even asked you when you were here last time. What do your parents do?"

I rubbed my fingers together until they were sticky with honey and all I wanted was to get up and wash them off.

Mitch opened her mouth. "Annie Lee's—"

"My daddy's dead," I said, my words cutting in front of hers. Short. Sharp. Hard. Filling up the kitchen

around us with invisible bubbles of guilt and awkwardness. Nobody ever knew what to say to a girl whose
daddy had dropped dead playing basketball at church
one day, so I mostly stayed away from talking about it.

From the corner of my eye I could see Ms. Johnson's
eyes widen just a little, but when she spoke, her voice was
smooth and even. "I'm so sorry to hear that."

Everyone was always *so sorry to hear that.* But none of
them were as sorry as I was.

Mitch cleared her throat. "So, we'd better get brain-
storming, right?" It had already been three days since
Mr. Barton gave us the egg-drop assignment, and we
hadn't done anything so far. I didn't like big projects
like this one, where you did a demonstration in front of
the whole class. It just meant there were more people to
see you fail.

"Yeah," I said, and jumped up to rinse my sticky
fingers in the sink. From here, I could see through a
doorway into another room, sunlight spilling through
tall windows onto the glossy ebony of an upright piano.
Something snagged in my chest. I could almost see
Daddy sitting at that piano, like in my dreams. He
would've liked Mitch's house—liked all the books, liked
the way Mitch's mom and grandma sat at the table talking to me and Mitch like we were grown-ups.

Ms. Johnson stood. "I'll be in my study, so you girls

go ahead and take over the kitchen table for your project. If you need any help, let me know."

"Mmph," said Mitch's grandma, following her daughter-in-law. "*I'm* gonna go check if I've got any hits on my online dating profile."

I felt my jaw drop down at the same time that my eyebrows shot up, exactly like when a cartoon character is surprised. *Online dating?* I mouthed to Mitch. When she nodded, a giggle started somewhere around my belly button and rose up and up until I had to plant my hands over my mouth to stop it escaping and echoing all the way up the staircase to where Mrs. Harris had disappeared.

"I *know*," Mitch whispered, giggling herself. "And you should *see* it. It's so much worse than what you're imagining."

"Did she wear those glasses in her profile picture?"

"I *wish*. She has another pair that makes those look like nothing. And she wore at least three huge chunky necklaces *and* an electric-green scarf, too. She looked like an old-lady version of Professor Trelawney."

I leaned back against the counter and buried my face in my hands, the giggles taking me over.

"Girls!" Mitch's mama called from her office down the hall. "Aren't you supposed to be doing something?"

That just made us laugh harder.

* * *

Later, after we'd written up a list of weird contraptions we thought might protect our egg from its drop, Mitch's mama popped back out of her study, stretching her arms above her head and yawning.

"Friday! Thank goodness. We should celebrate! Annie Lee, what time is your mama coming to pick you up today?"

"Soon. She gets off at six o'clock."

"Mr. Harris is bringing a movie home with him in a few minutes—want to stay for dinner and watch it with us afterward?"

I opened my mouth, the *yes* dancing forward to the tip of my tongue, but then closed it again. I thought of Mama after our hike, saying that about jellyfish.

Losing your daddy—it was like being wrapped up in those tentacles, Annie Lee. Sometimes it still is.

There was something in this kitchen, here, folding itself around Mitch and her mama and me, a web of love and happiness like I hadn't felt for months. It was tempting to stay right where I was and let that love and happiness soak right into me, filling me up.

But being filled up that way just made it hurt more down the road, when something bad happened.

How had I let my invisibility cloak drop so much this

month? First Ray, then Queenie, then Mitch: I was letting people see me more and more each day, forgetting that invisibility was my only chance to never again be hurt as much as I'd been when Daddy died.

"Annie Lee?" Ms. Johnson asked. "Everything okay?"

"I can't stay," I mumbled. "My mama wouldn't like it."

Mitch's mama's smile sank a little. "Oh, I'm sorry to hear that. Maybe another day."

When Mama knocked on the door a few minutes later, I jumped up and had my arms into my backpack straps faster than anyone could react. Mama, though, wasn't in such a hurry to leave.

"Hi there," she said, coming inside to shake Ms. Johnson's hand. I tried hard not to notice that Mama—with her used-to-be-blond hair slicked back into a ponytail and her pink polo with a big stain on it where she'd splashed some kind of cleaning product on herself—looked poor and plain next to Mitch's mama, who wore a comfy-looking striped maxidress and stylish tortoiseshell glasses. "I'm Joan Fitzgerald."

"Lisa Johnson. I'm glad our girls have become such good friends. Mitch just loves Annie Lee. Things were a little rough at her last school—I'm glad the two of them connected this year."

"*Mom*," Mitch groaned from inside the kitchen, where I could see her sneaking the last slice of her nana's bread. "Can you not make me sound like a five-year-old, please?"

Ms. Johnson rolled her eyes, and Mama laughed—a nervous little laugh that didn't sound exactly happy, but was better than I'd heard for months, anyway.

"I'm real glad they're friends, too," Mama said.

"Well, Annie Lee is welcome over here anytime."

I closed my eyes, silently begging Mama not to return the invitation.

"I know she appreciates it," Mama said, her lip puckering a little as she chewed the inside of it. "It's hard for her, being home all afternoon while I'm working."

"Annie Lee told me about her dad," Ms. Johnson said, her voice taking on the soft gentleness that people always had when they heard about Daddy. "I'm so sorry to hear that."

Mama swallowed hard. "Thanks."

Mama pulled me close as we walked toward her car. "I'm glad you have a friend, honey. Mitch and her family seem nice."

"Yeah," I said, wishing so hard it hurt that our home felt more like Mitch's, filled with love and light.

22.

Sometimes at night when I lay in bed trying to fall asleep, I'd picture what it would feel like to sit at the piano the way Ray did, letting my fingers whisper against the keys exactly right so the sound that came out of them was pure magic. I could *feel* it, there in my bed, the way the music would pull itself out and heal all the broken parts inside me. I could feel it in every muscle from my fingertips to my shoulders.

But every time I managed to sneak away to Brightleaf to practice or get another lesson from Ray, it wasn't one bit like that those twilight dreams.

After my lesson last week, Ray and I had agreed to meet again the next Tuesday. I'd shown up early today and found Ray at the piano in the atrium, playing something sad and sweet while a few passers-by—Queenie included—lingered to listen. The melody was the kind that reached right into my heart, and I didn't think I'd ever felt anything before that was more comforting and uncomfortable all at once, the way it held me up but laid me bare at the same time. Ray's magic lights rose and fell like ocean waves in blue and silver, and I couldn't look away.

By the time he'd finished playing, I didn't even know if I was breathing anymore.

"Gracious, that man has a gift," Queenie said when Ray had finished. "You ever hear anything quite like that, Annie Lee?"

"Never ever. I guess since you've known Mr. Owens so long, you've gotten to hear him play a lot."

"Sure have. I used to be friends with his wife, Margie, before she passed away. When Mr. Richardson, the mall owner, was looking for a musician to bring an 'ambience' to the mall ten or so years back, I suggested Ray. It was a good thing, too, because it was only a few years later that Margie died, and not even a year after that that he got injured and had to retire as a roofer. It's just the tips he makes here and the disability payments from that fall that get him through now. I'm grateful to have him here, though. Anytime he's out here playing, if I haven't got a client in the salon, I come to listen." Queenie let out a long, satisfied sigh, like everything in life was just the way she'd hoped. "How's your mama doing, child? She get off work soon?"

"Oh," I said, trying not to let my heart race too much. "She's fine. She'll be off in . . . uh, a little while."

"You oughta bring her by sometime after her shift, if she isn't too tired. I'd like to meet her. I'm a little surprised she hasn't been by already," Queenie added with a pucker of her forehead. "I figured for sure she'd want to meet Ray, maybe sit in on your lessons once or twice—"

My skin prickled all over. "She, uh—I don't know, Miss Queenie. She works so hard, and she's always real tired. She usually doesn't have energy for much extra. Hopefully she can come soon, though." I was lying about Mama working at the hotel, but not about this. It was the plain truth: Mama *was* tired, and she *did* work hard. Me and her may not have known quite how to be around each other without Daddy there to draw us together, but even I could see how hard Mama was trying.

Queenie clucked her tongue. "Poor woman. Ray told me about y'all's lesson schedule, how you can't have them on regular days because her shifts are so unpredictable. That's tough on anyone."

"Yeah." I curled my fingers into my palms. "Anyway. I gotta go have my lesson now."

"See you later, shug." Queenie headed back to her salon, and I went over to Ray.

"Annie Lee," Ray said as he collected the coins from his baseball cap and put the hat on his head. He slid over, patting the bench next to him.

An old man with ruddy, white skin and a newsboy cap on his gray hair pushed a long broom into the atrium. "'Lo, Ray," he called over to us. "You okay? How's the arthritis?"

Ray waved his cane. "Hasn't claimed me yet, though it's trying, Stan."

Stan chuckled. "Takes more than arthritis to do in an old cuss like you."

"Okay, Miss Annie Lee," Ray said as Stan disappeared around a corner. "Take it from the top. Maybe we'll see if you're ready to start the next piece today, too."

I unfolded the sheet music for "Russian Folk Song in G" and played through it, my fingers like elephants on the keys, until I got to the middle and things snarled up so bad I let both my hands smash down on the keyboard in frustration, making a sound like the piano's last dying wail.

Through the big window of a music shop nearby, I

could see a teenage clerk jump and drop the cell phone she'd been scrolling through. I scowled.

"Now, come on," said Ray, and I wondered if he ever in his life had gotten truly mad about anything. "It didn't sound half-bad."

"How can you *say* that? It was *terrible!*"

"Nah. It's coming right along."

I closed my hands into fists and banged on the keys again, short and sharp. The music-store girl winced. So much for my invisibility cloak.

"I'm never gonna be any good, Ray. I might as well give up now."

"Aw, don't give me that, now. It just takes practice, don't it?"

"What's the point? I'm hopeless. I'm—" I paused, looking down at the keys, cool under my hands. "I'm all broken."

"I don't know, Miss Annie Lee. I guess I kinda think it's our brokenness that makes us beautiful—makes us who we are—and not our perfection."

I let my fists slide off the keyboard into my lap.

"Think about the courtyard out there," Ray continued. "All those bricks making up the path. Have you ever noticed how the weeds push up through them anyway, all green and brave and strong?"

I nodded.

"It's like that, Annie Lee. You can think how you want, but it's my personal opinion that everything's more beautiful when it's had to fight hard to come up the way those weeds have. The way I see it, Annie Lee, avoiding risk is no way to live. You can get hurt no matter what you do—if you take chances or if you don't take them. But think of all the good parts you'd miss."

I thought of Ms. Johnson asking me to stay for dinner the week before, and Mama saying, *Her family went to the beach a few weeks every summer, and she said she still kept swimming. I don't think I could've done that.*

"But doesn't it just open you up to get hurt *more*, when you take risks like that?" I told him about Mama's friend and the jellyfish.

"I read once that a man-of-war sting feels like getting cut all over with a hot knife. How could Mama's friend risk that again?"

"Sounds like she was pretty brave, your mama's friend. Brave enough to go off and find her joy, even if it had cost her pain in the past. And wise, too. Just think of all the things she'd have missed if she'd stayed away from the water her whole life. You ever been to the beach, Annie Lee? You ever felt that silky salt water against your skin?"

I hunched my shoulders, pulling into myself like a turtle.

"I dare you to tell me something, child. Tell me what *you'd* do right this very minute, if you were ready to be the bravest, wisest version of Annie Lee Fitzgerald you could be."

I swallowed. "There's a girl at school."

"Oh yeah?"

"Her name's Mitch. She's my friend, I guess. Maybe my best friend now."

"Mm-hmm?"

"Sometimes it feels like there's a cage wrapped around my heart, ever since my daddy died." I laced my fingers through each other, hard and tight like bars. "Like this."

I thought with a pang about what it had been like when Mitch hadn't shown up to school the week before—like I'd been twice as alone, twice as invisible, as before. A few days ago in English class the teacher had read a poem about two roads diverging and how the writer had to choose which one to take. In some ways, everything in my life right now felt like that poem: like I was stuck between two different roads and I didn't know which one was better.

Down one road, there was just me, invisible Annie Lee who couldn't be hurt or broken anymore. But it was awfully lonely and boring, too. And *that* Annie Lee was the one who couldn't remember how to smile, or have fun, or what it even felt like to be happy.

Down the other there was Mitch, and Ray, and Queenie, and even Mama—the happy, smiling Mama who'd taken me hiking at Eno River State Park the Sunday before. That road had note-passing in science class and sitting together at lunch and piano lessons and smiles and friends. *Love.*

But that road was scary, too. Because what if all those people disappeared? Like Daddy? Like the M&Ms?

If I was really brave and wise, maybe I'd know how to stop holding on so hard to Daddy. Maybe I'd figure out how to let go of the "pro" section on that pro-con list about the ghost in our apartment. Maybe I'd be ready to live my life the way it was, instead of the way it used to be.

I didn't know how to say any of that to Ray, though. Instead, I took a deep breath. "If I was really brave and wise, I'd figure out a way to open up that cage and let Mitch in. And . . . maybe other people, too."

"That would be brave and wise indeed," said Ray. "And you know what, Annie Lee? I bet you could do it. I'm sure of it. You just have to stop thinking about what's hiding in the water and get out and swim."

"Yeah," I said quietly. "And—" I stopped, squeezing my laced-together fingers so hard they hurt.

If I was *really* brave, I'd go all in. Take my invisibility cloak all the way off.

"Yes?"

"There's something else I'd do if I were brave, too."

"Oh? What's that?"

Slowly, I pulled my right hand away from my left one and reached into my pocket. The paper was still there, where it had been for weeks now. It was fading fast from rubbing against the inside of my shorts and from being washed once or twice.

I took the paper out now and spread it out on the piano in front of me.

Cash prizes. Beginners welcome.

Ray studied it for a minute, his expression never changing. When he'd finished reading it, he nodded. "I've heard good things about this competition, Annie Lee. I'm not a member of the association, of course, but I've got a friend who is, and I bet he'd help me register you for the competition if you liked. So—if you were brave, you'd enter it, is that right?"

My chin jerked up and down, so quick it was hardly a nod at all. I couldn't meet Ray's eyes.

"Well, then," said Ray quietly. "Are you sure about quitting today, or are you ready to be brave?"

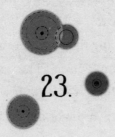

23.

I went to Mitch's house again on Friday after school.

"You know, pretty soon we're going to have to actually start dropping these things and seeing if any of our theories work out," said Mitch.

"Maybe we can divide and conquer—we each take half. We can work on them this weekend."

Today we were supposed to be writing up paragraphs on why we thought each of our different designs might protect the egg from impact—*a demonstration*, Mr. Barton had said, eyebrows bristling harder than ever, *of your comprehension of the scientific method*. The presentations were starting in less than two weeks. Even though ours wasn't till close to the end of October, exactly three weeks away, I was beginning to have the itchy feeling that Mitch and I had spent a little too much time creating theories and not enough time actually practicing.

Mitch wrote furiously in our notebook. Her handwriting was kind of like her face—unexpectedly sweet, the kind of thing you only noticed if you could get past her scowl and beanie and sidle in close. All the letters were even and round. I half expected her to dot her *i*'s with little hearts, the way Meredith did.

Or used to. I had no idea what Meredith did now.

"There," Mitch said, writing a ferocious final period. "That's done. I say we call it good for today. So, reader girl, do you ever do anything but reading and falling off longboards?"

Sometimes when a moment hits that might change the course of your life a little bit or a lot—it sort of comes over you in a prickling flush, starting at your toes and making all your hair stand on end. This was one of those moments. I sat in my chair, my heart all full up of Ray's words from a few days before:

What would you do if you were ready to be the bravest, wisest version of Annie Lee Fitzgerald you could be?

I took a deep breath, just like I had when Ray had asked me that question to begin with.

"I'm learning piano."

"Cool," said Mitch.

"I can show you how, if you want. I mean, if you're interested. If you don't already know. Which you probably do, since you have a piano and everything."

Mitch shrugged. "Nope. The piano is Nana's. She used to teach lessons and play in concerts and stuff, but Dad never learned and when Nana tried to teach me when I was six, she gave up and said I was as stubborn as a twice-cussed ox and had the musical ear of a warthog."

"Wow. She said all that to your face?"

"Yep. Did I mention I was only six?"

I pictured Mrs. Harris five years younger with fire in her eyes. "Scary."

"Nana can be a dragon when she wants to."

Maybe that's where Mitch got it from.

"C'mon. Show me what you know." Mitch jumped up from the table and swept our egg-drop notebook and all the other stuff we'd had spread out into her backpack, like a hurricane that left things cleaner in its wake instead of messier.

Mitch's brother, Jacob, was lying on the floor in the living room when we got there, a giant hidden-picture puzzle spread out in front of him. He'd circled five hidden objects so far: a comb disguised in a horse's tail, a firework hidden in a sprinkler, and a couple other things I couldn't identify.

"Scoot," Mitch said, nudging him with her toe. "We're going to use the piano."

Jacob scooted. I followed Mitch and sat down next to her at the piano bench. The wood was warm and glossy. For just a minute, I wondered what it would be like to be Mitch: a family with enough love for lifetimes, a little brother who hung on everything you ever said.

A mama who didn't just ask how you were doing over cereal in the morning while her eyes drifted to her phone, but who actually sat down with you on purpose and met your eyes and *talked* to you. *Every* day, not just once every few months.

I swallowed hard.

"So, what can you play?" Mitch asked, flipping open the piano's lid. The keyboard suddenly seemed bigger than the one in Brightleaf. Shinier. Scarier. I thought of Ray again, telling me to be the bravest, wisest version of Annie Lee Fitzgerald.

"Hardly anything yet. I'm learning a song by Beethoven, but I'm not too good at it yet. And I just got sheet music for a new one, a minuet in G Minor by Bach, but I only played that once and messed it up pretty bad. I gotta practice, though, because my teacher entered me in a piano competition in December." I thought about adding that practicing was easier said than done, since I had to sneak out to Brightleaf to do it or content myself with pretending my kitchen table had a keyboard, and that thinking about competing against students who had pianos in their homes that they could practice on anytime they liked made me feel kind of sick to my stomach.

But I didn't know if I was ready to open my heart up *that* much yet.

"What do you have to play for the competition?"

"Those two pieces and two scales. One major, one minor."

"What, like snake scales?"

I stared at Mitch. "You're kidding, right?"

"I told you, my nana gave up teaching me a long time ago. I don't remember any of it."

I placed both my hands on the keyboard, finding middle C and the C one octave below it. The ivory felt like warm silk. "So, every piece of music has a key signature," I said. "That means the set of notes that you play in that piece—whether there are any black keys, what note you start and end on. Like, in the key of C, there aren't any black notes at all, and you start and end on C."

"Okay."

"So, a scale is when you play all the notes in that key

in order. Up and then down again, like stairs." I played the C major scale: one-two-three, cross my thumb under, one-two-three-four-five—then back down again five-four-three-two-one, cross my middle finger over, three-two-one.

"So . . . what's the point?"

"It helps get your fingers used to playing, for one thing. And it trains your ear so you know what things should sound like when you're playing a song in that key signature. Like, the new song my teacher gave me is in G minor, right? So the first thing he had me do, before I even looked at the music, was to learn the G minor scale. Like this. This one has two black notes, see? B-flat and E-flat."

"It sounds spooky," Mitch said.

"That's because it's in a minor key. In a minor key, you lower the third, sixth, and seventh notes in the scale. It can sound sad or spooky."

"Huh." Mitch paused, looking at my hands on the keyboard. "What made you want to learn piano?"

I put my hands in my lap, scratching at the skin around my nails.

What would you do if you were ready to be the bravest, wisest version of Annie Lee Fitzgerald you could be?

"My daddy," I said. "He loved music, all kinds of

music, but especially piano. He couldn't play very well—he had a really hard time reading music, said the notes didn't stick in his brain. He had the same problem with math. But he loved to sit and mess around. And he had all these old records of his favorite piano songs. He used to listen to them a lot."

"I bet you miss him."

"All the time."

"What was he like?"

"He was . . . funny. Everyone loved him. He was one of those guys who walk into a room and everyone looks toward them. His name was Robert, but everybody called him Fitz. For Fitzgerald. He had the kind of laugh that filled up a whole room."

Mitch was still and quiet on the bench beside me.

I had hardly said anything about Daddy for months, but once I started, it was like I couldn't stop. "He always called me Al, too. You know, for my initials—*A* and *L*. Sometimes he would sing me that old Paul Simon song, you know, 'You Can Call Me Al.' He loved old music, especially the kind that sounded a little bit sad. And he did magic. Magic tricks, I mean. He'd been collecting all these different tricks—all these props and stuff—my whole life. He had trick cards and that kind of thing. And this."

I pulled the two-headed quarter out of my pocket and showed it to her: heads up, either way you turned it. Mitch laughed. "That's cool. You keep it with you now?"

"Yeah. It's kind of like my good-luck charm, I guess."

"Hey. Reader girl." Mitch's gray eyes met mine square on.

"Yeah?"

"Thanks for telling me."

Then she reached out her right hand and played a C major scale, just the way I'd showed her.

I flipped the quarter between my fingers: *heads*, *heads*, *heads*, and thought about Ray.

It felt kind of good, being the brave, wise version of Annie Lee Fitzgerald.

No invisibility cloak required.

Mrs. Garcia was out on the landing that evening, watering the plants she grew in pots outside her front door, when Mitch's mom took me home. Mama had texted to say she'd be a little late, and I should go ahead and get dinner.

"Hi, Mrs. Garcia," I said. It felt like the bubble of happiness from Mitch's house was still inside me, warm and soft and nice.

"Annie Lee!" said Mrs. Garcia, smiling. "I was

beginning to think you weren't my neighbor anymore. You've been gone so much in the afternoons! Your *mamá* said you have a new friend?"

I smiled back. I felt more like the old Annie Lee today. "Yeah. We're doing a project together for school, so I've been going there a lot to work on it."

"I'm glad for you. It's no good for a little girl to be alone so much. Better to have friends."

I gave a little wave and let myself into the apartment. The radio was on, the soft guitar notes of "Annie's Song" harmonizing with John Denver's liquid voice while he sang about his senses being filled up.

But right now, even the ghost couldn't wipe the smile off my face. I turned off the radio and opened the fridge.

Mrs. Garcia was right, I thought as I made myself a turkey sandwich (dry, because we'd run out of mayo and Mama said we didn't have money for any more until her next paycheck came in). Ray was right.

Better to have friends.

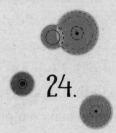

24.

"What're you doing, honey? You sure look like you're concentrating hard."

Mama came up behind me and put her hands on my shoulders, like she was about to give me a massage. I shrugged them off. I was packing an egg into a plastic container filled with cotton balls—the third idea from my half of the list of theories that Mitch and I had agreed to test out the day before yesterday.

Ideas number one and two had already resulted in big, fat splatters.

"Trying not to break more eggs," I muttered as I sealed the Tupperware carefully, adding a little bit of duct tape to the rim just to be sure. When Mama and I had bought this carton of eggs at the store last week, we'd paid two dollars and ninety-seven cents for a dozen, which meant that—according to the calculator on my phone—each egg had cost us nearly a quarter. I'd already cracked half a dollar on the complex parking lot, dropping my contraptions off our balcony. I still had three ideas left to test after this one, and then probably more, once Mitch and I figured out ways to make our prototypes stronger.

How many dollars was this project going to eat up before I was done? Probably more than mayo. Or a load of wash at the Laundromat. Or any of the other things Mama had said we couldn't afford. We should be putting this money into Mama's New Washer Fund instead of splattered eggs.

I finished taping up the lid and carried the container out to the balcony. Mama followed. I closed my eyes and held the Tupperware out over the railing.

Then I opened my fingers and let the container go.

It hit the ground a minute later with a muffled thump. Even from this high up, I could see the yellow of the yolk leaking through the cotton balls.

This had been one of our best ideas. How could anything be safer than a whole lot of padded plastic?

I gripped the balcony railing hard.

"What's the matter, Annie Lee?"

I'd seen the way Mama's lips had gone thin every time

she'd gotten the mail to find more bills. I'd seen the big dark bags underneath her eyes when she came home from working all day cleaning other people's houses. I'd seen the way she checked her email and her phone messages over and over again, hoping each time that the district secretary would be there, telling her they'd found the proof that the life insurance company owed us five times more than what they'd paid.

I clutched the railing until my hands went white, the blue veins popping out on them like roads on a map. "I just—keep—wasting—*eggs*! I'm too stupid not to!"

"Learning always takes some practice, honey. That's what science is all about—finding all the things that *don't* work, so you can figure out what *does*."

Practice. Just like Ray had said the day we'd talked about the Durham Piano Teachers Association competition. It seemed like just about everything in life came down to practicing. But what were you supposed to do when you *couldn't* practice? When eggs cost money and pianos cost even more?

I looked down at the Tupperware, now starting to leak yellow yolk through to the pavement below. "I'll pay for the eggs, I promise. I'll figure out a way to get the money. Maybe I could walk dogs, or—"

"Annie Lee Fitzgerald, you will not," said Mama,

sounding more woke-up than she had maybe since the day Daddy died. "I won't allow it. We're not so bad off that I need to take money from my eleven-year-old. I promise, a few dollars' worth of eggs isn't gonna break our bank, honey. I know I've been pretty stressed about money. With the life insurance, and me trying to figure out if I'm going to be stuck cleaning houses forever, and all that—I get that money's been stressful around here. But you listen to me, Annie Lee." She snaked an arm around me and pulled me close. "Those are grown-up worries, okay? Let me handle them. In fact—"

Mama turned and disappeared back into the apartment, but not before I caught the tiniest hint of a grin on her face. A real, true *grin*. When was the last time I'd seen her smile that way? When was the last time I'd seen her look like anything except a sleepwalker? Mama had always been quieter than Daddy, more prone to nervousness and stress. But before he'd died, she had smiled more than she'd frowned and laughed more than she sighed.

When she came back out, she had the carton of eggs in her hand. With almost theatrical slowness, she set it down on the tiny patio table, opened the lid, and drew out an egg, holding it up for me to inspect.

"See this?" she asked, and before I could nod, she'd

raised the egg up high over the railing and thrown it down to the asphalt below. *SMACK*.

Mama giggled and pulled another egg out. *SMACK* again.

"See?" she said, still laughing like she was my friend, not my mama. Like Queenie might have laughed with me. Like *Daddy* might have laughed. "Now I've wasted a pair of eggs, too. And it was kind of fun."

Mama had left the sliding door half-open, so we could both hear when the oven beeped its preheat warning, and smell when the scent of butterscotch cookies rose up in the kitchen and wafted its way out onto the patio. We looked at each other for a long minute, our faces mirroring each other: eyebrows up, mouths in little O's of confusion.

I hadn't put any butterscotch cookies into the oven, and I was pretty sure Mama hadn't either. But they'd been Daddy's very favorites.

Ever since that day in June, I'd been clinging to the memory of Daddy as hard as I clung to his two-headed quarter. Moments like this felt like he was clinging right back. But somehow, all that clinging didn't make me feel closer to Daddy; it made him feel further away, like every memory the ghost turned real just served to show how gone he really was.

Without saying anything at all, Mama slipped through the door and opened the oven with a face like *she* was the one who'd been turned into a ghost.

The oven was empty.

All the breath in my chest turned to ice, like it had forgotten how to move in and out of my lungs. Was Mama going to burst into tears, there in front of the empty oven? Was I?

But instead, Mama closed the oven door and hit the power button hard, and then she looked up at the ceiling and shook her fist at it, like she was berating someone who lived just upstairs.

"*Not* this time, Fitz," she said, and her voice didn't sound like it was full of tears at all. It sounded strong, and angry, and brave. "You just leave us alone today, you hear me?"

And then she came back through the sliding door onto the patio, and closed that door so hard that it bounced off the frame and she had to close it again. But when she looked up at me again, her hands were steady and the smile on her face looked like a *real* smile, like it held the memory of the way she'd been laughing before.

Had I ever seen Mama smile quite like that? At *me*?

She pulled out another egg from the carton and pressed it into my hands. "You try it."

The egg was cool and heavy in my hand, smooth with just the littlest hint of grit. Monica had told me once that that grainy feeling was the pores of the egg, the teensy holes that air and moisture could pass through so the growing chick inside it could breathe. The Hsus had had chickens, of course, and on mornings after she and I had had a sleepover, we'd go out together and collect any eggs the hens had laid, so that Mrs. Hsu could scramble them up for a breakfast that tasted like sunlight and fresh air.

I lifted the egg just the way Mama had and then brought my arm down hard and quick, so that when the egg hit the pavement, it was going way faster than any of the ones I'd tried and failed to slow down. *SMACK*.

A grin inched its way onto my face. I could see why Mama had giggled—it was strangely satisfying, that great big smack, the way the egg pooled out from its shattered shell in a glistening creep.

"See?" Mama asked, but her voice was quiet and gentle. "No harm done, honey. I promise you that."

I wasn't certain if she was talking about the cost of all the eggs my project had broken so far or the ghost with its butterscotch cookies.

"Now, I'll tell you what," she went on. "This project seems like the kind that might need a rest for tonight so your brain can think on it. What do you say after we hose off all those broken eggs, we pull out some ice cream and do something fun instead of finishing up homework? Just for tonight." Mama paused, and I could tell she was thinking hard. "Maybe we'll watch a movie, or—I don't know, paint our nails, or something. Isn't that what mothers and daughters do?"

Before Daddy had died, *he'd* always been the one organizing fun family nights: movies, or trips to the mini-golf course, or ridiculously dramatic magic shows where he wore a tall silk hat and swirling purple cape and had Mama and me both in stitches the whole time. I could tell that Mama didn't really know, any more than I did, what mother-daughter bonding was supposed to look like.

But tonight, just the fact that she was *trying* was enough to send a little thread of warm light all through me.

I leaned into her, smelling her soap-and-vinegar Mary's Maids smell. "I'd like that a lot."

"Me too, Annie Lee. I'd like it, too."

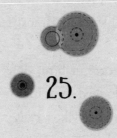

25.

Clara was waiting outside Brightleaf when I went for my next lesson, a Wednesday afternoon right after I'd gotten home from school. Her leash was looped around a pole, her paws folded under her chin as she watched the world with her warm-honey eyes.

"Hey, girl," I said, dropping to a crouch and scratching behind her ears. Clara closed her eyes in appreciation. "Such a pretty doggy. I bet Ray loves you a whole lot."

Clara opened her eyes again and looked soulfully at me, like she knew what I was thinking. Dr. Hsu had always said that dogs were experts at picking up cues from their humans, and that was why they made such excellent companions for people with blindness or epilepsy or anxiety. Could Clara sense Ray's pain, the way his arthritis ate at him all the time? Did she worry, just like I did, when he stretched out his fingers or rubbed at his legs or stumbled and almost fell on the polished wood mall floor?

"We gotta take care of him, don't we, girl?" I murmured, and Clara looked right into my eyes and made a low rumble in her throat like a cat's purr.

I wandered into the mall, pausing to peer in Queenie's window. She wasn't with a customer today—she sat behind a desk, looking over some papers with a pair of little half-moon glasses like Dumbledore's perched on the end of her nose. I didn't think I'd ever seen her sitting down before, or quiet like this, except when she was watching Ray. She looked older, but softer, too.

I knocked on the glass, and she looked up and saw me, waving her hand in big strokes to tell me to come on in. The salon was warm and perfumed, with jaunty pop music playing from a speaker somewhere. In the back, one of Queenie's stylists—a bald white man with black studs in his ears—was chatting with a customer while he gave her highlights.

"Aren't you a sight for sore eyes," Queenie said, getting up from her desk and hugging me. She smelled like shampoo and hair spray, and her silky shirt was soft against my cheek. "How you doing, Annie Lee?"

"Good." For once, it was actually true, too.

"You off to another lesson with Mr. Owens?"

"Yeah."

"He told me yesterday y'all were coming right along. Said he registered you to enter a competition in December. I wasn't half proud!" Queenie beamed so big I could tell she *was* proud—like I was her own daughter, not some stranger she'd met less than half a dozen times.

Was there anyone in the world Queenie didn't love?

"How's your mama? It strikes me I don't even know her name."

The nervous fluttering started up again in my chest. Talk about Mama was dangerous territory. "Joan Fitzgerald, Miss Queenie, ma'am," I said, praying that Queenie had never met anybody named Fitzgerald in her life.

As if she could hear the little shake in my voice, Queenie's gaze sharpened, the brown skin around her eyes crinkling into a suspicious squint. "She usually walk over to pick you up after she's done?"

"Well—no. I go meet her there."

"I still hope I get to meet her one of these days. I'm not trying to judge her, Annie Lee, but doesn't she worry 'bout you coming here to have lessons with somebody she doesn't know?"

"She trusts me," I said. It was true, but I knew all that

trust would be shattered if Mama had any inkling of where I was right now. "I'm very responsible. Anyway, I'd better go. Bye!"

Queenie watched me for another minute, a thinking sort of expression on her face, before the glass door of the salon closed between us and I made my escape. I walked to the atrium still feeling like something was trailing me, some kind of shadow I could only catch out of the corner of my eye. Part of me wished I'd never said a word to Queenie, no matter how nice she was.

How much longer could I go on like this before Queenie sniffed out all the lies I'd been telling? Before Ray did, too? It was only two weeks into October—there was a lot of time left until December and that competition.

What if Mama found out what I was doing before then? What if I lost my chance to play for those judges because Queenie was so friendly, cared so much about me and about my mama, who she didn't even know?

By the time I got to where Ray was waiting at the piano, my hands were cold and clammy and I was having to work hard to take deep, slow breaths. Sitting on the shining black piano bench helped, though, and so did putting my hands on the keys and playing through both scales I was practicing for the competition, C major and G minor.

After I'd finished, I pulled my sheet music out and put it on the piano music stand, and lifted my hands up to start it, but Ray put his hand on mine so I couldn't. His skin, only a few shades darker than the ivory on the white keys, was rough and dry. Then he looked right into my eyes just the way Clara had, his eyelids drooping down at the corners.

"I've got something special I want you to focus on today, Annie Lee. Today, I want you to let yourself forget a little bit about the things you've been practicing—the fingering, the rhythm, those things. You'll still be working on those same pieces, but today, I want you to concentrate on the way you feel in *here*"—he tapped his chest—"and let that feeling come out through your shoulders, your arms, your fingers, and into the keys. Like this."

He leaned forward and played "Russian Folk Song in G," the very same notes I'd been playing for all these weeks of practicing—but the way he played it was different. It was light and playful and sweet. Some notes tripped and some notes swayed; if I closed my eyes, I could almost see the crackle of candlelight, lords and ladies in fancy dress moving in time to the music.

"I'm never gonna be able to play like that," I said, panic rising back up like acid in my throat.

"Of course not. That was from inside *me*. Now you

show me what's inside *you*."

I put my hands on the white keys and let them sit there a minute, their satin coolness flowing into my fingertips and up my arms. *Joyful*, I thought. *Peaceful. Light.*

I closed my eyes. The music was sitting there in front of me, but I'd played it so many times in the last month that I didn't need it anymore: the notes were inside of me, running through my veins alongside my blood.

And for the first time since I'd asked Ray to teach me, I wasn't thinking about the competition or even the bit about *Cash prizes*. I wasn't thinking about anything but the music.

I played.

And even though I'd been coming to Brightleaf for weekly lessons *and* extra practices for more than a month, and even though I'd played that dumb old Russian folk song every single time, today was different. Today it *was* joyful, peaceful, light. Today my fingers didn't slip or trip or clump like elephants. Today, they spoke all those words my heart could never figure out how to give voice to.

Today, that music came from me.

Ray was quiet when I'd finished, lifting my hands gracefully from the keyboard just the way he'd shown me to and then letting them drift into my lap. He was silent so long I turned to look at him, a little of that burning panic back. Was he okay? Was I? Had I done something terrible?

But he was breathing just fine, and the look on his face wasn't shock or frustration. It was something golden and lovely, something that poured all through me like autumn rain. When he spoke, his voice was tight and scratchy.

"Well now, Miss Annie Lee," he said, and I could've sworn his eyes were brighter than normal. "Well now. I'd say that was just exactly as it should be."

I didn't even need him to tell me to pull out the Bach minuet and try that one, too.

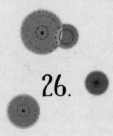

26.

By the time I got back from school that Friday, the message light on our house phone was blinking double time. I hit the button as I took off my backpack and rummaged through the kitchen looking for a snack. *"You have three new messages,"* the smooth recorded voice told me, before beeping its way into the first message.

"Hello, Joan, this is Patricia with the school district office. I'm calling on behalf of the district superintendent. If you could give me a call back as soon as you get this, I'd appreciate it. Thanks."

The machine beeped a second time. *"Hi, Joan, it's Patricia. Just checking in again to let you know that the superintendent would still like to speak to you as soon as possible. Please call me back when you have a chance."*

My hands stilled on the banana I was peeling. *"Hi there, Joan, this is Patricia. I'm really hoping to get in touch with you before the workday is over, as Mr. Shepherd's message is fairly urgent. Please give me a call back right away. Thanks."*

Patricia with the school district office. Was this the secretary Mama had been calling and emailing ever since the life insurance people told her to?

Mama's contract with Mary's Maids stated that she was never allowed to make or take personal phone calls when she was at jobs, or even between them, because the people who owned the company didn't want to run the risk that their employees might try to talk on the phone and drive at the same time. And Mama *never* took off work early—anytime she did, she didn't get her pay for those hours and had to pay a fine out of her other wages to cover the cost of sending another maid over. In the three months she'd been working full-time at Mary's Maids, I hadn't one single time asked her to do anything that might've resulted in that fine.

But if this urgent message was about what I thought it was about, it might just be worth it.

I pulled my phone out and texted Mama. *Secretary* had been a spelling word in fifth grade, but I was a little fuzzy on *superintendent*. I hoped she'd get the point.

I scratched the skin near off my knuckle waiting for her to get home. By the time I heard Mama's key in the lock, I'd come close to throwing the coffeemaker out the window when it wouldn't stop burbling and smelling of Daddy's Panama blend, and kicked the record player twice when it had started up with John Denver singing how he felt like a sad song without his girl. The record player hadn't even been plugged in.

It was like Daddy's ghost could feel the tension in the air, the way our whole apartment was holding its breath.

Sometimes, the ghost appeared in important or happy moments, like the first day of school, or the day me and Mama were throwing those eggs off the balcony—like Daddy wanted so badly to be there celebrating with us, and this was the only way he could think to do it. Other times, the ghost showed up when it was lonely and quiet, like in the afternoons while Mama was still at work.

But nothing seemed to make the ghost more agitated than stress. Like the day Mama and I had come home from our hike at the Eno and she'd gotten that bad email and the TV had turned on two different times, like Daddy was trying to reach out from wherever he was now and reassure her.

Except the only thing the ghost ever succeeded in

doing was making everything worse.

I squeezed the lucky quarter in my pocket.

Mama came through the door and hugged me, still in her pink polo that was damp with sweat and cleaning spray, and then went right to the message machine without a word. She listened to the first message, then the second, then the third.

Then she picked up the phone.

"Hello?" she said after a minute. "Patricia? Yes, hi, it's Joan Fitzgerald. Yes, of course I'll wait . . ."

Mama didn't look at me and I didn't look at her; the hope rising in that kitchen was like a soap bubble, bigger and bigger and bigger, and one breath could've made it pop.

"Yes, hello," Mama said again. "Yes, it's nice to talk to you too, Mr. Shepherd. I know, it's been awhile. Mm-hmm . . . yes . . ."

Mama's side of the conversation devolved into murmurings that didn't make much sense without knowing the other half of it.

But her face was getting tighter, her eyebrows pulling together and her mouth going thin. She wasn't saying, *Oh, I'm so relieved* or *That's so good to know. Thanks so much, Mr. Shepherd.*

Mama finally finished the call with an "I appreciate

you letting me know," and put the phone back on its cradle. She had to try three times before she could get it where it needed to be, her hands were trembling so bad.

"There isn't any more life insurance." She floated into the family room and sank onto the sofa. She looked puffy, like her skin wasn't fitting her bones the way it should. "They looked all over. All through the computer system. They finally found his personnel file. It had a typo—two *L*s in 'Fitzgerald' instead of one—which is why they couldn't find it. Can you believe that? All this time, a little extra *L* was the only thing keeping us all in the dark. Once they found the file, though, there wasn't any record of him paying extra for more life insurance. The way we'd talked about. *The way we'd agreed.*"

Mama was breathing fast, her chest sucking in and out. "Nothing on his pay stubs. Nothing anywhere else. They even called the insurance company manager back just to quadruple-check. There's no more, Annie Lee. No more coming. Ever."

No more life insurance. No more money. Nothing at all for us except Mama working all day every day but Sunday for Mary's Maids and coming home smelling like sweat and vinegar and sadness. Never moving out of our haunted apartment. Probably no new clothes for me this winter, which meant I'd have to dig out my too-small clothes from fifth grade and wear them again and hope nobody laughed.

No new washer.

No new anything.

"What are we going to do, Annie Lee?" I might've thought Mama would cry, but she didn't. She just sat there on that sofa like she was the one who had died, shaking her head over and over again and talking to the empty air. "What are we going to do? How in the hell are we supposed to keep making ends meet? How am I supposed to afford the things you'll need for school?"

I thought of the DPTA competition. *Cash prizes. Beginners welcome.* A hundred dollars wasn't much, but if I could win that prize money, maybe we could at least get a new washer, at least have one thing in our life that worked okay.

Mama was still talking. "Who's going to take care of you, honey? I feel bad every single day, letting you get off the bus and spend all afternoon in an empty apartment. Maybe I should let Mrs. Garcia watch you the way she offered, but I don't have any money to pay her and it just seems like such an imposition to ask of a neighbor we hardly know. . . ."

Guilt wriggled inside me as I thought of the secret life Mama didn't know about—all the trips to Brightleaf, all those afternoons with Ray at the piano. Queenie in her salon, living out the life Mama might have had if she'd learned to be a hairstylist instead of getting pregnant with me.

"What about going to beauty school?" I asked.

"I don't know, honey. It would take money. I just can't see that far into the future yet." The white skin around Mama's lips was extra pale, her chest still going in and out like there wasn't enough air in the world. Was this what hyperventilating looked like? Did I need to call an ambulance or get her to breathe into a paper bag or something like that?

"It's just like Fitz to have been too busy living in the moment to make sure things would go on smoothly after he was gone. It's the fuel pump all over again. That man never *could* keep the important things straight." Mama rubbed her hands over her face hard, and I couldn't tell if she was trying not to cry, or wishing she could.

I thought of the day the fuel pump broke, how Daddy had built that fort and played records of all the things we'd have heard at the symphony if the car hadn't broken down. About how we'd all ended the night feeling twice as happy as if we'd made it to the concert in the first place.

This time, Daddy wasn't here to make things up to

us. He'd always been uncomfortable with things that took paperwork and filing, especially things that were about the future.

Look at me, Al, he used to say sometimes, a grin on his face. *I'm in the prime of my life right now. A beautiful wife, a beautiful little girl who's gonna be a concert pianist someday. The job of my dreams. Why on earth would I want to spend any time worrying about stuff that's far off on the horizon, when I could use up my energy being happy right now?*

It had never bothered me before when he'd said things like that, because life with Daddy was one big adventure, filled with laughter and surprises and spontaneous fun. Even Mama couldn't ever stay mad at him too long, because Daddy's happiness was infectious, the kind that crept into you and changed you from the inside out.

I had a feeling if he'd been here right now, Daddy would have argued that he was *great* at keeping the important things straight. He'd have said that me and Mama were the important ones, not some old fuel pump. But he'd have been wrong. Because things like car repairs, like paperwork—those were the things you were supposed to do to take care of the people you loved. And right now I wished, harder than I'd ever wished anything in my life, that Daddy had used a little of his endless energy to make sure me and Mama would be okay when he was gone. How could he just *leave* us like this?

I shrank away from Mama, tucking myself into the corner of the sofa, pulling my invisibility cloak tight around me.

How could I be the brave, wise Annie Lee when the whole world seemed out to hurt me?

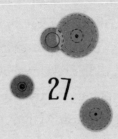

27.

I could hear Mama crying in her room for a long time that night, her sobs rising and falling like waves in the ocean. I scrunched my eyes hard and rolled over and pulled a pillow over my head, but I could still hear.

When I finally did sink into sleep, I dreamed about Daddy, back in that same place with the bright sky and the rainbow umbrellas hanging over us like charms and the rolling melody of the piano. "Annie's Song." His favorite.

"Daddy," I said, and this time he didn't squint at me or act like I was hard to hear—he stopped playing and turned to look at me straight on, in a way that sent prickles from the top of my head down to my knees. It may have only been a dream, but he was *here*, and this time, so was I.

"Al," he said, his voice all choked. He slid his hands off the keyboard and into his lap. On the piano, where the gold letters usually said something like *Yamaha* or *Baldwin*, this one spelled out *Fitzgerald*.

"How come you didn't take care of Mama and me?" I said, the words tripping over themselves before I could stop them. I could half hear Mama's crying even in my dream. "How come you didn't leave us life insurance or anything like that?"

Daddy's mouth twisted. "I'm so sorry, Al. So sorry."

This was the first time I had been able to really talk to my daddy in more than three months, even if it was only a dream, and I couldn't shut up about the stupid life insurance. "You didn't leave us *anything*. Not a single thing except magic tricks. And now Mama has to work all day every day, and comes home looking like wrung-out laundry, and—"

Daddy was shaking his head. "I wish I had, Al. You have no idea how much I wish I had."

He patted the bench beside him. "Want to play with me?"

All the anger and frustration that were knotted up tight in my chest unfurled like a ball of yarn rolling itself out. I stepped forward. "Yeah."

Daddy grinned, the kind of smile that was better than

chocolate, and slid over to make room—

But before I could touch the warm gloss of the piano bench, I woke up.

I lay there in the darkness of my bedroom for a long time, wondering what it would've been like to play a duet with Daddy. Wondering if I'd be able to play the way he did in that bright umbrella place—with careless freedom.

After we were done, would he have picked me up and twirled me around like he used to, crushing me to him like I was still his little girl?

Would I have been able to feel him?

My cell phone, next to my bed, buzzed, making me jump just about out of my skin. The little strip of screen you could see through the flip case glowed blue.

A minute later, it stopped. The notification screen said *MISSED CALL*.

I opened it with shaking hands. The number wasn't one that had ever been programmed as a contact into this phone, since my only contact was Mama—but it was a number I recognized anyway, one that had been burned into my brain from all the times I'd called it on our home phone.

I remembered the way Mama had cried and cried the day she'd disconnected it.

It was Daddy's cell number.

I threw the phone so hard it smacked into the wall. In the bedroom across the hallway, I could hear Mama startle, her bed creaking as she turned over.

I didn't get back to sleep that night.

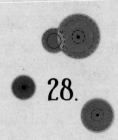

28.

The night before the first egg-drop presentations, a cold snap settled over Durham. October was usually sunny and mild, a second summer that went on and on. Most years, the weather didn't think seriously about cooling down until the Thanksgiving pies had been put away.

But on that Tuesday, I woke up to air that wanted long pants and jackets instead of the shorts I'd been wearing to school for the last month and a half. I pulled a hoodie and some blue jeans out of last year's clothes bin.

Both were too short, and the sweatshirt was tight across my chest in places it hadn't been last year. Meredith and Monica had both gotten new bras over the summer, one after the other. I didn't think Mama had even realized that I might be ready for something more than a training bra. Even if she had, she wouldn't have had the money. How much did a real bra cost? Five dollars? Ten? More than a box of name-brand macaroni and cheese, that was for sure.

At the bus stop I joined all the other kids waiting there and tried to ignore the cold whisper of the wind on the exposed skin at my wrists and ankles. It had been such a strange season—long and short, full of goodbyes and not many hellos. I didn't think I'd been to the pool once, or laid out in the sun, or eaten so much as one Popsicle.

Mr. Barton's class felt like a party, with kids laughing and tossing paper airplanes at one another as Mitch and I settled into our seats. The plan was to have the first four oral presentations, and then we'd all troop outside and watch the presenters drop their eggs off the school roof. The roof was one of those strictly off-limits places, the kind that had a big heavy door with a regular lock and a padlock too, and excitement zinged through the whole classroom at the idea of going up there, even if most of us wouldn't be getting our turn today.

"I understand that our agenda for today has imbued this classroom with a frisson of electricity," said Mr. Barton, the brown skin on top of his head gleaming in the fluorescent light. "Still, I expect perfect quiet and utter politeness as our first two teams present."

From the front row of the class, tater-tot-throwing Malik muttered in a not-very-quiet-voice, "I still don't get why we can't all just go up and toss our eggs at the same time. Ka-POW!"

"I understand your position, Mr. Larson. It would indeed be thrilling, had we time enough to launch all of our projects at once. Quite, as you say, 'ka-pow.' Unfortunately, the main purpose of this project is to demonstrate your grasp of the scientific method itself, and as such, we must put a priority on the oral report as well. Now! Team one! You may take the floor."

The class was quiet but twitchy all through the four presentations, and when they finally finished and Mr. Barton motioned that we could get up, we sounded like a herd of elephants.

Mitch linked her arm through mine, a move that seemed oddly un-Mitch-like. Then again, the more I got to know her, the less I felt like I had her pegged. "Think they'll work, reader girl?"

I shrugged. Mitch and I had worked our way through our whole list of ideas, and every single one of them had smashed to yolky smithereens on the pavement. Now that the presentations had started we weren't allowed to come up with any new designs, but Mr. Barton had said we *could* revise them as long as we didn't use ideas from other teams, so we were adding everything we could think of to make them safer.

"Let's just say it's a good thing none of us are responsible for making sure astronauts enter the atmosphere safely," I said as we shuffled through the front door of the school. Mitch laughed, a dog-bark of a laugh that made me laugh, too.

It felt good, making people laugh. There hadn't been much laughing in my house since the Bad Day, except for the night Mama and I smashed the eggs. I wished we'd been able to hold on to that lightness, that laughter, but the call from District Superintendent Shepherd had stolen that barely-begun smile away from Mama faster than the chilly air stole the heat from our bodies as we gathered outside the school building.

"All right, scholars!" Mr. Barton waved from the roof. He'd borrowed a bullhorn from the gym coach, which made me suspect that deep down, he was just as excited about this as the rest of us were. "Here comes our first demonstration. Team one: let it rip!"

Black-haired Kavya Lahiri, half of the first team, stepped cautiously to the edge of the roof. She held up her contraption—a Dixie cup filled with cotton, the egg nested into the middle of it, a plastic grocery bag tied to the cup's top to act as a parachute. Kavya waited for a moment, the cup and bag in her hands, like she was afraid to let go.

And then she dropped it.

The cup went fast at first, until the plastic bag ballooned out and started to slow it down. It fell, rocking once or twice in the wind, all the way down to the blue tarp Mr. Barton had laid out on the pavement to catch the fallen eggs. The cup tipped gently onto its side, a few of the top cotton balls slipping out onto the ground.

Like a beast with seventeen heads, all of us kids on the ground moved toward the tarp. Tonya and Shonda were nearest to the downed parachute, their best-friend necklaces gleaming in the cold sunlight. They hovered close as Kavya's team partner, a tall girl with skin almost as creamy as the egg Kavya had dropped, picked the contraption up. Her hands cradled the Dixie cup like a newborn puppy as she pulled the cotton balls out, and then the egg.

It was whole.

Shonda, standing behind the girl from Team One, cheered. "Not a crack!" she yelled, loud enough that Mr. Barton and the teams on the roof could hear it.

Everyone cheered.

"All right, ladies and gentlemen," Mr. Barton called

through his bullhorn a minute later. "I appreciate your jubilation. That was indeed an auspicious beginning to our demonstrations. Now, it's time for our second team to take their turn."

The dropper from the second team—a blond boy named Chris, with a black hoodie that looked like an exclamation point against the blue October sky—stepped to the edge of the roof, holding up his team's egg. It was encased in a complicated cube made from what looked like toothpicks.

He let it go.

This one fell a lot faster than the first, hurtling corner-over-corner toward the pavement. I slipped my hand into my pocket and rubbed my quarter hard.

The contraption landed with an audible crash, the toothpicks collapsing with the impact as they hit the ground. I didn't even have to see the yellow yolk oozing out over the blue tarp to know that their egg was toast.

A few students hooted, and somebody yelled out, "Anybody want an omelet?" Everyone laughed. Up on the roof, Chris huddled into his hoodie like a turtle retreating into its shell.

The egg from the third team broke, too, but without the dramatic *splat*—it looked fine until the team member on the ground held it up and we could see a crack in the side, leaking sticky egg white. The fourth egg was perfect, smooth and whole and completely protected by the hollowed-out grapefruit they'd taped it into. I wished Mitch and I had come up with *that* idea.

"My friends," said Mr. Barton from the roof after the fourth egg had been retrieved, "alas, it is time to return to our classroom. We shall meet you there posthaste."

The aide who had stayed with us in the parking lot moved forward to gather up the tarp, and the rest of us started shuffling back into the school. I took my quarter out and flipped it over and over in my fingers, *heads, heads, heads*. What if our project turned out the way Team Two's had? What if our egg splattered into smithereens, and everyone in the class laughed at us, too?

I rubbed the quarter harder.

After we'd settled back into our seats and Mr. Barton was giving the homework assignment for the day, Mitch reached over and flicked a note onto my desk when he wasn't looking.

It's okay, the note said, her little round letters more cheerful than any words that ever actually came out of Mitch's mouth. *Our project is going to be THE BOMB.*

As long as it doesn't just BOMB, I wrote back, my quarter warm in my other hand.

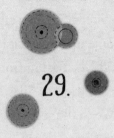

29.

"Hang on a minute—don't get that out quite yet," said Ray Thursday afternoon, after I'd finished playing my scales and reached for the sheet music for the Bach minuet. He gestured at the sheet music—his fingers trembled a little and he was breathing harder than normal, like maybe he wasn't feeling so well. He opened his mouth to keep talking, but coughed instead.

"Mr. Owens—I mean, Ray. Are you feeling okay?"

He waved my concern away. "Just got a touch of the allergies this week. Won't seem to quite leave my chest."

"Would it be better if I come back some other time?"

"Nah, Miss Annie Lee, I'll be fine. But leave that sheet music put away for now. We're gonna try something different this time."

I pressed the heels of my hands into the piano bench. My daddy had been the kind of person who loved "different." He'd driven home from work a different way every day, just to keep things interesting, he said. When we went to church on Sundays, he couldn't bear to sit in the same part of the chapel every week. At dinnertime, if he was the one setting the table, he'd never put any of us in the same chair two nights in a row.

Mama, on the other hand, wasn't a big fan of "different." She liked patterns, organizing things, a place for everything and everything in its place.

I chewed on my lip. I wanted so, so much to be like my daddy, full of fun and adventure. Or like Ray, joyfully living his life even though he didn't have much money and always hurt. Or like Queenie, so filled with love and light that she positively glowed.

But I knew I took after Mama the most: liking things the same way every time, getting nervous when big changes came along. Never quite brave enough to reach out and try to catch things that seemed just a little out of my reach.

"What do you mean about trying something different?"

Ray coughed again, a deep, throaty kind of cough. "Oh, that's nothing to worry about. You're ready for it,

I know. When you came to me back in September, you said you wanted to learn to play piano the way *I* do."

I nodded. "Yeah. The music. And the lights."

Ray leaned forward and slid his hands onto the keys high up on the piano, closing his eyes and playing a few chords that sounded like chimes in the wind, like memories and what it felt like to be a kid and sad things that were somehow happy, too. A wisp of purple sunset light glowed in the air above his fingers.

I swallowed.

"You asked me before why some could see the lights and some couldn't," Ray said.

"You said that people seem to see them when they need them."

"Exactly. I've been playing my whole life but never had seen anything like those lights until my Margie died. I was at a concert one night, feeling right sorry for myself, and there was a solo violinist on the stage. Every time he set bow to string, music came out of that instrument like nothing I'd ever heard. And when he played, light swirled in the air above his fingerboard. I thought at first it was part of the show—thought it had been rigged up by the lighting techs. But then I started seeing them other places, too. When a musician was truly opening themselves up, playing the truth inside of them, there would be light coming from their fingers."

"Why?" I asked. "Why could you only see it after Margie died?"

"Things were pretty dark for me in those days. I'd just lost my soul mate, and it wasn't long afterward that I fell off that roof and ended up losing my job, too. I didn't know which way to turn. Didn't know if I even wanted to keep on living. I think those lights appeared when they did because I needed to know it was possible to be happy again. I needed to know it was worth being like those musicians—learning to open myself back up to life the way they did. Music, it takes courage, Annie Lee. That kind of vulnerability can be scary. You've got to be willing to let go, to let the audience see a true, deep part of you. Otherwise, you might as well just plug some tones into a computer and call it Mozart."

"You have to take off your invisibility cloak," I whispered.

"That's exactly it. You can't have secrets from the piano."

"But what if you . . . get hurt?"

Ray looked at me with an expression as gentle as his dog Clara's, and just as wise, too. "Sometimes you will, Annie Lee."

"But isn't that scary?"

"'Course it is. Every time I sit down at this grand piano and start playing, it scares me. But that's the choice I make. Opening up to the music, making yourself so anyone can see what's in your heart . . . it means you're willing to get hurt, if that's what it takes to experience the magic."

I smiled without quite meaning to, looking down at the keys.

"Now. You want to learn to play the way I play? You gotta practice that, just like we practice the other things," Ray went on. "Remember how you played your competition songs last time so pretty it near about made me cry? That's what you got to do, Annie Lee. But this time, with *your* music." He tapped his chest. "The music that lives right here."

My whole body was perfectly still, still as stone, still as glass, still as the ivory on the piano keys themselves.

"But—" I licked my lips. "What if I don't have any music? Or what if it sounds bad?"

"Oh, it will. Don't everything new sound bad at first? But in time, it'll come. Just try it out."

"But—the competition. Don't I need to focus on practicing the pieces I've got for that?"

"Sure, and we'll do that today, too. But trust me when I say that finding your own music will just make you that much more able to play Bach's and Beethoven's stuff. Now, try it out. Close your eyes and let it come. Be that brave, true version of Annie Lee Fitzgerald that I know's hiding out in there."

I took a deep breath, let the air travel down my arms, to my fingers, till the skin of my fingertips was light and tingly. I didn't want to do it—but at the same time, I did.

I lifted up my hands, closed my eyes, and did my best to open up my heart, the way Ray said.

The notes were jangly at first, like stumbling feet. My pulse thumped in my fingers, hammering *bad idea, bad idea*.

It took everything I had to keep my eyes closed, to keep my fingers on the piano.

But then I found a few notes that sounded good together. And then some more, and some more after that. My fingers were slow on the keys, but that was okay. The song really *did* sound a little bit like the things inside me: tentative, fearful, nervous, all wrapped up in a gossamer string that felt like hope. And even though it still felt like I was on a cliff's edge and any minute the wrong note might send me spiraling down to the rocks below, I kept on going.

Next to me, I could feel Ray holding his breath.

I played on and on, my fingers creeping up the keyboard to the chime notes and then back down to the ones that were deep as the sea. Here and there, I even played a few notes that sounded just a little bit like summer nights when I was a kid, with Daddy in my dusky bedroom singing "Annie's Song" as I fell asleep.

I played until the melody had gotten too complicated and my fingers tangled over themselves. I stopped and opened my eyes, breath coming out of me in a long sigh.

And as I opened my eyes, I caught just the faintest hint of light like pale gold, shining in the air above the piano keys before it winked out of existence.

"See that, Annie Lee?" Ray asked, turning aside to cough again. "You've got great things inside of you, child, if you can just find a way to open up and let them through."

"But I messed it all up."

Ray shrugged. "So? There's a little mess in all of us."

I stared at my reflection in the shining ebony of the piano. I was small and faraway and watery, wisps of hair flying around my face. Playing like that, like Ray did, had been scary—terrifying, even. My fingers curled into fists at the idea of trying it again.

But it had been amazing, too, listening to that slow, beautiful song coming out of *me*, telling the world who

I was. Telling the world about my daddy. About all the things that scared me. About all the things that gave me hope.

I'd always thought it was silly when books described people's eyes as *twinkling*, but as Ray looked at me right then, the blue in his eyes seemed extra bright, like he was laughing on the inside. "All right, then. Thanks for humoring an old man. You can take out that sheet music now. And I want you to remember what it felt like, playing like that, and see if you can take a little bit of that feeling and put it into these two pieces. If you play like that at the competition in December, child, I'd put my money on you walking home with a prize."

I unfolded "Minuet in G Minor" and set it on the piano stand.

But even as I started picking out Bach's melody, I couldn't stop thinking about how it had felt, playing my own.

30.

The next day, a week before the day Mitch and I were supposed to present our egg-drop project, I did something even scarier than playing my own music for Ray: I asked Mitch if she wanted to sleep over at my house.

Mama had been more excited than I'd ever seen her when I asked if it was okay. Her eyes had gotten big and her mouth had the kind of genuine, delighted smile that hadn't been there for months.

"Of course, honey," she'd said. "Let's do something fun! We could make cookies, or go see something in the theater, or—"

I shook my head fast. "We'll just hang out here." Mama deflated like a four-day-old balloon. "Maybe cookies," I added, and she perked back up a little.

It wasn't like we could've afforded the cost of a movie in the theater, anyway. The last time we'd gone, a few weeks before Daddy died, I'd overheard him telling her that the three of us together for a matinee had cost over twenty bucks.

Mitch, when I asked her, was calmer, her too-cool-to-care attitude pulled around her like a sweater. But I could see the way her lips tugged themselves up into a smile when she turned away from me.

"It's a little weird," I said, thinking about the ghost.

"No *way* is it as weird as my house," said Mitch. "It's you and your mama, right? All I'm saying is, at least we won't wake up to Jacob rubbing mustard on our faces."

"Did he—"

"Yup. He heard my dad saying it was good for burns or something. I couldn't convince him it would be bad for pimples."

Her mom brought her over that night after dinner, once Mama had gotten home from work. Mama and Ms. Johnson chatted for a while, their smiles stretched into their cheeks and their voices bright as tin, until Ms. Johnson pulled Mitch into a hug and then waved good-bye. She was out the door and down the steps before half a breath had passed, and then it was just me, Mama, and Mitch.

And Daddy's ghost.

Earlier that afternoon, I'd gone over to where Daddy's record player sat in the corner as soon as I got home from school. Of all the places in our apartment, it seemed to be the one that held the most of Daddy left inside it. I'd sat down by the record player and put on a record of John Denver's greatest hits, letting the soft guitar notes of "Annie's Song" fill the family room.

"I don't know if you can hear me, Daddy," I'd whispered, letting John Denver's voice cover my own. "But if you can, can I ask a favor? My friend Mitch is coming over tonight for a sleepover. Our first ever. Can you keep things quiet around here till she leaves? It's really important to me."

I'd felt weird all over as I'd said it, and been glad Mama wasn't off work yet so there was nobody home to see me making a fool of myself. But I'd been desperate enough to try anything.

When "Annie's Song" had finished playing, the record player had made a scratching sound and the song had started all over again.

I really hoped that had been Daddy agreeing with me.

Now, Mitch and I sat at the kitchen table while Mama fluttered around, too excited to sit down. I hadn't seen her trying this hard to act like a regular person for months. "I'm so glad you could come over tonight, Micheline."

"*Mitch*, Mama," I said through my teeth. "Her name is Mitch."

"Oh—yes. Sorry." Mama laughed, and even though she was still trying too hard, the laugh was real. "Well. Do y'all want to work on your project first, or break out the cookie dough?"

Later, after we'd baked pan after pan of gingersnap cookies and eaten them dipped in milk, we went out to the balcony to test our latest egg prototype: a pyramid-shaped contraption made of dozens of drinking straws and duct tape.

"Who should do the honors?" Mitch asked.

"You can." I didn't want to be responsible for spilling any more yolk on that parking lot.

"Okay," said Mitch, both of us barely breathing as she held the pyramid out over the railing. "Ready?"

"Ready."

I waited for the *smack* against the pavement as Mitch threw the egg as hard as she could toward the ground.

Instead, there was silence.

"What happened?" Mitch asked, staring down into the darkness of the parking lot below. The streetlight closest to our apartment had gone out two weeks before and the landlord still hadn't fixed it, so our part of the building was shrouded in gloom as soon as the sun went down every evening.

"I don't know," I said, going inside and rummaging through Mama's catchall drawer for a flashlight. "Let's go see."

When we got down the creaky metal stairs, we found the drinking straws pretty smashed out of shape, with one of the strips of duct tape flying free. But the egg inside was whole and uncracked, shining white in the light from my flashlight.

"We did it," I whispered.

"We did it!" Mitch whooped, jumping up and down so that her curls bounced under her beanie. "We did it, Annie Lee! We're getting an A on this one for sure!"

I scooped up the mess of straws and tape and still-intact egg and carried it upstairs. Mitch trailed behind me, and even though I couldn't see her face I had a feeling she was grinning just as broadly as I was.

Mama was waiting for us in the doorway when we got back to the apartment. The skin between her eyebrows was puckered up, and she seemed distracted. "Annie Lee, honey. Mrs. Garcia just came over to see if we wanted any of her pears before they all went brown. While she was here, she mentioned that she stopped by to check on you after school yesterday, but nobody was home."

I froze with one foot inside the apartment and one foot still in the stairwell. I'd been at Brightleaf yesterday, with Ray.

"I was wondering why she said that," Mama went on, "since I was at work yesterday afternoon, so you should've been here. Care to explain what was going on?"

I just stared at her. What could I say? How could I possibly get out of this one? I couldn't say I'd been playing outside the complex—Mrs. Garcia could've seen me. But no way could I tell Mama I'd been all the way over at Brightleaf Square, taking piano lessons from a man she'd never met.

Mitch cleared her throat behind me and nudged me into the apartment. "I can explain that one, Mrs. Fitzgerald," she said brightly, closing the door behind her with a loud *snap*. "Me and Annie Lee had to stay after school awhile. Everyone who has presentations next week did, to work on some stuff with the egg-drop project. We had to get our final designs approved by the teacher."

I stared sidelong at Mitch. How had she come up with that whopper so easily?

All the tension went out of Mama's shoulders, like the wrinkles being shaken out of a bedsheet. "I see. Thanks for letting me know, Mitch. Annie Lee, I hope you know that next time something like that comes up, I expect a phone call about it in advance. I may not be able to be here after school, honey, but I'm still your mama, and I still need to know where you are at all times, understand?"

I nodded. "Yeah."

"Good. I forgive you—this time. So, how'd your egg do?"

I looked down at the remains of our prototype; I'd forgotten all about it when my heart had nearly stopped at Mama's question.

"Oh." I cleared my throat, pasting on a smile. "It worked!"

Mama flung her arms up into the air cheerleader-style. "Yes! I knew y'all could do it, honey!"

The smile on my face shifted into something real.

"If you can manage to get that egg free of everything else," Mama said, "go on and put it back in the fridge. Omelets for breakfast tomorrow seems appropriate, doesn't it?"

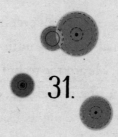

31.

Later, after we'd all celebrated the successful egg-drop with one more cookie, Mitch and I blew up the air mattress and got into our pajamas.

It had taken awhile for my heartbeat to return to normal after Mama's comment about Mrs. Garcia. I had come so close, *so* close to losing everything—Ray, Queenie, Brightleaf, the thrill of feeling piano notes roll out under my fingertips. If Mitch hadn't jumped in to save me, I'd be grounded for the rest of my life. No piano. No Ray. No little thread of hope for the first time since the Bad Day in June.

But Mitch *had* saved me. And slowly, so slowly I almost didn't realize it was happening, my shoulders had loosened up, the wound-up tightness that always seemed to hold me in its grasp these days slipping away like sand in an hourglass.

The ghost had been quiet all evening, like my plea to the record player had worked—until Mitch and I were brushing our teeth. I heard the record player whir to life in the family room, the soft chords of "Annie's Song" starting again. Just like the nights Daddy had sat by my bed and sung to me in the darkness until I was sleepy.

Mama was sitting at the kitchen table—our apartment was so small that the table was barely ten feet from the bathroom door. My eyes met hers across the hallway. Neither of us went over to turn the song off. We let it play all the way until it was done, until the last sad guitar note had faded and the record player clicked itself off.

"That was pretty," Mitch said as we climbed into our beds. "What song was that?"

I swallowed down the lump in my throat. "It's the song my parents named me after. It was Daddy's favorite. It's called 'Annie's Song.'"

"Cool," said Mitch. "I liked it."

"Yeah," I said. "I do, too. Hey—" I paused, my words hanging in the air between us. "Thanks for covering for me earlier. With my mom."

Mitch shrugged. "I figured you had a good excuse."

"Sometimes it's just too hard staying here all by myself

every day while Mama's at work. I have to get out, or I feel like I'll pull apart at the seams. There's just too many . . . memories."

"I can see that. Where do you go?"

I hesitated. Mitch had lied to Mama for me earlier—but all the secret details of my piano lessons and how they'd come to be felt too big, too dangerous, to share, even with a friend. A best friend. "I just go ride my scooter around the neighborhood. Not too far. Mama's just really overprotective."

"I get that." Mitch had taken her trademark white beanie off sometime earlier that evening, and her curly hair flew around her face like wings, all staticky from the hat but still pretty. It made her look two years younger and not nearly as tough.

"You look different," I said. "Without your hat on. Your uniform, right? How come?"

Mitch shrugged, rolling onto her stomach and hugging a pillow to her. I thought suddenly how it was the first time I'd had a sleepover with anyone at all since before Daddy had died. It was strange, like if I turned around I would see Monica or Meredith out of the corner of my eye, their presence prickling all over my skin.

But for maybe the first time since June, being memory-deep like that felt different. Somehow, thinking about the M&Ms didn't sting nearly as bad as it had a few weeks ago. It was like they were friends from another lifetime. Like maybe, just maybe, I could be okay without them in this one.

"My mom found it on clearance a week or two before school started," Mitch said, and the ghosts of Monica and Meredith snapped out of being like a blink. "I liked the way it made me feel. Kind of . . . strong. Different. I don't know."

For the first time, I wondered if maybe Mitch's beanie, her tough attitude, were all her own version of an invisibility cloak. Maybe Mitch had figured out that if all she showed to the world was her strong outside, nobody would ever see through to her soft inside.

Mitch hugged the pillow harder. Her face was a pale smudge in the darkness of the bedroom. "People . . . they aren't really my strong point. I get nervous when I'm around big groups. And it's hard for me to, you know, go up and talk to somebody if I don't know them."

"You came and sat by me at lunch."

"You looked so lonely sitting there with your book. And, I don't know, I know what that feels like. So I figured we'd have something in common."

"Thanks," I whispered.

"Anyway. Kids were pretty mean, back at my

elementary school. I went to this little private school for artsy professors' kids. Everyone there made fun of me for my name, for the clothes I wore . . . everything, I guess. Anything they could think of. People thought I was stuck-up and rude, because I had a hard time opening up. And then, last year, in fifth grade, a bunch of the boys were really awful. I had to, um, get a bra before a lot of the other girls, and this group of boys were always snapping the straps and saying awful things about me. And some of the girls started spreading rumors. Calling me a slut. Saying I'd done a lot of things I hadn't."

"That sounds awful."

"Yeah, it kind of was. I told my parents I wanted to go to a regular middle school for sixth grade. And I promised myself it would be different."

"But don't kids still—"

"Oh yeah, they're all still jerks," said Mitch, but she was grinning in the darkness. "But now I don't care. When I put the hat on, it's like a reminder. That it's okay to be me. That nobody else matters. That I can be angry if I want, or quiet, or loud, or shy, or wild."

"Like my quarter. Carrying your own luck."

"Yeah. Kind of like that," Mitch said. A minute later, her voice twice as quiet, she added, "Do you miss him a lot?"

"My daddy?" My fingers slipped over to the night-stand to rub at the quarter. "Yeah. A lot a lot. Sometimes it feels like I don't know how to keep breathing with him gone, and I don't think Mama does, either."

"I bet." Mitch was quiet. "Sometimes my family drives me crazy. All of us shut up in that house—Dad, Mom, Nana, Jacob. Our own little five-ring circus. But I can't imagine any of them being . . . not there anymore."

I pulled my hand away from the quarter, not meeting Mitch's eyes. "Anyway, I think you're pretty cool. With the hat or without it."

It was like my words were keys, reaching inside and peeling back the layers of my stony heart, opening my fingers up so that my own invisibility cloak fluttered off my shoulders and left me there alone on the bed. Me. Just Annie Lee. The way I'd always been, or maybe the way I was just starting to be.

I felt lighter. I hadn't realized until now just how heavy all that invisibility sitting on my shoulders could be.

"Thanks," said Mitch. "You're pretty cool yourself, reader girl."

32.

That weekend, the October chill that had started the week before deepened into the kind of cold that we didn't usually get until more like December. By Monday, as I rode my scooter to Brightleaf, it felt chilly enough for frost to settle into my skin, making tracks of silver dust along the blue of my veins.

It made me think of Monica and Meredith—how once, when we were eight, there'd been a freak snowstorm in Durham the week before Thanksgiving. Our parents had let us all sleep over at Monica's for two whole days while school was out. We'd gorged ourselves on hot chocolate and sledded down Monica's hilly street until we'd worn all the ice off the road, then lay on Monica's trampoline with our heads together, my yellow hair mixing with Monica's black hair mixing with Meredith's curling red.

Let's make a solemn vow, Meredith had said, her voice dramatic as always. I didn't know exactly what a solemn vow was, but it sounded important. *No matter what happens, we will always be best friends forever.*

Deal, Monica had said, and I'd agreed. Meredith had jumped down off the trampoline and run into the house to get paper and pens, and when she'd come back outside, she'd written up a contract and had each of us sign it, promising that nothing would ever come between us. It had felt magical, sitting on that trampoline with my two best friends, like the three of us made something so strong and tight that nothing could get inside it to hurt me.

Now, as I rode toward Brightleaf Square, the memory was a little hitch in my breathing, a small pluck at my heart, like hitting the wrong note in a piano piece. But it didn't slam into me like it might have before school started. It was more like I could feel that little prick of sadness and then move right along—like the sleepover last weekend with Mitch had begun to fill in the M&M-shaped cracks inside me.

It was a good feeling.

The mall was quiet when I got there, only a few people

ambling in and out of the shops or lingering in the restaurants, their voices drifting out into the atrium like smoke. I went in through a different door than usual so I didn't have to walk past Queenie's shop. I couldn't get the way she'd looked at me last time out of my mind, like she was working out exactly who I was and where I came from and where my mama wasn't.

I missed Queenie, but I couldn't risk seeing her. Not today. Not with so many weeks still between me and the piano competition.

The atrium itself was empty when I got there, the grand piano crouched and waiting, shining in the skylight. I had never gotten to the mall before Ray. My piano lessons were never on the same day—it always depended on homework, and I couldn't come too often for fear that Mama would find out I was riding all over town while she was gone—but we always agreed in advance on when we'd meet next.

I'd never known Ray to be late.

I hung around for a few minutes, like maybe if I stayed still enough, I'd blink and then he'd explode into being right there on the piano bench, music and light pouring out of his fingers like water.

But he didn't. The piano just sat there, silent. It was like a seven-foot magnet, unspooling an invisible string across the floor to me, looping somewhere behind my knees and then tugging. *Come*, the gloss of the ebony whispered.

Come here.

I looked around once, twice, three times just to be sure. The atrium was empty.

I walked forward, toes first so that my shoes didn't make any sound on the tile of the floor.

On a whim, I took my phone out before I sat down, resting it gently on the piano's music stand and hitting the record button.

The wood of the bench was cool under my legs, but the ivory keys when I rested my fingertips on them were warm, like somewhere inside it the piano breathed.

I'd been playing on this piano for weeks now, but somehow it felt different, being here without Ray, without Queenie, with people walking past who might hear anything I played. Even though nothing had really changed, the air was charged.

Like me sitting down on that bench was the same as me choosing to open my heart right up for anyone to see.

The first notes of Bach's "Minuet in G Minor" were wispy and thin, and the left-hand accompaniment was off by two whole notes before I slid my shaking hands to where they were supposed to be.

I almost stopped. My hands paused, hovering like butterflies barely brushing against the ivory. But then I thought of Ray last week, saying, *There's a little mess in all of us*, and instead of lifting my hands up, I pressed down harder.

And a minute later, when I'd come to the end of that minuet, I let my fingers keep on going, wandering their way up and down the keyboard.

My music wasn't like Ray's. It didn't have any of his power, or his control, and it didn't sing out into the atrium like it was giving voice to the soul of every person who heard it. My music was small, and a little bit tentative. There were wrong notes sometimes, and other times notes that weren't really wrong but didn't sound very nice, either. I didn't use the pedal the way Ray did, pulling my song into beautiful swaths the way the Milky Way pulled in the stars, because I didn't know how yet.

My music still sounded like beginner stuff.

But it was *mine*.

And as it poured out from somewhere inside me, that so-faint-you-could-hardly-see-it shining gold light rose up and danced above the piano. My very own musical light show. My heart, spun out of my chest like the straw in "Rumpelstiltskin," glowing there for anyone to see.

I put everything I'd been thinking and feeling for the last three and a half months into that music: the way it had felt to see Daddy lying cold and still in the hospital. The way Mama cried every morning. How it had seemed like the M&Ms took pieces of my heart away with them when we drifted apart. What it was like when Mitch came to sit next to me, and then kept coming back every day. The way joy had sung through my bones when we'd thrown our egg off the balcony Friday night and it hadn't even cracked.

And I put in Daddy's music. A little bit of "Annie's Song," wistful and sweet, the way Daddy used to sing it to me. The jumping, funny notes of "You Can Call Me Al," reminding me of how Daddy had turned the volume up and danced around the house with a pretend microphone. The slow melodies of "Carolina in My Mind" and "Like a Sad Song"—Daddy had liked to put those ones on during rainy afternoons. *Sad music is good for a crying sky*, he'd always said.

I played until I lost track of time, until the song told me it was ready to be over, and then I let my fingers slow down and creep into something that sounded like an okay ending.

When I lifted my hands off the keys, somebody walking past clapped.

Still, there was no sign of Ray. I checked my phone: I'd already been here an hour. The recording had timed out more than forty-five minutes ago. If I didn't get home quick enough to do all my homework before Mama got back she'd get suspicious, and my secret would be smashed to bits, just like all the eggs that had met their deaths on our apartment parking lot.

I swallowed down a twinge of unease and slid off the piano bench. I went the regular way out this time, slinking past Queenie's. With that great big shop window, she must know everything that happened in the building.

Would she have seen Ray come or go today?

But even that wasn't enough to give me the courage to push her door open, and so after a few minutes I just left, pulling my jacket tighter as the cold outside air hit me.

Did the cold make Ray's arthur worse? Had he hurt too much this morning, maybe, to get up and come meet me like normal? Last week he'd seemed sick. Had it really just been allergies, or had it been something else?

As I rode back toward my apartment building, the whir of my scooter against the pavement sounded like a murmuring voice:

Ray. Ray. Ray.
Lost. Lost. Lost.

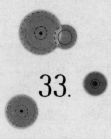

33.

Mama was crying when I woke up Wednesday morning. As summer had eased its way into autumn, she'd cried less—it wasn't *every* morning now, only four or five times a week. But even on the days her eyes were dry, they looked sunken, the lines around her mouth getting so deep they might as well have been carved there like the lines on Mount Rushmore. At least before the district person had called with the news that there wouldn't ever be more money from the life insurance, Mama had had a spark of hope inside her, even if it was smaller than a firefly's light.

Now, she seemed like maybe one of these days she'd wink out of existence altogether.

I reached my hand over to my nightstand the way

I always did, my fingers itching to rub Daddy's lucky quarter.

It wasn't there.

I sat up in bed, wide-awake now. The wood of the nightstand was cool under my fingertips. Cool and empty.

I slid to the floor, hardly registering the sound of Mama cleaning down the ghost-infested bathroom sink and turning on the fan, and ran my hands over the carpet, the bed frame, even poked my fingers in between the mattress and the bed.

Nothing.

Nothing.

And nothing in the rest of my room, either, after I'd stood and turned on the light and started shaking out all the pockets of my jeans and pulling the drawers from my dresser, just to make sure it hadn't slipped down behind one of them.

"Annie Lee?" Mama called, knocking twice on my door. "You fighting a bear in there, honey?"

"No," I said, the whole world tipping up around me. Where could it have gone? How could I have lost the one thing I had left that still made it feel like Daddy was here, wrapping his arms around me the way he used to?

"You sure?" Mama said.

"Yep." There wasn't enough air to breathe in my bedroom. How could I go to school without the quarter? How could I be sure Ray would be at Brightleaf when I went over there this afternoon, if I couldn't carry luck with me, the way Daddy always said? What if it stayed lost, and I didn't have it with me when Mitch and I did our egg drop on Friday, or when the DPTA piano competition rolled around in December?

I took a deep breath, then another, then another. My skin buzzed all over, like maybe I'd float away or explode any second.

If Mama saw me like this, she wouldn't understand. She'd just tell me to get ready for school, not realizing that I *couldn't* go to school without my piece of luck, *couldn't* face the world without that little connection to Daddy.

I'd have to figure out a way to get to the bus without her noticing anything strange.

I'd have to figure out a way to go all day without feeling like the pieces of my life that had only begun to fit back together after Daddy's death were ripping right down the middle.

I finally gave up looking for the quarter when Mama shouted that I only had ten minutes before the bus came and if I wanted breakfast, I better get it fast.

"What do you need washed this morning?" she asked as I sat down and poured myself some cereal. "I don't have time to do a lot."

With no washer, we never did laundry in big loads anymore—it was just little dribs and drabs, a few shirts one morning, some jeans the next.

"My gym clothes and my blue shirt." The blue shirt was my favorite, one of the few that still fit me right— not pulling too tight across the chest or riding up over my hipbones. It was the color of the ocean, somewhere between teal and turquoise, and it made me feel strong and brave. I'd need it for our egg drop Friday morning.

Mama rushed off into my room and then hers. When she came back, she had a bundle made of both our clothes in her hands. She filled the sink with hot water, poured in some laundry soap, and started scrubbing. Our clothes never got as clean these days; it was harder to get rid of stains and sweat and dirt without a washing machine to do it for you. It made me understand better why the pioneers had those washboard things to scrape clothes against when they did their laundry.

In the kitchen, the CD player made a crackle-pop sound and started playing, something mournful and quiet. At the sink, Mama threw her wet hands up, splashing water all over the counters, then trudged to the CD player and yanked the plug out of the wall.

"Is this supposed to make us feel better, reaching back here to play some depressing music? Because it never does," she said, but I didn't know if she was talking to me or to the ghost. Her eyes glistened—from frustration, or sadness, or maybe a tangled-up ball of both—and she rubbed a wet hand across her forehead. "I wish we were all a little better at letting go."

When she plugged the CD player back in again, it stayed silent.

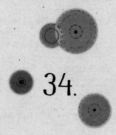

34.

When I showed up at Brightleaf again that afternoon after school had ended, Ray was nowhere
to be found. It was like the whole mall echoed extra
without him there—like instead of feeling expansive
and filled with light, those high ceilings and dark brick
walls were cold and shaded without the spark of Ray's
piano magic.

Ray wasn't in the atrium, or in any of the restaurants.
He wasn't outside in the courtyard, where the chilly
afternoon air made blood prickle into my cheeks like
needles. I even checked the other warehouse, the one
I'd never seen him go into. Ray's red-faced friend Stan
the janitor was pushing his broom along the shiny floor
there, and he gave me a little wave as he passed by, but

Ray himself was nowhere. I wandered back to the warehouse with the grand piano, feeling like I hadn't lost my piano teacher—I'd lost my own self.

For the first time since he hadn't shown up for my Monday lesson, I thought about just getting on my scooter and riding all the way out to find his home. I knew he lived pretty close to Maplewood Cemetery. But that was far—farther away than anywhere I'd ever gone by myself, and on a road that took you right on a bridge over the freeway. Mama would've had my hide if she ever found out I'd spent months wandering around Old North Durham all on my own, but she would have more than that if I tried to cross the freeway. She'd take my head right off my shoulders.

"Hey. Kid. You okay?"

I jumped. The girl who worked in the music store stood in the doorway of her shop, the silver stud in her nose winking like a star in the dim light.

"Yeah," I said. I'd been so upset, so lost in thinking about Ray, I hadn't even made sure my invisibility cloak was in place.

"You need something?" Music Store Girl asked, leaning against the doorway like she, too, was tired, like this cold snap that had crept through town had pulled away a little bit of everybody's soul along with it.

My fingers went into my empty pocket, wishing for my quarter. "Well. Maybe. I'm just looking for my friend. You maybe know him? He's here a lot? His name's Ray Owens?"

Music Store Girl rubbed the back of her neck. "He the one who's always out here with you?"

I nodded.

"I mean, I know him a little bit. He always says hi, and sometimes he comes in to chat after he's done playing the piano. But I've only worked here since the spring. Sorry. I haven't seen him around the last few days, if that helps."

"Do you know when you saw him last?"

"I dunno. Maybe last time you were out there together playing on that thing."

Thursday, then—the day of my last lesson. Six days ago.

"Thanks anyway," I said.

Music Store Girl ducked back into her store, letting the door swing shut behind her like a breath.

Most evenings, Mama was home by six, and I didn't need the buzz of the reminder alarm on the phone in my pocket to tell me it was past time I got heading back so I could get to the apartment before she did.

But I couldn't leave without knowing more about Ray's disappearance than I already did.

I stood in front of Queenie's big glass window, my heart ticking like a metronome turned all the way up, *clickclickclickclick*. I hadn't talked to her at all since two weeks ago. She'd been asking me more about Mama then, the piano lesson before last, with that look on her face like the gears in her head were sliding into place.

I couldn't get that look out of my mind. How much did she suspect about what I'd been doing behind my mama's back? I'd avoided her ever since, always coming in through the door that didn't go right past her shop. I kept to the shadows, invisibility cloak pulled tight, if I noticed her in the atrium.

But right now, my problems were bigger than me, bigger than the Vesuvius-level eruption that would come out of Mama if she found out how I'd been sneaking off to take piano lessons from a strange old man for the last two months.

I had to talk to Queenie about Ray, even if it gave her more chances to figure me out. I couldn't worry about the competition today, or my lies. My worrying was used up by Ray's disappearance.

I pushed my hand against the swinging salon door before my brain could freeze my feet up with fear.

A little bell tinkled above the door as it opened, and Queenie looked up from where she was writing something in a ledger at the salon's front desk. Her smile was like daffodils and hot chocolate and sunlight and the whoosh of summer rain, the way it went through you and traveled deep down to your toes.

"Annie Lee!" she said. "I haven't seen you in a hot minute, child! Where you been?"

I cleared my throat, wishing for the millionth time that I had my quarter back.

"It's about Ray," I said.

"I noticed that piano's been quiet this week," said Queenie.

"He's missing," I said, the words like cut glass in my mouth. "He was supposed to be here Monday, but I haven't seen him since my lesson last Thursday. I've come twice already this week. I don't know where he could be. I thought with the two of you being such good friends, you might know where he was. Or maybe you'd have seen him through your big window. Or maybe you'd gone out to hear him play, and . . ."

Queenie's lips pulled in together and her forehead wrinkled up. "I can't say as I've seen him this week, either. At least not since Friday. We actually got in a little bit of an argument, if you could picture the two of us old fuddy-duddies arguing. He was sneezing and coughing like all get out, and I was on his case to go home instead of finishing out his shift. He said I was being a busybody and that nothing was wrong with him that a dose of NyQuil couldn't cure. He was pretty crabby with me by the time he left—didn't even say goodbye. I was kinda glad when he didn't show up Monday, to be honest, since I figured it meant he was taking it easy like I'd told him to. I'm surprised he missed your lesson, though. That's not like him."

All the air trickled out of me, through my skin and my scalp and my fingertips. "Has he ever been gone this long before?"

"Sure, he'll miss a few days here or there, if he's got a little cold or had something else come up. And sometimes he goes down to Georgia to visit his brother, though he usually he lets me know if he'll be gone so I can feed his dog. I know he's got some neighbor kids to tend her before, though."

Maybe he had a cold. Maybe he'd been coming down with it last Thursday during my lesson, and that's what was wrong with him Friday when Queenie told him to go home. But would a cold have kept him away for nearly a week?

"Tell you what, Annie Lee. Ray'll call me an old

busybody again, but once I'm off work I'll drive over to his place and take a look around," said Queenie. "I'd call, but he hasn't had a phone for a while now. Couldn't keep up on the bills."

"You've been to his house before?"

"Plenty of times. His neighborhood's out by Maplewood Cemetery—that's why Margie's buried there, so he could stay close to her. Now it just takes a little walk through the woods for him to visit her grave."

So that's why he'd been in the woods when I'd seen him at the cemetery all those weeks ago.

"We'll get to the bottom of it," Queenie said. "Meanwhile, it's awful late. Your mama gone be off her shift soon?"

I nodded.

"Ray will be okay," said Queenie gently, looking into my eyes like she could beam comfort right into my heart. "Promise. Us old folks, sometimes we just get a little forgetful."

"I hope so," I said, and slipped back out of the salon, letting the glass door swing closed between Queenie and me with a rush of cold, cold October air.

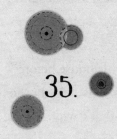

35.

Thursday went exactly the same way Monday and Wednesday had.

I spent all day at school trying to focus when Mitch passed me notes in science class or sat next to me at lunch, trying to pretend my thoughts weren't a million miles away with Ray, wherever he might be.

I took the bus home and tried to ignore Mrs. Garcia's worried eyes as I went into my apartment. "You okay, Annie Lee? You seem sad. Is something the matter with your new friend?"

I shook my head no, but I couldn't bring myself to put on even a weak smile.

I snuck off to Brightleaf as soon as I'd heard Mrs. Garcia's door close, creeping past her windows and praying that she had her back turned and couldn't see me leaving. The last thing I needed was her saying something else to Mama to bring Mama's suspicions roaring right back.

By that point, I'd given up trying to convince myself that I was doing anything except obsessing over where Ray might have gone. My homework sat in my backpack, untouched; yesterday afternoon, I'd hardly made it home from the mall before Mama got off work.

The next day was Mitch's and my turn for our egg-drop presentation, and at this rate my own brain was as scrambled as a shattered egg.

I went right to Brightleaf that afternoon and didn't even wait for the customer Queenie was blow-drying to leave before I pushed through the door into her salon.

"Be with you in a minute, honey," Queenie called to me. "Just take a seat."

I fidgeted in one of the chairs in the tiny waiting area, thumbing through an old copy of *Seventeen* until Queenie finished up and her customer paid and left.

"What can I do for you, Annie Lee?" Queenie asked, coming to sit next to me, looking glad of the excuse to be off her feet for a few minutes.

"Did you get a chance to go by Ray's place yesterday?" I asked. I couldn't handle small talk, not today.

"I did, but he wasn't there. I knocked a couple times, even rang the bell, but he never answered."

I scratched at the skin around my nails. "Where could he have gone?"

Queenie shrugged. "I wish I knew. He could be still feeling sick and avoiding me because he hates hearing me say *I told you so*. Or he could've gone out of town. Like I mentioned yesterday, he's got a brother down in Georgia he's real close with."

"But you said he usually told you if he was going out of town."

"Usually, sure, but there's been times he's decided to go last minute and I haven't known 'til after."

"Does he have a car? How could he get to Georgia?"

Queenie shook her head. "He sold his car years ago, when he lost his roofing job. He couldn't keep up the insurance. He usually walks over here—says it's good for his heart. Times he goes down to Georgia, he takes the bus."

"You said he couldn't keep up on his phone bills, though. Could he afford the bus?"

"I don't know, honey."

"Are you sure there isn't *anything* else we could do? Could we fill out a missing persons report?"

"I'm not sure the police would take us very seriously

if we said we wanted to fill out a report because somebody didn't show up for their volunteer job for a couple days. And I don't know yet that I think that'd be the right thing to do, anyway." Queenie laid her hand on my arm. "Let's hope for the best. He probably saw it was me through the peephole yesterday and decided not to answer because he was still all up in his feelings. Mr. Banks can be the same way when he's sick—they're both stubborn old cusses, never wanting to admit they're only human and sometimes need to sit back and take a break."

"But—how do you *know* that's what happened? What if he got sicker? Don't you think you should go by his house again?"

"He'd just say I was meddling if I did. Let's give it a little more time and see if he shows up. I promise if he's not back by next week, we'll do some more investigating." Queenie pulled me into a hug, her arms just as warm and soft as I'd always known they'd be. "You're a real good friend, Annie Lee. Ray would be touched to know how much you care."

"I just hope he's okay."

"Me too, honey. Me too. Now I got a few appointments to finish up this afternoon, so I'll see you another day, okay?"

I nodded and disentangled myself from the hug.

A minute later, when I'd made it out of her shop and looked back through the window, I could see Queenie still in the same chair. She'd told me not to worry; she'd seemed sure Ray was just being stubborn. Stubborn enough to stay away from the mall without even thinking to cancel the lesson we'd scheduled first.

But looking through the window, I could see worry written out in lines across her forehead and pulled into puckers around her mouth.

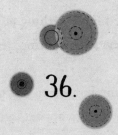

36.

I dreamed that night about the place with the colorful umbrella sky, the place where always before I'd seen Daddy at the piano.

Except tonight, it wasn't a dream. It was a nightmare.

The sky behind the umbrellas was bruised and purple, weeping rain that stung my skin and ran off the ebony of the piano in shining, sorrowing rivers. The umbrellas themselves were ripped, their spokes bent at awkward angles, like a giant had tried to swat them out of the sky.

Daddy wasn't there. The whole strange dream place was empty, empty, empty.

It was the kind of emptiness that had been on Daddy's face, the night before the funeral when they'd laid him out in white clothes in the glossy coffin. He hadn't looked a thing like himself, lying there in that box with his eyes closed, like the mortician was pretending my daddy would wake up any second.

He hadn't looked like anything at all—only a memory. Only a hollowness, a wanting. Just like this dream place was tonight.

I tried to open my mouth, to call out to him, to will my voice into making him appear right there, his hands running up and down the keyboard and making the kind of music he'd always wished to play. But my words were swallowed in silence before I could even get them out.

It was worse than being invisible. It was like being wrapped up in four or five invisibility cloaks, until I was so faded that nobody even remembered I'd ever existed.

When I finally woke up, I could hear James Taylor playing somewhere in our midnight apartment, even though all the lights were off and I knew Mama was asleep. I pictured the ghost, sitting there in the darkness of the living room as the nonexistent record spun its way through the player over and over and over.

And for the first time in maybe months, I shoved my face into my pillow and cried, and cried, and cried, until all my tears were gone but my body still shuddered like it wanted to keep on going.

37.

The next day, Friday, Mitch and I were scheduled to do our egg drop.

I didn't go to school.

Mama took me to the bus stop, hovering until the bus pulled up and I climbed on. I slid into the seat beside Mitch—our usual row, halfway between the front and the back.

"Listen," I said in a low voice, so nobody else could hear. It wasn't hard, since the rest of the bus was loud and rowdy anyway. "I need your help with something."

Mitch looked up from the book she'd been reading with her eyebrows raised.

"I have to get off the bus early," I whispered as fast as I could, before I could chicken out. "I can't go to school today. I need you to cover for me."

I unzipped my backpack and pulled out the egg-drop supplies I'd brought: notes for my half of the oral presentation, a box of straws, and an egg—wrapped in a towel so it didn't break in my backpack. Mitch had the duct tape, since it was the most expensive thing on our list.

"Tell Mr. Barton I had a family emergency and that I'll talk to him about it on Monday," I went on. "If you need to, you can tell him to give all the credit to you, not me."

Mitch stared at me, not raising her hands to take the egg and the straws from mine. "Are you freaking kidding me right now?" she hissed, each word like a sharp little dart. "You're seriously going to sneak off and leave me to take the fall for this? It's the *biggest day of the semester*, Annie Lee. You heard what Mr. Barton said about participation and attendance for this project! It isn't enough just to give me all the stuff—we'll both end up getting our grades docked if you're not there."

"I know. I know." The back of my throat burned with unshed tears. "I'm sorry. I *have to*, though. It's really, really important." I closed my eyes. "Listen. Remember what my mom said at the sleepover, about how I was gone when our neighbor came by?"

Mitch nodded warily. "You said you were just out riding around your neighborhood."

"Well, remember how I told you a few weeks back I was taking piano lessons? And how I've been working on stuff for that competition in December?"

"Yeah . . ."

"Well, I am. Except, my mom . . . kind of doesn't know about it."

"What do you mean?"

I closed my eyes. "I was telling the truth when I said I went off on my scooter when Mama was working, but there's more to it. The week school started, I rode over to Brightleaf Square mall, and I met this man. His name is Ray. He plays the piano like nobody I've ever heard before—it's magical."

"Girl, this story is *not* going to have a good ending," Mitch interjected.

"I know it sounds bad, okay? But he's really nice. He's old and has trouble getting around sometimes because of his arthur—I mean arthritis. But everyone at the mall knows him, and they all love him. He's been volunteering there for a long time."

"So you just asked some strange old man for piano lessons and he said yes?"

"Well . . . yeah."

Mitch whistled. "That is pretty messed up, but keep going. What does any of this have to do with our project?"

"He's missing. He hasn't been in his usual place for a week, and nobody knows where he is. My friend Queenie—she works at the mall—she thinks he's just avoiding her because they had a fight, but I've got a bad feeling about it all. Last time I saw him he didn't seem like himself. He was coughing pretty bad. I'm real worried about him, Mitch. I think something happened to him."

"So, what exactly are you saying?" Mitch looked down at the bus floor, where my folded-up scooter sat beside my backpack. "You're seriously telling me you're going to get on your scooter and ride out to . . . wherever this dude lives? By yourself? You realize that's how horror movies start, right?"

"I don't know what else to do."

"Tell somebody! An adult!"

"My mama would straight-up *kill* me, Mitch. She wouldn't go after him. She wouldn't make sure everything's okay. And I've already talked to some of the people at the mall, and none of them are doing enough about it. *Please*, Mitch. I can't wait until this afternoon. He lives a lot farther away than Brightleaf, farther than I've ever been on my scooter, and I don't know if I could get to his place and back before Mama got off work. And—I just can't shake the feeling that something's really, really wrong. That he needs me *now*." The tears had finally spilled over my eyelids and were rolling down my cheeks now. I caught a glimpse of the blond eighth-grade girl in front of us staring at me. "Please help me."

Mitch looked at me like I'd grown an extra head. "Are you for real right now, Annie Lee?" She shook her head. "Look. You know how hard it was for me to come up and sit by you at lunch the first week of school? I already told you how much trouble I have making friends. You know, I've never told another single soul all that stuff I told you at the sleepover. About my old school? You know you're, like, the first *real* friend I've had since kindergarten or first grade?"

"Yeah," I whispered.

"I even covered for you with your mom last week, and now you're telling me you weren't even honest about *why*?"

I squirmed in my seat. "Yeah."

"You know, I've been thinking for months that if I just gave you some time, if I just tried as hard as I could to be a friend, you'd eventually act like a friend in return. But you know what? All you ever do is ask, Annie Lee. All you ever do is ask for help, like it's never even occurred to you that maybe I needed things, too."

Ever since I'd met her, Mitch had seemed like the strong one, like I was the one who needed her to help me stay steady. But maybe I'd been wrong. Maybe it went both directions; maybe we were both strong and we were both weak, and we both needed each other in different ways.

Maybe I'd been too stuck inside my own grief over Daddy and the M&Ms to realize that until now.

Still, I couldn't make my plan work without Mitch's help.

"I'm sorry," I said. "I'll make it up to you, okay?"

"No."

"Please." I was crying again. "Please, Mitch. I don't know what else to do."

"You're going to end up getting murdered!"

"I won't. I'll be fine, okay? But I need you to cover for me with Mr. Barton."

Mitch looked at me for what felt like a hundred years. She was paler than normal, her freckles like dark stars across her face. "Fine, Annie Lee Fitzgerald. I'll do it." She took a breath. "But you might have to find yourself another lunch seat from now on."

Her words were an earthquake; part of me was surprised the bus didn't break right apart beneath us.

Could I really do that? Trade Mitch for Ray?

I thought of the way Ray's hands had trembled at our last piano lesson. The way he'd coughed and I'd heard it echo all the way down to his lungs. Even Queenie had said he'd been under the weather last time she'd seen him; I couldn't get the picture of him, sick and alone—maybe in serious trouble—out of my head.

I didn't have a choice.

"I'm sorry," I said again, and jumped forward to give Mitch a hug. Her bouncy curls were soft against my cheek.

She didn't hug me back.

If I'd had my lucky quarter, would I have been able to make her understand why going after Ray was so important? If I'd had my lucky quarter, would I have been able to keep them both?

The next time the bus stopped, I got up and told the driver that I'd gotten an emergency text from my mom and she was waiting for me in this neighborhood, and he let me off.

Then I sped all the way back to the apartment, dumped my school stuff out of my backpack and filled it with a water bottle and a couple of granola bars, slung it over my shoulder, and left.

I'd looked at the map on the computer earlier, using a pen to trace its lines on the back of my hand just in case I forgot. I recited the street names to myself: *Mangum. Chapel Hill. Duke University Road.* It seemed easy enough—no different from all the other days I'd ventured out into the city without anybody being the wiser, just my scooter and me fading into the world around us.

Except it *was* different, and nothing I told myself

could take away the snake of unease that curled and twitched in my insides.

As I rode, I tried hard not to think about anything: not about Ray, or what might have happened. Not about Mama, and how she'd react if she knew that I was playing hooky and wandering the city alone.

And definitely, *definitely* not about Mitch. Would she say a single word to me ever again after this?

I tried hard not to think about her getting up in Mr. Barton's class and stumbling through my half of the speech, and tried even harder not to think about her alone up on top of the school roof, waiting to see if our design worked without a best friend to wait with her.

No matter *how* hard I tried, I couldn't stop hearing the wet *smash* of the egg as it hit the parking lot below. It echoed in my ears with every sidewalk crack my scooter wheels ran over. *Snap. Crunch. Snap. Crunch. Smash.*

Our prototype had worked, and we'd thought it was so strong.

But I'd also thought Mitch and I would be friends forever—or at least all of sixth grade.

And I'd never expected Ray to disappear.

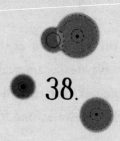

38.

The city around me was busy in a different way in the morning than in the afternoons, when I usually rode: the streets were filled with cars that crawled like insects in a row, herded through stoplight after stoplight.

As the forgotten neighborhood where Mama and I lived eased into the bustle and shine of downtown, the sidewalks, too, got busier, filled with people walking purposefully into tall buildings, their cell phones pressed to their ears or held in their hands like treasure maps.

Not a single person looked over at me, my invisibility cloak wrapped thick around my shoulders. I glided through the town like I was a ghost myself.

It took me more than twenty minutes to pass through

the heart of downtown, to the line that was a double-thick slash across the map on the back of my hand:

Durham Freeway.

The road I was on ran right over the top of the freeway like it was no big deal, cars rushing down it fast enough to make breezes that ruffled my short hair as I stood there on the sidewalk, one foot poised on the scooter.

This was it.

Now or never.

My hands shook as I kicked off and forward, slowly now, like the weight of all the rules I was breaking had wrapped around me, giant rubber bands pulling me back. It was claustrophobic, riding down that narrow little sidewalk on the overpass with cars blowing past beside me. A lousy little cement railing on my other side was the only thing between me and the scream of the highway below.

And then I was on the other side, and farther away from home than I'd ever been on my own.

It took me another fifteen minutes to get to the cemetery, nestled into its forest of trees and clipped grass that didn't seem to know how to grow dandelions. It was like another world there, all the chatter and roar of the town fading away into a deep, deep quiet, the kind that wove its way into every leaf and blade of grass.

I rode all the way to the edge of the woods, to the place where I'd met Ray and Clara back at the beginning of the school year—not even pausing to say hello to *ROBERT FITZGERALD, BELOVED HUSBAND AND FATHER*—and then propped my scooter against a tree and stepped inside. Leaves crunched under my feet, loud in the cemetery hush. It was still way colder than a Carolina October had any right to be, and even colder in the shade of the forest. I huddled into my hoodie, wishing I'd brought something heavier.

How far in did these woods go? How far was it to get to Ray's neighborhood? I'd looked at the map enough to know that Maplewood Cemetery was in the middle of the city, folded into the straight streets and grand old houses that hugged the Duke campus.

Still, out here between these trees, I could've been the last person on the whole earth.

I followed the trail for a few minutes, my ears straining for the sounds of cars, people talking, anything besides the chatty robins that hopped through the forest and scolded me when I came too close.

Finally, after I'd walked long enough to feel sweaty and nervous, the trees thinned. I stumbled out onto a narrow, quiet street with no sidewalks and just a couple of small, old houses clustered together. I'd tried to look Ray's address up online that morning while Mama was in the shower, but the website I found wouldn't give me his information without a credit card.

Which one of these houses was his?

I walked along the ditch that ran in front of the row of houses, trying to be like a detective on one of those mystery TV shows. Ray wouldn't live in the house with the little pink bike in the front—he didn't have any kids. He wouldn't live in the one that had two cars in the driveway and a sign on the front lawn advertising that a landscaping service kept the yard up, either. And he wouldn't live in the one with empty windows and a *For Sale* sign by the mailbox.

That left two others, both squat brick houses with painted shutters and weedy lawns.

I walked slowly past the first one. I could knock on both doors, but what if somebody asked me where my parents were or why I wasn't in school?

I thought of Daddy, flipping the two-headed quarter over and over in his fingers. *It always pays to carry your own luck, Al.*

That quarter was gone. But today, I had to figure out a way to *make* luck—for Ray, not just for me.

I was halfway between the two houses when I heard a

sound that made me freeze.

Barking.

It was coming from the last house on the street, the one with green shutters and a crookedy mailbox that looked like it had been rear-ended at least once in its lifetime. It was faint, but I could still hear it—barking. From somewhere inside.

Clara.

I ran up the long driveway and pounded my fist on the door. The barking got louder and more frantic, until I was pretty sure the dog was right on the other side of the door, but nobody came to open it.

"Clara?" I called. "Is that you, girl?" The dog barked even harder. She sounded more than just excited to have somebody knocking—she sounded like she was trying to tell me something.

Where was Ray? He may have been avoiding Queenie, but why would he ignore *me*?

The feeling of *wrongness* I'd been trying to shake all week grew even stronger.

"Hang on," I shouted, hoping hard that dogs really *were* just as smart as Dr. Hsu had always said they were. "Good girl! I'm coming!"

I tried the doorknob, but it was locked. I could hear Clara pawing at the other side of the door, her nails scratching like she was trying so hard to get to me.

I took a few steps back, scanning the house and yard. The grass was long; I figured Ray probably couldn't mow much on account of his arthur. A tall wooden fence separated the front yard from the back.

I thought about all the times I'd slept over at Monica's house. With all those pets, Mrs. Hsu usually left the back door unlocked, so that if they needed to get up to take a dog out during the night, they didn't have to mess with the locks.

Besides, I figure any burglar who's willing to climb an eight-foot fence isn't going to be stopped by a little dead bolt, she always said.

I stepped back toward the door. "Hang on, Clara," I called. "I'm going to try something else, 'kay?"

Clara barked back.

I ran around the side of the house to the wooden gate. It was locked from the other side, but I pulled a broken wheelbarrow that was lying by the side of the house over and turned it upside down, like a funky step stool. I climbed on the wheelbarrow and breathed in deep, thinking of the summer when I was nine. Me and Monica and Meredith had spent all of June making obstacle courses in Meredith's backyard, pretending we were on *American Ninja Warrior*, until Meredith fell off the rope ladder we'd made ourselves and broke her wrist and her mom made us take down the whole obstacle course.

I'd climbed and jumped over way harder things that summer than one wooden gate.

I'm coming, Clara, I thought, and grabbed the top of the gate and pulled myself over.

It was a long drop to the ground on the other side. I landed hard, the shock traveling through my feet and all the way up to my hips, but I hardly even noticed the pain. I went right to Ray's back door and jiggled the knob.

It opened under my fingers, the door swinging into the house in one try.

I stood in a small room with a couch and an old-fashioned TV set on an end table. It was dark and cold inside—almost as cold as it was outside. "Hello?" I called. "Ray? Clara?"

There was the sound of nails scrabbling on wood and then Clara rocketed into the room. She was barking louder and harder than I'd ever heard her, darting back and forth in front of me like she couldn't settle down.

I dropped to my knees. "Shh, girl, shh," I whispered, looking right into her warm-honey eyes. They were deep enough to fall right into, like they held all the secrets of the whole world. Clara looked steadily back, silent now, though her whole body was quivering and her ears were up. "What's the matter, girl?"

Clara barked again—one sharp, short bark—and turned and padded back out of the room.

I followed her down a little hallway, toward a kitchen with a humming refrigerator. The smell hit me as soon as I got close enough: a putrid, foul stench laced through with the scent of metal and sweat. I slapped a hand over my nose and tried not to gag.

Ray lay on the kitchen floor, his skin sheet-white, groaning and clutching his leg.

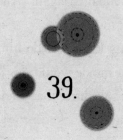

39.

His leg was bent in a way it shouldn't be, and his raggedy jeans were stained with something dark. *Blood.* Clara burst into a frenzy of barking and barreled into the kitchen, licking at Ray's face and hands and any part of him she could reach, nudging him with her nose.

But I couldn't make myself unfreeze. I just stood there, watching as Clara yapped and yapped and Ray tried weakly to calm her down, my thoughts crystallized into one big *NO NO NO NO NO NO NO—*

It was like every nightmare I'd had since the summer was coming true all over again, like every time I'd closed my eyes and seen Daddy lying motionless on that stretcher was repeating here in real time.

The whole world around me forgot how to work. The

refrigerator stopped humming. The room faded out.

And then Ray moaned again. And just like that, I could move again, too.

I dropped to my knees beside him, trying to think what a person in a movie would do. I pushed my shaking hands together, wishing that Daddy's lucky quarter was sitting warm in my pocket the way it had been since summer began.

Clara licked at Ray's face.

"Good . . . girl," he said, his voice brittle and thin.

"Ray? Are you . . . are you okay?" I tried not to look down at his messed-up leg, and all the other things that showed just how dumb my question was.

Ray blinked and turned his head toward me, slow as tree sap. "Annie Lee?"

"It's me," I said, my own voice barely a whisper. "You were missing. All week long. I didn't know what had happened, so I came here."

Ray's eyes drifted closed. I reached out and grabbed his hand—anything to keep him there with me, to keep him from going wherever it was Daddy had gone in June. His skin was made of flame and coal, so hot and dry it was almost painful to touch. When he breathed in and out, the sound was one long rattle.

"Stay with me," I said.

Right then, my phone buzzed in my pocket. It was so unexpected, so shocking in the middle of Ray's dark, cold house, it made me jump.

"Annie Lee?" Mama asked, her voice angry and frantic, as soon as I said hello. "I just got an auto-call from the school saying you didn't show up to your first class. Where *are* you? Why aren't you at school?"

"I need your help," I said, and on *help* my throat cracked open and the tears came. "I need you to come get me."

"What's going on?"

I breathed short and hard, trying to stop the sobs, but it didn't do any good at all. "I'm in a neighborhood on the other side of Maplewood Cemetery. The street is called Matilda Road. It's a brick house with green shutters on the end of the street."

"What?" In the background, I heard something thump to the ground. What had Mama dropped? Some client's expensive vacuum? A spray bottle filled with all-purpose cleaner? "You better tell me what's going on, young lady."

"I'll explain everything," I said, hoping she could understand me through the crying, 'cause I could hardly understand my own self. "Just come get me, okay? And you need to call an ambulance, too. I've got a friend here and he's hurt real bad, and sick, too. He needs to get to the hospital quick. I'll explain everything once you get here."

There was a long pause on the other end of the phone, but then Mama said, "Okay."

"My mama will take care of it all," I told Ray as I hung up, though I couldn't tell if he heard anything I'd said. He was awake but seemed confused, like he wasn't quite sure what was going on around him. "She's coming, and the paramedics, too. You just have to stay with me until then, okay, Ray? Just stay with me."

I squeezed his hand. Weak as a whisper, he squeezed back.

"They'll take good care of you at the hospital," I said. My eyes were wet, tears clumping in my eyelashes and running down my face, so that it looked like I was seeing everything through a rainstorm. "You'll see. Just concentrate on me and Clara."

"I'll . . . try . . . ," Ray said.

I sat there, holding his hand and talking about anything I could think of until I started to feel hoarse. I told him about going to Brightleaf the last few days, about how on Monday I'd played the big piano and somebody had clapped for me. I didn't dare stop talking.

I talked and talked and talked, until finally, *finally*,

Clara started barking again and a minute later I heard somebody pounding on the front door.

"Annie Lee? Annie Lee?"

"Here! We're here!" I yelled back, and Clara barked even harder. "Just a minute," I said to Ray, and let go of his hand so that I could race to the front door and unlock it.

Mama stood on the doorstep with somebody so unexpected that I had to blink three times to recognize her. Her black salon apron was gone, but her smart black slacks and silky burnt-orange shirt couldn't have seemed more out of place in Ray's run-down old house.

I sniffled hard, shocked right out of my tears. "Miss Queenie?"

Queenie nodded, a little half smile on her face.

"You know her, too?" Mama asked sternly. I nodded.

"Couldn't hardly sleep last night," Queenie said. "Thinking about Ray, how he'd disappeared without telling either of us. The more I thought on it, the less sense it made. I rescheduled my morning appointments so I could come over. I was just getting out of my car when I met up with your mama."

Right then an ambulance pulled into Ray's driveway, sirens wailing. Two people hopped out—a black man and a white woman, both in navy scrubs, with a stretcher between them and identical confused looks on their faces.

The man cleared his throat. "Excuse me, miss. Are you the one who's hurt?"

I shook my head and led the whole group into the house, where Ray lay unmoving on the kitchen floor.

"Oh my Lord," Queenie whispered, hand on her bosom.

Mama's fingers were claws on my shoulder. "Annie Lee. Who. Is. This?"

"His name is Ray Owens."

As I spoke, the paramedics set down the stretcher and crouched beside Ray, taking his pulse and feeling his leg until he made the most miserable agonized moan I'd ever heard.

"Broken," the girl paramedic murmured. "Open fracture. Maybe a tib-fib. Going to need surgery."

"Breath sounds are severely decreased," the other paramedic said back. "Could be pneumonia." He cleared his throat and looked up at me. "Do you know how long he's been here?"

I shook my head, wishing I could rub my missing quarter and blink the whole thing away, go back to it being me and Ray in the sun from the skylight at Brightleaf, music pouring out of him like waves in the ocean.

"Maybe a couple days. I don't know." I bit my lip. "He has arthritis. I don't know if that makes a difference."

"It does," said the girl paramedic, and she smiled at me. I felt the tiniest bit of my heart loosen up, like one of the strings tied around it had been cut. "Thanks, hon. It's a good thing you found him. He's going to be okay, but we need to get him to the hospital ASAP."

"Thanks," I whispered.

Clara whined and came over to rub her head against my leg as the paramedics lifted Ray onto the stretcher and then picked it up. He moaned as they moved him, his leg crooked and wrong, blood soaked through his pants and crusted in layers of brown and red, old and new.

In silence, Mama and Queenie and I followed them out of the house. Clara walked with us, her ears tipped forward and her eyes never leaving Ray's stretcher.

"It's a good thing you came by," the guy paramedic said as they loaded Ray into the back of the ambulance. "Sometimes things like this happen when old folks live by themselves—they get injured, can't get help. They don't always get found in time."

That settled into my stomach like a rock.

"Y'all aren't his next of kin?" the paramedic asked as his partner jumped into the ambulance and pulled the doors closed behind her.

Mama shook her head. "No, sir. I've never seen him before today."

"He doesn't have any family close by, but we're his friends," said Queenie. I tried not to notice how Mama's whole face tightened up at that *we*.

The paramedic nodded, meeting my eyes steadily. "They're probably not gonna let you in to see him right away at the hospital, but if y'all give me your names, I'll make sure that they know you're his contacts."

"I don't think I'm comfortable with that," Mama said.

"Mama, please—"

"I'm sorry, Annie Lee. I don't have a clue who this man is, or what you've been doing with him. I appreciate that he's in bad shape, but I'd rather you stay away from him from now on." She was wringing her hands over and over, scrubbing them together the way she washed clothes in the sink. I felt the tears welling up in my eyes again, sliding down my cheeks.

"If it helps, Miz Fitzgerald, I can vouch for Ray," said Queenie quietly. "He's a real gentleman. One of the kindest souls I've ever met. I think your Annie Lee has done him a lot of good, too. He's been awful lonely since his wife died about eight years ago."

Mama's nose was flared a little, like a skittish horse.

"I'll think about letting Annie Lee visit sometime. But I'm still not comfortable putting our names down as contacts."

"That's just fine," said Queenie, her voice calm and smooth, even though I could see the sadness and hurt in her eyes plain as day. She turned back to the man paramedic. "Thank you, sir. My name's Queenie Banks. I run a hair salon in Brightleaf Square."

If I hadn't been looking in Mama's direction I never would've seen it, the tiniest raise of the eyebrows and drop of the mouth when Queenie mentioned what she did for work. Queenie didn't notice. She was busy giving the paramedic her phone number, and Mr. Banks's name and number too, just in case they couldn't reach Queenie. The paramedic nodded and climbed up into the cab of the ambulance.

A minute later, the ambulance disappeared down Matilda Road.

40.

"Thanks for coming," I said to Mama and Queenie, staring at my shoes—still the same taped-up silver ones I'd been wearing since school started. They were getting tight around the toe, but I didn't have the heart to tell Mama.

"I guess I had no need, after all," said Queenie, a laugh in her voice. It was obvious she could feel the thick-as-butter tension between Mama and me but was too nice to say anything about it. "You're a real brave girl, Annie Lee, honey. You probably saved Ray's life."

Clara barked at the mention of Ray's name. I'd almost forgotten her sitting there patiently, I'd been so busy watching the ambulance leave and wondering if Mama would ever let me see Ray again.

Queenie knelt down and ran a gentle hand over the dog's head. "Hey, pretty girl. What we gone do with you while your human's in the hospital, hmm?"

She sighed and clambered to her feet, then looked for a long minute at me and Mama, like she was weighing in her mind if she should ask us to take Clara with us. *Please don't*, I tried to say with my eyes. Even if we could somehow keep a dog in our apartment for a few days without the manager figuring out, I had a feeling that asking Mama if we could watch Ray's dog would be the thing that made her explode.

Queenie read my message right. "I expect I could come by for a few days and keep Clara fed and walked. I can't take her home with me, 'cause my husband, Elijah, is allergic, but we can make it work for a short time."

"Thanks," I said, so quiet it was almost a whisper.

"Tell me," Mama broke in, her voice knife-edge sharp even though there was a smile on her lips. "How do y'all know each other?"

Queenie stuck her hand out. "I'm Queenie Banks, Miz Fitzgerald. Me and Ray go back a long, long time. I was friends with his wife before she died. My salon is right near where Ray and Annie Lee play at Brightleaf. I've never had the privilege of listening in on her lessons, but Ray tells me she's getting along real well, and what I

267

can hear sounds pretty great."

"Lessons," Mama repeated.

Queenie nodded. "Ray says your girl has a real talent, Miz Fitzgerald. Says he hasn't seen many kids who've made as much progress in such a little time. He's real excited about that Durham Piano Teachers Association competition in December—he thinks Annie Lee has a shot at a prize."

"Up at Brightleaf Square."

"Uh-huh. Well, no, the competition's at some church, I think. But Annie Lee's lessons are at Brightleaf—of course, you know all that. Speaking of, I've got to run! I've got a long coloring appointment in a few minutes." She fished a business card from her pocket. "But Miz Fitzgerald, you keep this card, all right? Maybe this isn't the time to bring this up, but Annie Lee told me about her daddy. It's not anywhere near the same, but ten years back my husband lost his job, and I had to go back to school to get my cosmetology license. I did well enough in those first few years I've got my own place now, and me and Mr. Banks are doing just fine."

Queenie patted Mama's hand gently as she handed her the business card. "I don't know what your plans are moving forward, but if you ever decide to do something like that, you call me up, sugar. I don't know how much help I can be, but I could talk you through the application and recommend some scholarships they've got."

There were so many expressions on Mama's face that it looked like the sky on one of those sun-rain-cloud days: irritation chased by surprise chased by something that looked suspiciously like a tiny glimmer of hope. I thought of her the day we'd learned that Daddy had never paid for the extra life insurance, saying she couldn't even see a way forward for us, she was so stuck in the middle of getting by.

Right now, it looked like she was seeing that way forward.

Finally, Mama managed to close her fingers around Queenie's business card. "Thank you, Mrs. Banks. That's very generous. I—I'll keep that in mind."

Queenie smiled at Mama, wrapped her arm around my shoulders in a quick half hug, and hurried off to her car. As soon as she'd disappeared into the little red coupe, Mama turned to me.

"Car. Now."

I swallowed hard and followed her to my doom.

Mama waited until we were both inside, doors closed behind us, before opening the floodgates.

"Let me get this straight." Her fingers were white-knuckled on the steering wheel. "You've been sneaking out while I'm at work and just—*riding your scooter all over downtown*—for two months? Taking some kind of—*lessons*—from a *strange old man I've never met?*"

The last few words were punctuated with sharp little hits to the steering wheel, like firing the words themselves off hard as gunshots wasn't enough on its own.

"Piano lessons," I whispered. There wasn't anything else I could say. Sun sparkled on the windshield in front of me; it was too bright, too pretty a day for all of this.

"Annie Lee Fitzgerald! Do you even *realize* what you're telling me?" Mama gripped the wheel again, but even though her skin was white as flour, she couldn't stop her hands and arms from shaking. She sniffed, hard and angry.

When I peeked at her out of the corner of my eye, her eyes glittered.

"Honey," she said a minute later, and I could hear in her voice how hard she was working to keep those tears back. "Annie Lee. You know how much I love you, right? You know it would rip my heart into pieces if anything happened to you, right? What if you'd gotten hurt off by yourself? What if you'd been in an accident, or gotten kidnapped! What if Mr. Owens hadn't been a nice old man who'd wanted to teach you piano, but . . ."

Mama stopped, her breathing fast. I didn't know if

I'd ever seen her this angry in my whole life.

"It near about broke me in two when your daddy died this summer, Annie Lee. What would I do if something happened to you, too?"

I stared straight ahead, my teeth set so hard my jaw ached with it. *You aren't the only one who's sad.*

It was what I had wanted to say every day for nearly five months, every morning when I woke up to the sound of Mama crying as she washed the shaving cream down the bathroom sink, every single time her face went white when the TV would mysteriously flip on or the record player would spin through phantom songs.

In the seat next to me, Mama deflated, sinking in on herself, a balloon leaking air.

"You're right," she said. "You're right, honey. Sometimes, I guess I forget I'm not the only one who's broken by all this."

We sat in silence for a minute, both of us looking out at the cold late-morning sun hanging over Ray's house.

"It was wrong, you lying and sneaking out," said Mama quietly after a minute. "But it was wrong, too, for me to hold myself away from you the way *I've* been doing. I should've known things weren't all right, Annie Lee. I should've seen that before—before—" She waved her hand, sweeping the whole world up in the gesture.

"Before I got a call saying you were skipping school and found you across town, chasing a strange man through the forest by Maplewood."

"*Mom.* It's not like that. Ray's my friend."

"I know he is. And I know you aren't going to believe this, but I'm really trying to take your word for it that he's the kind of man you say he is. But still," she added, rubbing at her eyes with the heels of her hands, "you have to realize, this is the kind of thing every mother in the *world* fears."

"I know," I said, and closed my eyes. There, in the darkness, I could see every good thing the last two months had brought me—those afternoons at Bright-leaf, Ray's music, his smile, my fingers on the piano keys—slipping away into nothing.

Mama wrapped a stiff arm around my shoulders and pulled me toward her, kissing the top of my head. "I'm sorry, Annie Lee," she whispered into my hair. "I think we need to make each other some rules, okay? No more sneaking around, and no more lying. I don't know what they're going to be yet, but I'm going to have to come up with some kind of consequences for the way you've been behaving. But also—no more of me trying to hold all this grief inside myself and forgetting how much there is inside you, too."

She took a deep breath. "Let's go home now, honey. I'll take the rest of the day off work, and we'll spend some time together. Maybe . . . maybe I'll think about Mrs. Banks's offer. There's a couple beauty colleges not too far from here—maybe I'll see about applying to one of them. It would sure be a lot better than Mary's Maids.

"None of this is going to be easy, but we'll get through it together, you and me."

"Could we visit Ray tomorrow?" I knew it was pushing it, but I couldn't not ask. I couldn't get it out of my head, the way Ray had looked, getting carted off in that ambulance. I wished I had Daddy's two-headed quarter with me.

Mama hesitated. I could see the worry she'd carried around with her since Daddy died, wrestling with the softness that was trying hard to come out.

"Not tomorrow," she said finally. "But I'll think about it. How about . . . you can tell me the whole story of what you've been doing and what your friend Ray is like. And maybe . . . maybe we'll think about going to the hospital on Sunday. Okay?"

"Okay," I said, and when she turned the key in the ignition and backed out of Ray's driveway, the rumble of that engine somehow sounded a whole lot like hope.

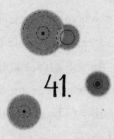

41.

It was quiet the next morning when I woke up, like a hush had fallen over our whole apartment. No bathroom fan, no sounds of Mama crying or stomping off to change into her Mary's Maids polo. The light filtering through my bedroom window was silvery; when I pulled open the blinds, rain sparkled on the parking lot outside and frost beaded the window glass.

Mama was in the bathroom when I got there. Not washing the sink or getting ready for work—she was sitting on the bathroom floor in her pajamas with her knees drawn up, a photo album spread across her lap.

The scent of aftershave was still strong in the air, the stubble still there.

Hello, Daddy, I thought.

In the other room, the record player whirred to life. "Annie's Song" hummed its way through the apartment.

Mama touched one of the pictures in the photo book, her finger soft and slow as she traced it. "He was so handsome," she murmured.

I sank down onto the floor next to her. She lifted her arm up and wrapped it around me, pulling me close to her, like she'd done when I was little and came into her bed with a bad dream. We hadn't sat like that in a long, long time.

The picture was one of Daddy and me the day I was born—white hospital walls in the background, little baby me wrapped in a white flannel blanket covered in elephants. Daddy held me like I was made out of glass, like if he breathed wrong, I'd shatter. Like I was the most precious thing the world had ever seen.

I couldn't say anything past the thickness in my throat.

Mama turned the page. More pictures of Daddy, of the three of us together—Daddy holding tiny toddler me on his lap at the piano, patiently helping me press down the keys. Daddy and Mama posing together on a trail at Eno River State Park, right where me and Mama had gone hiking last month. Daddy with a group of his English students, one of them holding up a stuffed raven with a speech bubble coming out of its mouth that said *Nevermore.*

"You know," said Mama, so quiet I had to lean even closer to hear her. "All these months, I've wished so hard that all of this"—she waved her hand at the sink filled with shaving cream— "would just go away. It makes it so much harder, some days, feeling like he's so close still.

"But in other ways, I think I've been holding on to all those little things. Because the only thing scarier than feeling like we'll never be free of that closeness is the idea of him being all the way gone."

"I know," I said, just as quiet. I thought of the rainbow umbrella dreams, of the way it felt to have Daddy so near, so reach-out-and-touch-able, and not be able to do anything at all about it. "Me too."

I thought of the pro-con list I'd made all those weeks ago. *PRO: With the ghost in the house, it was like a tiny piece of Daddy still lived there.* Had I been clutching that tiny little piece of Daddy all this time, even more afraid to let it go than I was to have it stay?

Mama sighed, a long, slow, sad sigh that wrapped its way around the bathroom and felt, strangely, like a hug.

"Sometimes I wonder if your daddy's had just as hard a time letting go as we have, Annie Lee."

"Me too."

Maybe all three of us were wrong to hold on like that.

For months, I'd felt like letting go of Daddy—figuring out how to move on and live a life without him in it, figuring out how to be happy without him around—would be a kind of betrayal. Like if I let go of him, it meant the love between us had never been as strong as I'd thought.

But maybe I'd gotten things backward. Maybe love was a little like that missing quarter: heads up either way you flipped it.

Maybe sometimes love meant holding on to somebody, but other times love meant letting them go.

"I think maybe it's time we all learned to move on," said Mama, like she'd read my thoughts. She rubbed my shoulder. "We're never going to stop loving your daddy, Annie Lee. But maybe it's time you and I figured out how to hold on to him a little less, and each other a little more."

"I'd like that," I said, and snuggled closer, breathing in Mama's cleaning-lady smell.

"I went on the computer this morning before you woke up," Mama said. "There's a new term that starts up at one of the beauty colleges right after New Year's. It's expensive, and it's a little longer than the other programs, but it's the kind of place that sets its students up to work in fancy salons and spas. The kind of job that could really help us make ends meet. It would mean tightening our belts even further for a couple months, honey. But I think if I could get one of those scholarships Mrs. Banks was talking about, we could really make it work."

I thought of Mama in a salon like Queenie's, wearing a black apron and calling her clients *honey* and *sugar*.

"You should do it," I said.

"I'll get in touch with Mrs. Banks later today."

"I want to show you something," I said, and flipped my phone open. The recording from that day at Brightleaf was still there, five minutes of my heart on the piano keyboard, and I pressed play.

This is for you, too, I thought, and hoped that somehow, my daddy could hear it.

I let it play all the way until it stopped—the little snatch of "Annie's Song," the laughing sound of "You Can Call Me Al." One tentative, hopeful note after another, holding the memory of the golden light they'd conjured up.

When it finished, Mama's eyes were wet. "Did you write that yourself?"

I nodded.

"That was really beautiful, honey," she said.

The bathroom light flickered off and back on, just once, like the ghost was nodding agreement.

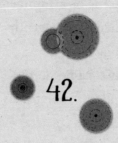

42.

The first thing I noticed when we walked through the doors Sunday morning was the smell, that sharp too-clean smell that brought back every moment of the horrible June day when Daddy died. Mama and I had followed the ambulance to the hospital, but by the time we'd rushed in through the glass doors that swooshed closed behind us and swept us into the antiseptic sorrow of the emergency department, the only thing we'd been able to do was identify the body.

Male. Thirty-eight years old. Time of death: Seven forty-two, June 8. Cause of death: unsuspected hypertrophic cardiomyopathy.

The doctor who'd read the chart had had black hipster glasses and a goatee and a voice like a stapler: cold, hard, abrupt. It had been the nurse, dressed in purple scrubs and carrying the scent of a summer evening with her like a cloud, who had spoken gently and folded Mama and then me into a hug.

Mama gave Ray's name at the lobby information desk, and the receptionist pointed us toward the elevators: fifth floor, west wing, general medicine specialties. As we rode the elevator up, Mama took my hand and squeezed it.

"It's hard, being back here, isn't it?"

"Yeah."

Mama took a breath. "But maybe it's good for us, too. I know I've avoided a lot of things these last few months, Annie Lee. Things that seem hard, or scary. Things that remind me of your daddy."

"Me too."

"I don't think I want to live like that anymore," Mama said.

When Mama had called Queenie last night to ask about scholarships, they'd ended up talking for a long time about Ray, too. Mama had asked so many questions it had sounded like she was training to be a detective, but I'd watched her face relax a little more with every answer Queenie gave. After she'd gotten off the phone, Mama had come over and given me a hug and said we could go see Ray in the morning. She didn't have to say it in words for me to understand what that meant: Mama trusted Queenie, and Queenie trusted Ray. And for now, that was enough for us both.

Queenie had told Mama on the phone that Ray had been admitted with multiple fractures in his leg and advanced pneumonia in his lungs. He'd be in for at least a week, with the possibility of discharge to a rehabilitation care center for up to two months after that while his body healed. The nurse had told Queenie that Ray was in *stable but critical condition*.

The general medicine specialties ward was flanked by heavy double doors that opened with clicks and whirs at the touch of a button. Ray was in a room right by the nurses' station, his door just the littlest bit open as we came to it.

It took a minute for my eyes to adjust to the gloom inside. When I did, I saw Ray, lying in a bed with rails, an oxygen tube snaking its way across his face. Beside his bed a bunch of machines blinked, tracking just about everything that could be tracked.

"Y'all checking up on Mr. Owens?" An aide with tan skin and a blue ponytail that swished when she walked paused by us. "He's been sleeping off and on ever since they brought him in. Poor man. You the little girl who found him?"

I nodded.

"Way I heard it, you saved his life, honey. You should be real proud of yourself."

I didn't feel proud, though. The hospital scent was thick in my nose so that I wanted to turn on my heel and run away into the fresh air.

Mama put her hand on my shoulder. "We're gonna be okay," she whispered, the way she had yesterday morning, and that was enough to remind my lungs how to breathe in just a little bit. I thought of what she'd said in the elevator: *I don't want to live like that anymore.*

I didn't, either. I stepped forward and sat down on the edge of a chair beside Ray's bed.

After I'd been watching him a minute, Ray's eyelids fluttered open. "Annie Lee?"

"Yeah," I said, like my voice belonged to somebody else. What else could I say? *Please, please don't die the way my daddy did?*

"Where's Clara?" Ray's hands twitched, casting around in his bed like Clara's leash might be laid across the hospital sheet somewhere.

"She's safe. I promise. She's at your house. Queenie's making sure she has food."

Ray relaxed back into the bed. "Thanks, child. Don't know what I'd do without that old dog."

Would Ray even be able to take care of his dog when he got out? How long could Queenie keep going over to his place to feed and walk Clara while Ray was in the rehab center?

"You been practicing?" Ray asked, the tiniest hint of a smile on his face.

I shrugged. "Kinda. Monday afternoon when you weren't there, I played on the piano while I was waiting. I tried playing the way you always do. *My* music." I blushed. "Somebody even clapped after I was done. And it made—" I waved my hand in the air in front of me. "Lights. Like yours does."

The hint of a smile turned real, stretching out under the oxygen cannula like the most beautiful thing I'd ever seen. "You musta opened up your heart pretty good for that to happen." Ray reached out and patted my hand, his skin thin and dry as the leaves on the forest floor. "You make me proud."

"I just wish I'd found you sooner."

"You found me in time, Annie Lee. I owe you my life."

From the doorway, Mama cleared her throat. "We'd better go, Annie Lee."

Ray turned his head slowly to look at Mama, his smile beaming out even brighter in that dark hospital room. "Now, Annie Lee, who's this lovely young lady you brought with you?"

Mama's mouth pressed into a thin line, but her eyes

were soft. Mama wasn't big on people who tried to flatter her, but it was impossible not to warm to Ray—you could tell that he was the kind of person who didn't say things just to make noise. Like his music, his words came straight from his heart.

"Ray, this is my mom. Joan Fitzgerald. She's the one who helped me get the ambulance to you Friday."

"Well then," said Ray, "I suppose I owe *you* my life, too, Miz Joan." He nodded, a gesture that somehow manage to be almost regal, even from a hospital bed where he couldn't hardly lift his head. "I appreciate it greatly. I expect you're real proud of your daughter, too. She's a good girl—and has the makings of a great musician."

"Hmm," said Mama, casting me a hefty dose of side-eye, and I knew that however much she might've liked the recording of my piano playing, it'd be awhile before I was forgiven.

I stood, reaching out real quick to squeeze Ray's hand, wishing it wasn't so bony and light-feeling. "I'll come back if I can."

"I'll look forward to it, Miss Annie Lee."

"You just get better, okay? You *better* get better."

Ray chuckled. "I'll do my best. I'd be afraid to do otherwise, with you around."

As we left Ray's room, the door swinging closed behind us, Mama put her arm around me. "You doing okay?"

I nodded, though I wasn't really sure. "I just want him to get better."

"I know, honey." Mama squeezed my shoulders. "I'm still pretty mad about the tricks you've been pulling this year, the risks you've taken. And I'm still not completely on board with your relationship with Mr. Owens. But I can see that he's a special kind of friend."

"Yeah." My voice split a little. "Really special."

Mama pulled me closer to her. "We'll do everything we can, Annie Lee. I promise, we'll do everything we can."

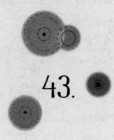

43.

I couldn't get Ray out of my thoughts the next morning. I sat on the bus alone, since Mitch had already been sharing a seat with Kavya Lahiri when I got on. Mitch's jaw was set and her eyes studiously avoided mine while I looked for a place to sit.

I leaned my head against the cold bus window, replaying over and over in my head what it had been like to find Ray lying on the kitchen floor, barely breathing. When Mama talked to Queenie Saturday night, Queenie had told her that Ray had been finishing up replacing a lightbulb that had gone out when he lost his balance on the stool and fell. He hardly remembered anything after that; nobody was even positive how long he'd been there on the floor before I'd found him.

"Can we go visit again this week?" I'd asked Mama earlier, while she waited with me for the bus.

"I don't know, Annie Lee. I think you need to focus on school for a while, all right?"

Mama had been so busy being mad and freaked out Friday when she found me at Ray's that she hadn't even realized I'd missed my egg-drop presentation until this morning. When she'd put two and two together, she'd looked at me with the strangest expression on her face— anger mixed with sadness, but blended up with love, like she was seeing me clearly for the first time since June.

"Things are going to be different from now on," she'd said at the bus stop. "I don't know exactly how it's all gonna fit together yet, but we're going to make some changes. We're going to build us a new life, okay, Annie Lee? And once we have some of those pieces figured out, we'll think about how Mr. Owens fits in."

Now I stared out the window at the streets whizzing past. Saturday, sitting on the bathroom floor with Mama, I'd thought of love like a two-sided coin: sometimes you have to hold on, sometimes you have to let go.

I wasn't sure I was ready to let go of Ray.

School that day felt like a hurricane of noise, with me as the quiet eye, the invisible center around which everything else swirled. I'd saved a seat for Mitch at lunch, but it had stayed empty the whole twenty minutes, except when Juan Diego Herrera accidentally dropped a granola bar onto it.

It was a worse kind of loneliness than what I'd felt at the beginning of the school year. At least then, I hadn't known any better.

I tried all day to catch Mitch in the hallway between classes, all the apologies I wanted to give pounding their way through my brain, but every time she saw me she set her jaw hard and disappeared into the crowd of students hurrying to their next periods. She wasn't even on the bus after school ended. Was she really so dead-set on avoiding me that she'd found another ride home?

Mr. Barton cleared his throat as I walked into the science room the next afternoon. "Miss Fitzgerald, a word, please?"

Dread poured its way from the crown of my head all the way down to my toes. From the desk next to mine, I could *feel* Mitch's glowering eyes on me. I dragged myself up to Mr. Barton's desk.

He steepled his fingers together under his chin as he looked up at me. "I understand from Miss Harris that you had a family emergency Friday."

I nodded.

"She had to present alone, as I didn't have enough advance notice to pair her with another student or team."

Another nod.

"Have you talked to her about what happened?"

I shook my head.

"I suggest you do that. She seemed considerably distressed."

"I'm sorry," I whispered. "Did we fail the project?"

"No. The two of you will have an opportunity to make the project up in private Thursday afternoon. You'll need to stay after school for one hour. Will that be possible?"

"I think so," I said, hoping it was true. Last night at dinner, Mama had laid out the new after-school rules: I had to go to Mrs. Garcia's apartment as soon as I got off the bus. Evidently Mama was less worried about taking advantage of a neighbor she didn't know that well now that the alternative was leaving me alone. I wasn't allowed to go anywhere else, or even be in our apartment by myself, without calling Mama on the phone and getting her express permission first. She was hoping that as soon as the term for the cosmetology program started, she could get enough money in scholarships and government grants that she could cut way back at Mary's

Maids—maybe even stop working there altogether—and be home in the afternoon with me.

"I will plan to meet you and Miss Harris here, in the classroom, as soon as school has let out on Thursday," said Mr. Barton, and then his stern expression softened. "I hope everything is all right with the circumstance that required you to be absent from school last week?"

I thought of Ray in his hospital bed, the oxygen cannula threaded across his face.

"I hope so," I said.

I slid into my desk right as Mr. Barton stood to start the class. I thought about taking his advice and slipping Mitch an apology note, but it only took one look at her, ignoring me like she was being offered a million dollars to pretend like I didn't exist, to think better of that. Instead, I caught up with her as she ice-queened her way out of class after the bell had rung.

"Wait." I grabbed her sleeve right before she could disappear into the hallway crowd.

The look Mitch gave me turned every bit of me into water. If only, like water, I could've washed myself away down the classroom floor and found a convenient drain to die in.

"Get. Your. Hand. Off. Me."

This was the Mitch I hadn't seen since the first week

of school—the Mitch made of stone and steel, the girl who could light the whole school on fire if she wanted to and walk away whistling as it burned.

I shrugged off the temptation to pull my invisibility cloak back on, trying to imagine that I was sitting on the shining ebony bench of the grand piano in the Brightleaf atrium with my fingers poised above the keys.

I didn't let go of Mitch's sleeve.

"Just give me thirty seconds," I said. It was taking everything I had in me to keep meeting Mitch's frozen stare head-on.

"Fine. Thirty seconds."

"I'm sorry. I'm so sorry. For everything. I shouldn't have ditched you like that last week. It was for an emergency, but I still shouldn't have done it. I shouldn't have made you carry things for me like I did."

"You realize it was completely *humiliating* to have to get up in front of the whole freaking class without my partner and BS my way through that egg drop, right? The egg splattered like Humpty Dumpty, by the way. Probably because I was so distracted I did a crappy job putting the straws together. It was pathetic."

Just for one second it was like the ice in her expression slipped and I saw something different on her face, something that made my heart stop. It was pain, and hurt, as raw and frustrated as anything I'd ever seen before.

I thought back to what she'd looked like when she'd taken off the beanie at our sleepover. What if maybe, all this whole school year, every time Mitch looked angry or disdainful or fierce, that was as much a kind of armor as her white hat? What if, this whole time, she'd really been just as afraid of being seen as I was?

Guilt slithered into my belly. "I'm sorry," I said again. "I'm so sorry. I can't say it enough times."

"I'm not your sassy sidekick, okay? I'm a *real person*. With *real feelings* of my own."

"You're right. And I'm—"

Mitch rolled her eyes. "I don't even want to hear it. Thirty seconds is up, reader girl. I've got to go to class."

Without another word, she whirled around and marched off down the hallway.

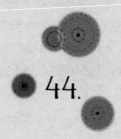

44.

We went to visit Ray again Tuesday afternoon after Mama's shift ended at work.

"There's a big part of me says I shouldn't be doing this," Mama said as we drove to the hospital. "Every time I think about you riding downtown all by yourself—every time I think about you having piano lessons alone with a stranger—"

"We weren't ever alone," I said. "There were always people coming and going in the mall. And they all knew Ray. Everybody there loves him. And Queenie's known him about a million years."

"Regardless, Annie Lee, you have to understand how it makes my heart freeze to think of what could've happened. There's a big part of me that thinks that I should turn this car around and forbid you from ever seeing Mr. Owens again. But," Mama went on before I could interrupt again, "I can see how much he means to you. I haven't seen you this worked up about anyone or anything since your daddy died. I know Mr. Owens is important to you."

"And music," I said quietly. "Music is important to me, too."

"I know, honey."

"Sometimes when I play, it's like I can feel Daddy there with me." I thought of the thread of golden light that had come from my fingers that day I'd played the grand piano at Brightleaf.

"I know, honey," Mama said again, and even though her eyes were fixed on the road in front of us, I could see that they were shiny with tears.

Ray was a little more alert today than he'd been on Sunday, the head of the bed raised a bit more so that he was mostly sitting up. "Miss Annie Lee!" he said as I came into his room, Mama behind me. "And Miz Fitzgerald! I don't know what I did to deserve such a good thing two weeks in a row."

Mama rolled her eyes, but she smiled, too.

Ray waved at the chair closest to the bed. "Sit down, Annie Lee. Tell me what's been happening in your world. It's got to be a far sight more interesting than this hospital room."

I told him about how badly things had ended with Mitch and about losing Daddy's quarter. Mama sat in the corner of the room, busy reading something on her phone with a little frown line on her forehead, not paying much attention to me and Ray.

"It disappeared right after you did," I said, working my fingers through a gap between the threads of the green hospital blanket that hung off the side of his bed. "It kind of feels like there's a hole in my heart every time I think about it. I can't stop reaching for it, like my brain can't seem to remember it's gone."

"I've had a hole in my own heart ever since my Margie passed on," Ray said. He looked a little better today, and although he still had the oxygen tube strung across his face, his breath didn't rattle quite so much. "I don't think holes like that ever really close up all the way. But I kinda think maybe we wouldn't want them to."

"Sometimes I think it might be easier." But even as I said it, I knew the words weren't true. It might hurt less if I forgot my daddy—but not remembering him, not remembering how wonderful he'd been, would be worse.

I picked at the blanket, making the hole big enough to

fit two of my fingers, then three. "Things always seemed easier with the quarter in my pocket. Like I was carrying around my own little piece of luck."

"I reckon you make your own luck pretty well, Miss Annie Lee. And I think you oughta make up with your friend Mitch before too much water gets under that bridge. She seems like the kind of friend you want to hold on to with both your hands."

A fourth finger went into the hole, the seafoam-colored threads rearranging themselves yet again.

"I already tried," I said. "It didn't work. She'd be right to keep on hating me forever." After our makeup egg drop was over on Thursday, I wasn't sure she'd talk to me ever again.

"Just do it like the piano."

"What do you mean? I haven't practiced in days. I haven't even done the fingering work on the table like you taught me to." I'd hardly even thought of the DPTA competition since I'd found Ray on his kitchen floor. Would Mama even let me compete at this point? Would I ever be able to practice again?

"No, child," Ray said. "I meant that you have to take off that invisibility cloak, Annie Lee. Open your heart up a little bit and let Mitch see inside it."

* * *

Mama agreed to let me stay after school to make up my egg-drop project Thursday. She even arranged to get off work a few hours early so she could come pick me up afterward, since there wouldn't be any buses leaving that late.

"Maybe we'll do something," she said as we waited at the bus stop Thursday morning. "We could go get a movie from the library and pop some popcorn. Maybe even unpack some of those boxes."

"We could go visit Ray again," I said.

Mama gave me a sidelong look. "Don't push your luck, Annie Lee."

"A movie sounds nice," I said.

"I've been thinking—maybe we need some new traditions, you and me. I know I'm not always the best at being—I don't know—*fun*."

"Me neither," I confessed.

"I think maybe you and I need to learn to get better at that," Mama said gently. "Without your daddy here, it's up to us. We could have a weekly movie night, maybe. We haven't seen hardly any of the things that've come out this year—we could make a list, take turns choosing the movie."

"I'd like that."

"I love you, honey," Mama had said as the bus

pulled up, brakes hissing to a stop. "I hope you know, baby girl, you're my whole world. Through this whole horrible year, you've been the only thing that's kept me hanging on even a little bit. I know I've been mad at you about the sneaking out, and obviously there's going to be some consequences for that. You've lost some of the freedoms you used to have in the afternoon now that you're going to Mrs. Garcia's. But I think— I think part of it is that we need to figure out a way to spend some more time together. We're all we've got now, Annie Lee. It's time we figured out how to be a family again."

"I love you, too," I said, and hugged her quick before I climbed on the bus.

As we pulled away from the bus stop, Mama waved. I thought of the morning right after school had started, when I'd gotten onto the bus so filled with anger and frustration and hurt that a traitorous little voice inside me wished it had been Mama who had died that day in June, not Daddy.

I didn't feel like that anymore.

Mitch ignored me all day. When the final bell rang and we both went to Mr. Barton's classroom, Mitch only looked at me long enough to ask coldly whether I had brought the thumb drive with our PowerPoint slides.

"All right, ladies," Mr. Barton said after he'd pulled up our presentation on the projector. "You have ten minutes."

I cleared my throat. Mitch and I had agreed to split the presentation into two equal parts: I'd start with an overview of what the egg-drop project was supposed to test, and then she'd share photos and descriptions of some of the prototypes we'd experimented with before coming to our final design.

"When an egg is dropped from a great height, there are a lot of forces that work to make it drop quickly," I said. My hands were shaking as they held the projector remote. "The law of gravity causes the egg to speed up as it heads toward the ground. Newton's first law of motion says that an object that is falling will keep falling unless something acts to stop it. So if there's nothing to slow the egg down or change the way it falls, it will break when it hits the ground. That's what went wrong with our egg last time. There wasn't anything to slow it down, and there wasn't enough to cushion it when it hit the ground, so it broke."

I met Mitch's eyes. "Sometimes, a person can make a choice that causes a lot of forces to work against something that's important to them. Like a class presentation.

Or a friendship. And if they don't do something to change the fall or cushion the landing, then those things might break, just like an egg. I'm sorry, Mitch. I should have realized the way you were feeling before Friday."

"Two more minutes, Miss Fitzgerald," Mr. Barton said, but his face was soft and sympathetic.

I chewed on my lip. Mitch didn't say anything at all.

How much more was I supposed to open up my heart?

I clicked the projector remote and kept going with my regular slides.

After we finished our oral presentation, Mitch and I followed Mr. Barton out of the classroom.

"Since you've already had a chance to do the drop, Miss Harris, I'd like you to be the observer this time," Mr. Barton said.

Mitch nodded but didn't say anything. She hadn't said anything except for what was on her presentation script. She hadn't acknowledged what I'd said during my part of the presentation at all.

I thought of the lost quarter with its two faces: holding on and letting go.

I wasn't ready to let go of Mitch.

It was windy on the roof. I held the egg in its duct-tape-and-straw pyramid over the edge while Mr. Barton gave a countdown.

When he got to zero, I dropped it.

Even from two stories up, I could hear Mitch's whoop of triumph as she picked up the unbroken egg and waved it in the air.

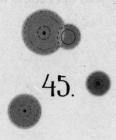

45.

On Friday the lunchtime cafeteria was even louder than normal. Voices clamored around me as I moved through the lunch line and got all my stuff. All the talking and laughing and yelling sounded like some other language I didn't know how to speak anymore. I was in a tunnel, a tunnel made up of sadness and guilt and grief and hope and I didn't even know what all else.

I sat at a table with an open seat and spread a book in front of my tray: *Bridge to Terabithia*, which seemed depressing enough to fit my mood lately. But even as I cracked the tab on my soda and let the pressure hiss out, I couldn't make my brain focus on the words.

Instead, I was thinking of Ray on Tuesday, there

underneath his sea-green hospital blanket. *Open your heart.*

I had never been the kind of person to do big, brave things. Between the three of us, that was always Monica. She was the smart one, the one who came up with all the best plans. Meredith was the gutsy one, who gave us pep talks and made us feel like we could make Monica's plans a reality. And me . . . I was the sidekick. The follower. The one who just went along with things.

But today—today needed to be different.

I put the book back into my backpack and slung the bag over my shoulder before picking my tray back up. It took me a few minutes of standing and letting my eyes wander over the cafeteria before I saw her, slumped in a corner with her head down, her white beanie like a signal flag.

The seat next to her was empty.

I gripped the sides of my tray so hard I could feel my pulse in my fingers as I walked toward her. When I slid it onto the metal table next to hers, the *thunk* was like an explosion.

I thought again of the piano at Brightleaf. *Open your heart up. Open your heart.*

"I want to tell you about my friend," I said. Mitch was eating mechanically, pretending like I didn't exist. "The one I had to go find last week. His name's Ray Owens. I was right, Mitch. He was sick—*really* sick. And nobody else in the world knew it."

This time I didn't just tell her about who Ray was—I told her about what he meant to me. I told her about the long, lonely afternoons while Mama was working, the way the apartment grew and echoed around me, so incredibly empty. I told her about the ghost, the way it would act up sometimes when I was home alone, the way it felt like the sadness would rip me right down the middle if I stayed there. I told her about my scooter and the way it had carried me all around Durham. To Brightleaf.

And I told her about Ray. About his music, the magic it made, the way I'd begged him to teach me. How I'd thought maybe playing piano like Ray did would help me feel closer to my daddy again. How Ray had gone missing last week and I'd worried more and more, until I'd finally skipped school Friday.

How I'd found him half-dead on his kitchen floor.

How he was still in the hospital, pneumonia eating up his lungs, his leg in a cast. How he'd be in a rehab center for at least a month after he got discharged from the hospital. I even told her about Clara—how lonely she must be without Ray, how much I worried that Queenie wouldn't be able to keep going over to feed and walk her for the whole time Ray was in rehab.

By the time I'd finished, tears were burning in my eyes right there in the crowded lunchroom. Somehow I couldn't seem to will them away like I always had done.

"Sorry," I said, sniffling, my head down. A fat tear rolled off my nose and splashed onto my lunch tray.

A napkin slid its way into my view, pushed by Mitch's freckled fingers.

"Don't be sorry," she said, the ice melted out of her voice. When I looked up, Mitch was biting her lip. "You can be done being sorry, okay? Honestly, you've said it enough times I'm getting really sick of that word. I think we both kind of screwed up. So let's start again." She reached her hand over. "Hi. I'm Mitch Harris."

I sniffed again, but laughed, too, as I shook her hand. "Annie Lee Fitzgerald. Nice to meet you."

"So. Your house is haunted, huh?"

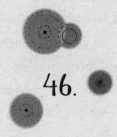

46.

Sunday morning, Queenie showed up at our apartment.

"I invited Mrs. Banks over for coffee a little later," Mama had dropped casually into our breakfast conversation. "She's going to help me with some scholarship applications. And she says she has good news for you about Mr. Owens."

Queenie brought the scent of floral hair spray and sunshine when she came. She seemed too big for our apartment—not because of her size, but because she had the kind of personality that filled any space she stepped into. Like Daddy had. The little braids she usually wore in her hair were pulled into one big, fat braid across her head today, and her dark skin glowed in the light that came through our apartment windows.

"Annie Lee, honey, I've missed seeing you round the mall," she said, gathering me into a hug. Then she hugged Mama. "And Joan, it's lovely seeing you again, too. I'm so glad you called."

"Mama said you have news about Ray?" I asked as Queenie slid off her shiny black clogs and set them next to the front door.

"*Good* news! I got the call this morning that Ray's doctors are discharging him tomorrow morning to the short-term-care facility. They're hoping he can be out of there in about a month, but they said he's in no condition to be living on his own yet. He'll need a lot of care these next few weeks while his leg and his lungs heal. It'll be awhile before he's moving around independently again."

"That's wonderful," said Mama. I couldn't say anything at all—my heart felt like a balloon expanding in my chest, filled with hope and happiness.

"Oh!" Queenie said, patting at her pockets. "That reminds me. I visited Ray yesterday and he gave me something to give to you." She handed me a piece of notebook paper, folded in quarters.

I unfolded the paper. It was a note, in Ray's spidery handwriting.

Dear Annie Lee,

It's going to be some time before I'm back to myself,
these doctors say. I don't know yet when I'm going
to be in any kind of shape to go back to playing at
Brightleaf. But I want you to keep your sights set
on that piano competition anyway. You find a way
to practice those songs, and remember: you've got
everything you need inside you. All you have to do is
be brave and let the music out.

Love, Ray

"What does it say?" Mama asked.

"He wants me to keep practicing," I said, not daring to meet her eyes. "He wants to make sure I still compete in the DPTA program in December."

There was a long moment of silence.

Finally, Mama spoke. "Honey, you can't go to Brightleaf by yourself anymore to practice."

"I know."

"And we can't afford to buy another piano right now."

"I know."

Queenie cleared her throat. "Joan, what if I was to offer to tend Annie Lee after school some afternoons? She could get off the bus closer to Brightleaf and come check in with me as soon as she got there. My shop's right by the atrium with the piano she plays on. If she did her practicing there, I could hear her and keep an eye on her, and when she was done, she could come sit in my salon and do her homework."

Mama pursed her lips. A trickle of hope ran through me. Silence wasn't a no.

"How would she get home?" Mama asked.

"The salon stays open till seven, but most evenings I leave around five—one of my stylists closes up. I'd be happy to give Annie Lee a ride home. Or if you got off earlier than that, I could keep her with me at Brightleaf until you could come get her."

I didn't breathe.

"I suppose that would be okay a few times a week," Mama said. "So long as you get your homework done and don't wander off, Annie Lee."

I threw my arms around Mama, like I hadn't done since I was a little kid, and held her tight. "Thank you," I whispered.

Mama hugged me back. "I know what music means to you, honey, and I don't want to take that away from you, even if it needs to look a little different from now on."

"Now that's settled," Queenie said, "I do have one other piece of news about Ray, but it's not quite so happy."

I let go of Mama and turned back to Queenie. My hand went to my pocket, looking for the quarter that wasn't there anymore. "What do you mean?"

"It's about Clara," Queenie said. "With Ray in a care center for at least another month, I think we've got to find another solution for his dog. I know she means the world to him, but I just can't keep getting over there every day to feed and walk her. And I wish I could bring her to live at my house, but like I mentioned, my husband's allergic."

I looked at Mama. She shook her head. "Don't even think about asking, Annie Lee. We'd get kicked out of this apartment right quick if we tried to bring a dog in here."

"I was thinking," said Queenie hesitantly, "we might need to find another home for Clara."

"Like, forever?" I thought of Ray in the hospital on Sunday. *Don't know what I'd do without that old dog.*

Queenie nodded. "I'm afraid so. Last night when I was visiting Ray, one of the doctors was there with him. He said that Ray will need a walker from now on, and he isn't supposed to walk long distances without somebody there, in case he falls again. I just don't know if he'll ever be able to take care of Clara all the way again."

Ray would hate the idea of Clara going to the shelter.

I could just picture the look on his face at that idea.

"I know, Annie Lee," said Queenie. "I don't like it either. I wish I could keep caring for her, but it's too hard to fit into my schedule. And I'm not as young as I was, either. I twisted my ankle up walking Clara two days ago and it hasn't felt the same since."

"Does Ray know?" I asked.

"I think so, yes," Queenie said gently. "He thanked me yesterday for taking care of her and said he knew I couldn't keep it up forever. I just wish I knew a good place she could go. Sending her to the shelter seems pretty cruel."

The seed of an idea, green and tender and bright, burst into my brain.

"I think I might have a solution," I said. "But I've gotta go send an email."

That night, I dreamed.

It was the umbrella place again, filled up with more light and color than it ever had been, the shaving-cream-and-paper smell of Daddy strong in the air. So strong, I realized, as soon as I realized I was dreaming—so strong because I was standing there beside the glossy grand piano with Daddy's arms wrapped warm and strong around me. As solid—as *real*—as anything I'd ever felt.

311

I breathed in deep, like maybe if I tried hard enough I could breathe Daddy right into my lungs, and then I burst into tears. Crying was all I seemed to be doing these days.

"Oh, Al," Daddy said, and I could feel the vibration of his voice against my hair. The same heart that had given up on him at the church gym all those months ago was beating slow and steady, *thrum-swoosh-thrum-swoosh-thrum*. "I miss you, baby girl."

"I miss you, too," I said, the words wobbly and weak. "I miss you *so much*."

Daddy pulled away, his arms on my shoulders so he could look at me. He looked and looked and looked, like he was drinking me all in, like maybe he wanted to breathe me just as much as I wanted to breathe him. I could feel it all, every bit of it: The pressure of his fingers against the bones in my shoulders, the breeze that snicked its way through my hair, the beat of the sun that shone somewhere above those rainbow umbrellas floating through the sky.

"What is this place?" I asked.

Daddy shrugged. "What does it seem like to you?"

I looked around. "Like nowhere. And everywhere. Like—" I hesitated, my words making even less sense than my thoughts. "Like a beginning and an ending."

"I think you're probably right." Daddy reached into his pocket and pulled something out—something that glinted quicksilver in the sunlight as he flipped it over and over.

"My quarter! Where'd that come from?"

"Didn't you say this is a place of beginnings and endings? Well, then."

I sighed. "Will I ever stop missing you?"

"I don't know, baby girl," said Daddy, hugging me quick and tight again. "But I know I won't ever stop missing my Al."

I thought of Ray, of the Margie-shaped hole in his heart. And I thought of just how hard I'd held on to the ghost, ever since Daddy died, even on the days I hated all the memories it brought us. I'd been holding on so hard all summer to everything I had lost—Daddy, the M&Ms, the way life had been before Daddy's heart had stopped in that church gym.

But it was time to let go now. I knew it, deep down near my belly button, in the same way I'd known that something was wrong with Ray.

Sometimes love meant holding on.

But sometimes it meant letting go.

I hugged Daddy even tighter, a couple of tears squeezing out from the corners of my eyes.

And then I let go.

"Now," said Daddy, sliding onto the piano bench and patting the space beside him. "What do you say we make some music?"

When I woke up the next morning, there was no stubble clogging the drain, no scent of aftershave.

The television, the record player, and the oven were all silent and still, and Mama was silent and still too, standing in the empty bathroom and looking at the clean, shining sink.

Without saying anything, she reached an arm out and tugged me in close. I didn't need to hear her say it to know, deep down in my bones, that the ghost was gone. It was a little bit sad and a little bit of a relief. I thought of what I'd told Daddy in the dream the night before:

Like a beginning and an ending.

For the first time in days, I found myself wandering into my bedroom and pulling from my nightstand the little piano contest paper.

Beginners welcome.

And somehow, in that same deep-down place that knew that the ghost wasn't coming back, I knew something else: Mama and me, we were going to be just fine.

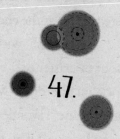

47.

"Do you remember how to get there?" I asked, my insides flipping like my stomach was full of tap-dancing butterflies.

Mama rolled her eyes. "Yes, Annie Lee, I do. Cool your jets."

Her hands, I noticed, weren't *quite* as white on the steering wheel as they usually were.

Clara whined at my feet. She'd come obediently when we'd picked her up from Ray's house, but I could tell she was just as nervous as I was. Her tail thumped once against the floorboards.

"It's okay, girl," I said, rubbing her ears. "It's okay. We'll only be a few minutes."

Mama drove along the highway until the Pizza Huts

and AutoZones had dropped away into tree-lined streets with huge lots, then pulled into a long gravel driveway with a green-shuttered house at the end. I unbuckled my seat belt and gripped Clara's leash, wishing I could swallow the butterflies out of existence.

I let Mama knock on the door. Monica opened it, her smile as nervous as mine; I wondered how she could seem so much like a stranger, after all those years of best-friendship.

"Come on in," she said, her voice too bright and cheery.

We followed her inside, Clara hanging back by my legs.

"Joan! Annie Lee!" Mrs. Hsu rushed forward to wrap Mama and I both into hugs, beaming. "It's been too long!"

"Jenny," said Mama, returning Mrs. Hsu's hug. "It's good to see you."

"And I suppose this is Clara," said Mrs. Hsu, crouching down to look Clara in the eyes and rub her face. Clara didn't pull away or bark. Dr. Hsu may have been the vet, but I'd never met an animal who didn't think Mrs. Hsu walked on water.

Mama looked at me, her eyebrows raised.

"Yeah," I said, trying not to squeak. "This is Clara.

Are you—are you sure you're okay taking her?"

Mrs. Hsu laughed. "Are you kidding me? She'll fit into our family perfectly." From somewhere else in the house, a parrot squawked, like it was agreeing. "We're delighted to have her. She's a beautiful dog."

"We'll take care of her, Annie Lee," said Monica, and when I looked up at her, the fake smile was gone and something tentative and serious and real was there instead. "I promise. And—and you can come see her anytime you like. And your friend Mr. Owens can, too, once he's out of the rehab place."

"Thanks," I said, and then it was my turn to crouch down and look Clara in the eyes. "You'll love it here, girl," I whispered, while Mama exchanged small talk with Mrs. Hsu. "It's great. It's the best place for you that I could imagine. And Ray and I will come visit you, all right? He'll be back home in a month, the doctor said. I bet he'll come see you first thing."

Clara barked, her liquid gold eyes filled with understanding. She licked my chin. For once, I didn't wipe it away—instead I wrapped my arms around her neck, hugging her as tight as you can hug a dog without getting bit. "We'll see you soon."

"Thanks," I said again after I'd disentangled myself from Clara and stood, looking at Monica and then at

Mrs. Hsu. "Ray feels a lot better knowing Clara's got someplace like this to be, where she'll be safe, and—loved."

I handed the leash off to Monica.

"I'll show her around the place," Monica said with a little wave and a half smile. "See you, Annie Lee."

"See you."

As she turned away and skipped out the back door with Clara beside her, I waited to feel that familiar stab of hurt and anger, the one that had been a part of me all summer and fall, every time I'd seen or thought of the M&Ms.

But it didn't come. It was like a whole different Annie Lee had felt all those things.

And when I said goodbye to Mrs. Hsu, the smile on my face was one hundred percent real.

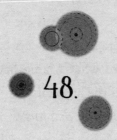

48.

That December was the coldest ever recorded for Durham. By the day of the DPTA piano competition, halfway through the month, there was still almost a whole week before school would get out for the holiday break, and we'd already had a dusting of snow, just enough to kiss the grass with white and give the whole district a snow day.

The morning of the competition was chilly and bright. I wore a red dress that we'd found at Goodwill, and I could hardly breathe for nervousness.

A month before, when Mama had found out where the piano competition was being held, she'd come close to making me pull out. "I can't go there," she'd said, her eyes dark and haunted. "Not for anything, Annie Lee."

I knew just how she felt, because I felt it, too. The competition was going to be held in the Presbyterian church we'd gone to since I was eight years old.

The church where Daddy's heart had stopped.

But I thought of what Mama had said when we'd gone to visit Ray in the hospital.

I don't want to live like that anymore.

"I don't want to always be so afraid," I said, and Mama smiled, the haunted look slipping away.

"You're right," she said, and pulled me into a hug. "You're exactly right, Annie Lee. It will be hard, but we can do it. We'll be brave together."

Now, as we stepped into the sanctuary, I thought of that conversation, and what Ray would have said to me: *Open your heart. Be the brave, wise version of Annie Lee Fitzgerald.*

I squeezed Mama's hand. It was trembling a little, but she squeezed back anyway.

The judges were sitting in the choir seats near the full-size grand piano at the front of the sanctuary. The piano was newer and nicer than the one at Brightleaf, so glossy I could see myself reflected perfectly in the ebony as I sat down.

The room was too quiet; it was too easy to hear my *whump-whump* heart, too easy to pay attention to my nervous skittering thoughts. Too easy to think about all the times I'd seen Daddy sitting in this room, heard his strong voice singing hymns. All those memories of Daddy just added to my nervousness.

"You may begin whenever you're ready, Miss Fitzgerald," said one of the judges, an Asian man whose black hair was graying around the temples.

I put my hands down on the keys. They were cool as water.

And then I straightened my shoulders, the ones that felt so much lighter without an invisibility cloak wrapped around them.

Invisible people couldn't be hurt, but they couldn't be loved, either. And even if my heart would always have a Daddy-shaped hole, I was starting to think that being able to let other people see what was inside me was worth the risk.

Be brave.

Be wise.

Open your heart.

I played my C major scale slow and then fast, and then went right into my G minor scale, my fingers only slipping once on the part where my thumb was supposed to cross under my middle finger.

When I was finished, I lifted my hands and then

started Bach's "Minuet in G Minor."

This time, I let everything that had happened over the last six months come out in my playing.

Daddy dying.

The ghost.

Mama using up all the room for grieving until there was no space left for me to be sad, too.

The M&Ms.

Mitch.

Ray and Queenie and Clara.

Finding Ray at the end of October, half-dead.

Helping him move back home after he was discharged from rehab, and giving him the picture of Clara that Monica had sent me, put into a nice frame and wrapped up with a bow.

All the people who were standing outside this room right now, waiting for me to finish playing: Mama, Mitch, *her* mama, Queenie and Mr. Banks, Ray. So many people I hadn't known I needed so bad. So many people who felt just like family.

As I finished the minuet and started into Beethoven's "Russian Folk Song," I could have sworn I saw somebody out of the corner of my eye, sitting in the pews. Somebody with red hair and an easy smile. Somebody with a singing voice that could fill a whole room. Somebody whose laughter was contagious. Somebody who loved music more than life itself.

I closed my eyes and thought, *This one's for you, Daddy.*

When I was finished, both the judges clapped, and I stood and bowed just the way Ray had shown me.

"Thank you, Miss Fitzgerald," said the judge who'd told me to begin when I was ready. "Competition results for your skill division will be available in a few hours."

As soon as I opened the sanctuary door, I heard clapping—clapping from everyone who was waiting for me.

"We heard it all," Mama said. There were tears in her eyes, but this time I could tell that they were happy ones. "That was beautiful, Annie Lee."

Ray limped forward, leaning on his shiny new walker. The doctors had told him that between the arthritis and the broken leg, he was never going to walk quite the same, but he didn't mind. He said the walker was "fantastic" because it had a built-in seat, and that it didn't matter so much that he couldn't walk from his house to Brightleaf, since he'd gotten set up with a special bus pass for "disabled old codgers" like him.

"That was real nice, Miss Annie Lee," he said now, wrapping an arm around my shoulders. His blue eyes were happier than I'd ever, ever seen them, and they looked suspiciously shiny, too. "I'm real proud of you, child. You're one of the bravest, wisest girls I've ever known."

"Thanks," I whispered, and hugged him back.

One month after New Year's, I sat on a different piano bench—this time at Ray's house, in front of the small upright piano he'd started using to teach lessons. It wasn't just me anymore; he'd had two *paid* students sign up already since the competition, *and* Queenie, who said she'd always wanted to learn. Ray wouldn't let me even try to pay him, though. He said since I was the student who'd taught him how to be a teacher, he owed me.

It had taken Mama a little while to get to the point where she'd agree to let me keep taking lessons from Ray, but eventually she'd come around. She'd gotten a scholarship and some government grants for beauty school—enough for that *and* a little bit extra, including a new-used washing machine—and enrolled in classes that had started right after the new year. Already she seemed happier than she had since the Bad Day. Now she sat in on my lessons, paying bills or reading a novel in a chair in the corner while I played. She'd even taken me to the music store to pick out an electric keyboard of my very own with the fifty dollars I'd received when I'd won second place at the competition in December, and she'd helped me set it up in a place of honor in our living room.

"You ready, Annie Lee?" Ray asked now.

I nodded and laid my hands down gently on the keys, closing my eyes and taking a deep breath and calling up that place deep inside me where the music lived.

And when I started playing, I didn't even need to open my eyes to see the thread of gold light that unspooled itself out of my heart with every note.

ACKNOWLEDGMENTS

Like Annie Lee, music was an integral part of my life growing up. Many of my most vivid memories of adolescence are centered around my time as a serious violinist and pianist—lessons, practice sessions, concerts, and competitions. Like Annie Lee, I regularly participated in Durham music competitions (and occasionally even won!). Like Ray, piano improvisation and composition has always been a deep and important creative outlet for me. And, like both of them, I've spent my fair share of afternoons performing in the unique and lovely Brightleaf Square mall.

There are so many people who supported and guided me in my musical journey, and I thought of each of them often as I wrote *Beginners Welcome*. First and foremost, my violin teacher, Stephanie Swisher, who not only taught me performance and competition skills but also nurtured my passion for teaching and gave me opportunities to assist in orchestras for many years. I'm so grateful to have had Stephanie's friendship, love, and cheerleading for the past two decades (!!!).

Other musicians who were integral to my music education were Sally Ehrisman, my first piano teacher; Susan Kosempa, who taught me how to seek excellence as well as how to shape my piano compositions into the strongest versions of themselves; Dorothy Kitchen, whose incredible Duke University String School was my second home all through middle school and high school; Alisyn Rogerson, who let me assist her as an orchestra conductor and showed me how much I loved pedagogy; Sean Johnson, who made me play pieces that felt too hard, but believed in me enough to help me succeed; and Sam Hammond, the most talented accompanist I've ever known, with whom I shared many wonderful conversations about books, music, God, and life. And my mom, Cindy Ray, who filled our home with everything from John Denver to *Les Misérables* to the *Well-Tempered Clavier*—and, of course, made me practice even when I didn't want to.

I am blessed with a vibrant and tenacious publishing

team, without whom this book would not be half so good. I can write a 64,000-word novel but still never have enough words to describe how grateful I am for my incomparable agent, Elizabeth Harding, who helped me revise *Beginners Welcome*, convinced me that the whole book really couldn't be Annie Lee skulking around in the shadows not talking to anyone, and spent hours via email and phone counseling me through every anxious, frustrated, or confused moment. I can't imagine not having Elizabeth on my side. I'm also thankful for the help and support from Sarah Gerton, Jazmia Young, and everyone else at Curtis Brown.

Alexandra Cooper is, hands down, the most talented editor I've ever had the privilege of working with. She understands my stories on a deep level, and without her, *Beginners Welcome* would still be a sad thing trying really hard to be a book but not quite managing it. Alexandra's passion for Annie Lee and Ray and her insightful suggestions were a light for me in the moments it felt like I'd never get this story right. I also benefited from the support of the whole HarperCollins team: Alyssa Miele, Allison Weintraub, Nicole Moreno, Gweneth Morton, and Valerie Shea. Harriet Russell, Erin Fitzsimmons, and Catherine San Juan created a cover so filled with life and color that I can't look at it without smiling.

So many people read drafts of this book through its long journey to publication, and I am so thankful for the feedback they gave as I struggled to shape Annie Lee's story into what it is today. I'm grateful for critiques from Heather Murphy Capps, Ashley Martin, Amanda Rawson Hill, Cory Leonardo (who is responsible for coming up with the title *Beginners Welcome*, which I love so much!), Jamie Pacton, Kit Rosewater, Mary Bader-Kaaley, Julie Artz, and Shannon Cooley.

I don't know how anyone gets through publishing without community. To my #TeamMascaraTracks kindred spirits; my Sisters of the Pen group chat; and Shannon, who models resilience and persistence better than anyone I've ever known: You make this writing life a joy.

Likewise, *Beginners Welcome* benefited enormously from the expertise and enthusiasm of many friends and relations. My brother Jason Ray put his brilliant scientific mind to the problem of helping me iron out the details of Annie Lee's egg-drop presentation. So many friends answered Facebook questions about everything from obscure car problems to school counselors to automated absence phone calls. My other siblings—Josh, Rachel, Jenna, and Jared—and my dad, Russ Ray, were tireless cheerleaders. My parents came to every single event for

Where the Watermelons Grow and seeing them in the audience each time was the best gift I could imagine. My new sister-in-law Ruth Ray earned a special place in my heart the minute she gushed to me how much she loved my first book. I also have been so lucky to have the support of my mother-in-law, Kathy Baldwin, and the rest of the Baldwin family.

I owe so many happy memories to Mallory Perry and Melissa Lewis, my best friends through my preteen years and the original M&Ms, who were far kinder than Monica and Meredith and included me in their circle from the moment I met them.

And, of course, I was buoyed so much in writing this book by every person who bought, read, reviewed, and loved *Where the Watermelons Grow*. I'm honored that so many teachers, librarians, and booksellers (especially the wonderful indie bookstore community!) embraced and shared that book with those around them.

Most important of all, I am forever grateful for the love and support I've received from my husband, Mahon (who sparked the initial idea for this book), and my daughter, Kate. Both have encouraged me to chase my dreams and—just like Annie Lee—to open my heart to the new experiences that come my way.

Keep reading for a sneak peek at
THE STARS OF WHISTLING RIDGE,
Cindy Baldwin's book about magic and sisterhood.

1.

In stories, the number three is important.

Three princesses.

Three woodcutter's sons.

Three tasks.

My story is the same, I guess.

Three sisters.

Three fallen stars.

And three disasters.

Mama always says that disasters are like blessings—both of them come in threes. They follow on each other's heels, the way starlight follows moonrise, so that you can't untangle them even if you tried.

This is the story of how I proved her right.

* * *

Everywhere we travel, word about the wishes gets around. You'd think that for a family who lives on the road 100 percent of the time we'd have to advertise, but somehow we just show up to a town, park our Winnebago—we call her Martha—and by that night we've already had at least one knock on the door.

They're all different, the wish-seekers. Sometimes it will be a young mother with tired eyes. Others, a granddaddy with a cane and a tightness around the mouth. Every now and then it'll be a teenager, shifting from one foot to the other on the RV front step like his shoes are full of fire ants.

But they all want the same things:

Happiness. Peace. Resolution. And while Mama never barters a wish without first cautioning about how wishes have limits, and rules, and don't always work out the way you expect them to, the wish-seekers always leave with a lighter step, like the world is finally turning their way. Sometimes we see them again; sometimes we don't. Sometimes their wishes work out for the best; sometimes they don't.

But no matter where we go, they find us.

The evening we pulled up in Silverwood, Oklahoma, the visit came from a grandmotherly lady with short blond hair and a way of holding herself that made me think of the Queen of England. She wore a navy skirt and blazer without a speck of dust on them—the kind of outfit you could only get away with if you had a regular house with a regular closet, a laundry room, and a full-size ironing board.

We'd been wandering our way north from where we'd been staying in the Louisiana bayou country, where Mama had spent a whole week trying to calm a well-spring of swamp magic that was pouring enchantment into the water and creating some *very* unusual alligators. When we'd packed up our things and gotten back on the road, Daddy had asked where to go next, and Mama had pointed to a map. Even though none of us had ever heard of Silverwood before, Mama was never wrong about that kind of thing.

And once we reached Silverwood, we had barely plugged Martha's power cord into the campsite's adapter before the stranger showed up.

There was no actual knock on the door this time, on account of the fact that we were all already outside: Daddy and Sophie were down at the lake fishing for our dinner, Elena and I were putting a tablecloth and dishes on the campsite picnic table, and Mama was crouched by the firepit, laying logs with more precision than most people build houses.

3

The visitor paused at the edge of our campsite, her feet together in their tan pumps, and cleared her throat.

"Hello," said Mama, standing up and wiping char from her hands. Her hair swished and sparkled in the afternoon sunlight.

Mama's hair was long and white. Not stringy and white like an old lady's, and not white like people say when they're describing hair that's so light a blond it's nearly see-through. Mama's was bone-white, star-white, milk-white, shot through with glimmers of silver, so that sometimes when she moved it looked almost like water. Everywhere we went, people stopped to stare at Mama, at her golden-brown skin and white hair and eyes the clear gray-blue of moonlight on snow.

Nobody in the world looked quite like my mama and her sisters, Aunt Agatha and Aunt Ruth.

"Can I help you?" Mama asked, lifting a hand to shake the visitor's. "I'm Marianne Bloom. These are my daughters, Ivy and Elena."

Beside me, Elena shrank into herself, her shoulders curling in and her arms folding across her chest. Elena sometimes reminded me of a mouse—bright and cheerful and energetic when she was alone, or with people she trusted, but trembling and quiet around strangers. Sometimes it got so bad she could hardly talk when people we didn't know asked her a question.

The navy-blazer lady only darted nervous eyes at us and then looked back at Mama, like she didn't want to say whatever it was she'd come to say where me and Elena could hear her.

They were often like that, the wish-seekers, carrying their secrets in tight fingers.

"Ivy honey, come here and get this fire going while I take our guest inside a minute," Mama called, and even though curiosity burned through me hotter than any campfire, I obeyed. The regal lady followed Mama into the RV, Martha's door swinging shut behind them with a bang.

For as long as anybody could remember, people had been wishing on falling stars. And over time, those wishes had grown heavy and solid and real enough to weight down tiny pieces of that stardust, and give them hearts that beat and wings that could carry them through the warm night air. Because fireflies had come from stars once, it didn't take much for a fallen star-woman to breathe the wishes back into them, reminding the fireflies where they'd come from and how they'd come to be.

All you had to do after that was whisper your wish as you released the firefly, and as it drifted up into the darkness it would take your wish with it, wrapping that wish up in its glowing golden magic.

"What do you think it's about this time?" Elena asked, relaxed again now that the stranger was gone, as I stuffed some paper into the log cabin Mama had built in the firepit and lowered the lighter down after it. My charm bracelet jingled, the little silver RV on it catching the light and making my stomach twist unhappily. For something that used to make me smile every time I saw it, that bracelet was sure getting to be an annoying reminder.

"Shh," I hissed. "Maybe we can hear." Sometimes we knew what the wish-seekers wanted, sometimes we didn't, but Mama always respected their privacy if they requested it.

Two clicks and a burst of flame, and the paper caught. I sat back on my heels, straining my ears to catch the conversation from inside the camper. Mostly it was just murmuring, indistinguishable as the ocean, but every now and then I'd hear something from the wish-seeker: *"Husband . . . fire . . . job."*

A few minutes later the door opened again, and the visitor stood on the front step with her hands cupped around a glass jar, like it was maybe the most precious thing she'd ever held.

"Thank you," she said to my mama, in that trembly half-there-half-gone sort of voice people often had when they were leaving with a wish in their hands. "Truly. Thank you."

"May it bring you joy. And remember the rules," said Mama, the way she always did. Standing there in the gloom of the RV, she glowed just a little bit, silvery-gold light rolling from her hair and skin.

The visitor stepped down. Between her fingers I could see a glimmer of light, there and then gone: the firefly in her jar, blinking its golden glow on and then off quicker than a whisper. With one last grateful look at Mama, those fancy pumps carried her out of our campsite.

A minute later we heard the sound of a car engine turning over, and then she was gone.

Still in the shadow of the doorway, Mama sighed, rubbing her face with her hands. "I hope it helps."

"Won't it?" I asked. Mama was the only one of her sisters who bartered wishes. Aunt Agatha and Aunt Ruth both had forever homes—in North Carolina and Montana, respectively—and Mama always said it was too hard to trade in wishes if you never moved on from a place, because you'd get too invested in fixing your neighbors' problems, and maybe you'd end up giving out wishes that were never meant to be granted.

Mama stepped out of the RV now and shrugged, her hair sliding over her shoulders like starlight. "I hope. But wishes aren't always predictable."

Mama and Daddy had drilled that into my head over and over again, until it was all I could do not to roll my eyes as I heard those words coming out of Mama's mouth for the zillionth time. *Wishes are unpredictable. Wishes are powerful. Wishes don't always work out the way you think or hope they will. Wishes aren't to be treated lightly or taken for granted. Wishes are to be respected, honored, earned.*

"The fire looks good," said Mama, dumping ingredients for skillet cornbread into a bowl and beating them together until they were creamy and yellow. "Thanks, Ivy Mae."

"You're welcome," I said. My full name was Ivy Mae Bloom, which was only one letter away from being a sentence. *Ivy may bloom.* Mama and Daddy named me Ivy because they liked it, and Mae had been my Grandma Bloom's name before she died, but still. You'd think that they would have thought about the possible psychological damage before filling out the birth certificate. It's like before I was even an hour old, my parents knew I'd spend my whole life looking for a place to put down roots.

As the fire I'd built burned down to coals, the air filled with the smell of charcoal and wood and smoke— smells so familiar that I had to pay attention or I didn't even notice them. Once, when I was Sophie's age, we'd stayed for a while somewhere in Kansas, and I'd been playing at a park one morning and met a little girl wearing a plastic tiara that glittered and sparkled in the light. When we'd first shown up, me and Elena with Mama pushing baby Sophie in a stroller, the tiara girl had run over to her mom and whispered, *She smells weird*, loud enough that we could all hear it.

The girl's mom had scolded her, and the girl had shot a guilty look my way. But still, that afternoon, I'd gone home and scrubbed my hair and skin with shampoo three times in a row, afraid that I'd never smell like anything other than campfire and the scent of the road.

Back then, it had been a small thing, one hurtful moment in a lifetime made up of adventure and fun. But the older I got, the more those bad moments seemed to crowd out the good. Everywhere I went I carried with me a notebook—my writer's notebook, so I could always have it handy to jot down inspiration or collect the definitions of words that sounded cool, or work on stories or poems or plays as the inspiration struck. And in the back of that notebook there was one thing that never changed, no matter how many actual notebooks I might go through: a list called *Things I Wish*. When I was little, they were pretty dumb, like wishing for ice cream for dinner or my parents to stop making me take showers. (Ew.)

But these days, that list of wishes looked different. In my current notebook, the wishes were mostly the kinds of things that no family who lived on the road full-time could ever have. Like *my own bedroom*, or *a tree house*, or *a library card*, or *the chance to see a whole year of seasons in one place*. I didn't know exactly *when* living in Martha, traveling all the time, had stopped being fun and become frustrating, but I knew one thing—the closer I inched toward my thirteenth birthday, the more I envied Mama's clients, who had a chance of their wishes actually coming true.

I thought of the rows and rows of glass jars inside the camper, each one with its glinting firefly, each one holding within its little light the power of one wish.

Wishes may not have been predictable, but even so: those wish-seekers didn't know how lucky they were to walk away from our campsite with the thing they'd hoped for cradled in their arms.